"I've slive. If you'll

Meical shook his head, but it only made him dizzy. The downy heat of her attraction to him vibrated through his body and eclipsed all else for a blessed moment.

He closed his eyes, soaking her up. "I'm warning you…"

"I'll consider myself warned, then. Shut up and let me get you inside where you can rest."

She opened the door and nudged him in. He literally fell onto the sofa. For a moment he fought the lethargy that sought to claim him. Was it the day-death? He couldn't hold his eyes open, just had to...

Sleep? After two hundred years of never resting... to rest in the way of mortals?

The bed dipped, and he felt Caroline close to him.

Heaven help her if she was within reach when he woke.

JANET ELIZABETH JONES

writes paranormal and fantasy romance for adults and teens. History, cybertechnology and the paranormal world provide the inspiration for much of her work as a writer, as well as her work as a computer artist and web designer. She currently lives in the Lone Star State with her family and "The Queen of the Universe," a feline majordomo who keeps the whole clan on schedule.

INCUBUS

JANET ELIZABETH JONES

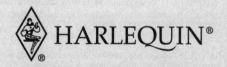

HARLEQUIN®

TORONTO • NEW YORK • LONDON
AMSTERDAM • PARIS • SYDNEY • HAMBURG
STOCKHOLM • ATHENS • TOKYO • MILAN • MADRID
PRAGUE • WARSAW • BUDAPEST • AUCKLAND

Recycling programs
for this product may
not exist in your area.

ISBN-13: 978-0-373-61851-4

INCUBUS

Dear fellow vampire lover,

Don't we love the very thought of vampires secretly sharing the long night of their existence with humanity? Sheltered in their world of deadly beauty, arcane wisdom and exquisite pleasure, these beings can be found everywhere, even–as in this book–in a snowbank in Pennsylvania.

That's where this story begins, but it has its origin in the historic town of Camden, Maine, home of the New England Enclave–one of the oldest surviving vampire communities. Meical (pronounced just like "Michael") is the silent one among them, acting instead on raw hunger and pure instinct. He doesn't consider himself a member of the family, and he plans to keep it that way.

So, how did elusive Meical Grabian end up deader than undead in a snow bank? He'd say it was a simple matter of keeping a promise. In truth, he craves the warmth and light of humanity as much as he craves blood. But it's going to take the love of a gifted, gutsy woman to rescue him from the cold dark.

If you want to know more about this vampire enclave, drop by my site, Romance for the Night Raven, at www.janetejones.com.

Janet Elizabeth Jones

This book is dedicated to my loving family, without whom I would not be the person I am today, and to my fellow writers who inspire me when my muse wanders off and forgets her way home.

Prologue

Alone. Neither dead nor alive.

But it was better than the pain. Meical Grabian drifted in the blackness, as wispy as a spiderweb. Nothing ahead of him, nothing behind and nothing left of him but his conscious mind.

Where was the power the Alchemist had promised? The chance to feel the sun's warmth again, after two hundred years of drinking blood and living in darkness?

Fool. He'd actually believed the Alchemist's potions and spells would work for him. Was *this* what he'd bartered away his existence for?

No. He'd done it for Ellory and Talisen, for their brood of fledgling vampires. He'd purchased the Alchemist's protection of them in return for his participation in this "experiment."

Sacrificed for the sake of vampire science and the future of his kind. Meical filled the silence with bitter laughter, and the sound echoed around him. A thousand Meicals in the darkness laughed back at him.

His laughter was shattered by a woman's scream. The sound shook him, claimed him. Who was she? How could her screams reach him here when nothing else could? Was she alone here, too?

Not anymore. He'd find her, and whoever was hurting her would beg for death before he was finished with them.

He followed her screams, drawn to her as if her life force had wrapped around his soul—a life force that weakened with every wail.

Two lights creased the gloom, one below him and one ahead. Meical looked down at a room that seemed miles below him, yet every detail was clear and sharp. He saw himself on the Alchemist's lab table, looking like a vampire made out of wax. His creator toiled over his lifeless body, pumping it full of various concoctions and murmuring arcane chants.

The woman screamed again, weak and hopeless. Meical turned away from the scene below him and flew toward the light ahead, peering through the darkness in search of the woman. He burst into a shadowy room, bringing his own murderous red glow with him. Two cloudy green blobs of energy towered over a pool of sickly yellow. Silver baseball bats rose and fell. He heard her bones crack, and she screamed again.

The instant Meical's feet touched the ground, the room took shape, and he found himself in a filthy basement lit by a single overhead bulb. The woman's assailants moved in for the kill, even as she tried to drag herself into a corner. Meical unleashed a tidal wave of rage. The men rounded on their heels and gaped at him. Their bats slipped to the floor, and they fled up a ladder.

He rose right through the basement ceiling to catch them on the floor above as they sprang out of the trapdoor. But when he reached for them, his hands went through them, leaving him grasping at dust and silence. The door of the house slammed behind them.

The woman's life force ebbed, vibrating through the floorboards under his feet, and fluttered in his chest. She had no time left. She'd die here and now if he didn't do something. And then he'd never know who she was, or how and why she was able to reach him in the void.

He shot upward through the rooftop, into a navy blue sky with a thousand stars, and halted when he was high enough over the little house she lay dying in, to see the lay of the land. Desert, for as far as he could see. The sky was so big it made him dizzy.

The headlights of a car twinkled on the dimly lit road that passed the house. As the car loomed closer, Meical focused his gaze on a tree in the front yard and stretched out his hand. A wave of heat exploded from him, jettisoning him backward. When he rolled upright again, the tree was not only enflamed, but so was the grass around it.

The car squealed as it slowed, lurched to the left and

sped up the driveway. The driver leaped from the car with his cell phone in his hand, slapping at the blaze with his jacket. A minute later, sirens broke the desert stillness. Meical watched the man eye the house with hesitation.

Hurry. Find her. Find her now.

The man paced a moment longer, then ducked inside. Just as the ambulance and fire truck arrived, he emerged with the unconscious woman in his arms.

An iron hand closed around Meical's soul and jerked him downward. *Where are you going, you ungrateful nit? Do you think I brought you this far to let you wander off and leave my work undone?*

Meical gasped and shivered as his physical senses returned to him. A stab of cold struck him speechless, followed by numbness that was worse than the day-death. He was in darkness again, but he could sense the Alchemist's presence.

"Neshi?" he slurred. He opened his mouth to speak again, but his lips were sluggish and his vocal cords made no sound. He called to the Alchemist in his mind. *I was under the impression there was nothing left of me to "work" with.*

No, everything is going according to plan. Your body must remain dormant and regenerate.

That woman...

You weren't ready for her yet. Still, it's indicative.

What's indicative, you lunatic?

How fast you found her. You're definitely doing better than my last subject. You might survive long enough for me to see something come of my efforts.

Meical snorted. *I'm sure you feel gratified. She'll be all right, won't she?*

Is that sympathy I hear in your voice, Grabian? For a human?

Answer me. Will she be all right?

That depends on you.

Me? Who am I to her?

By Ra, you're an idiot. Considering what you just went through with her, I should think you'd be able to answer that question yourself, if only in part. You don't really believe you merely happened upon her in her hour of need, do you? Not that it matters in the least. When next you wake, you won't remember any of this.

What do you mean I won't remember?

What you just did for her, as fortuitous for both of you as it was, will be part of your unconscious memory when you're restored to yourself. You may recall it later, with some help, but who knows?

For the first time since Meical had surrendered himself to Neshi's insanity, he felt truly afraid. *How much memory loss are we talking about?*

You'll remember who I am and what we're trying to accomplish with your transformation. You'll remember your previous life as a vampire—

I'm still a vampire.

Not for much longer. The next few months will be lost to you, naturally, since you'll be mostly dead for the duration.

Deeper than dead, actually. Deeper than the day-death, according to how Neshi had explained it to Meical.

I'm going to put you to sleep now, the Alchemist said. *Time will pass, and you'll heal. Or not. If you survive the regeneration of your body, you'll wake up in a few months, but you'll need sustenance immediately, or you won't last long enough to see your first sunrise. Understand?*

Sunrise. That was all Meical wanted. To feel the sun on his face. To see it.

Neshi's voice touched his mind again. *As an incubus, Meical, your power will be greater than ever before, and you will feed on the essence of the human heart. That is the key to your survival now.*

Even as Meical's body began to shut down, the thought of feeding on human passion made him burn in every vein, muscle and bone. This was a hunger more devouring than any he had known as a vampire. He thought of the woman, imagining her safe and happy and unhurt. And his. He thought of the warmth and life in her pouring into him, while her beautiful body danced beneath his. How he'd please her. She would never know another moment of pain again, and the men who had hurt her would rue the day they were born.

Even if he wouldn't remember her, if they were to meet again, would she remember him? Probably not. Not in the condition she was in when he saved her. She'd be lucky if she remembered none of that nightmare.

Meical heard Neshi's voice reverberate like distant thunder. *I'll make you a deal. If the two of you survive the next few months, I'll see that you're somewhere close to her when it's safe for you to be revived. We'll see how well you manage to call your prey when you're in a weakened state.*

You don't even know she'll hear me calling her. You don't know, Neshi.

That's why it's called an experiment, Grabian.

Chapter 1

Eight months later
The Poconos, Pennsylvania

Caroline drank down the deluge of emotions around her, soaked up the haggard feelings like gravy. Serene and resolved, she ignored the contorting shadows in her cabin, the dance of darkness with his coy mistress, light.

Emotion throbbed from the people who'd come to ask her help. She tasted the mother's fear, the father's skepticism and the sheriff's impatience. But there was also John's unwavering faith in her and Dash's tranquil, canine contentment. With a steadying breath, she opened herself to take in the emotions of those who lived beyond her cabin.

She swam in a sea of human nature. Greed, hope, lust, love, devotion, angst, gratitude, lust again. She sampled and plucked at every thread of feeling that came to her, like a harpist feeling for the right string. The chord she sought was abject terror. She found it in varying flavors, in every nook and cranny of the night, terror mixed with sorrow, rage and hatred. But what she was looking for was pure terror in a tiny package of confusion named Megan Feinstein: five years old, blond hair, green eyes, freckles, a Barbie flashlight with dead batteries and a tendency to stray from her parents when they weren't looking. Megan was lost and alone.

Caroline knew how that felt.

She weeded through the stream, her stream, and let it flow in, out and away from her. All the while her inner wall of mental protection trembled, threatening to fall and leave her open to the tide of humanity where she could lose herself. She shored up her protective barrier with the reminder that these emotions were not hers, and chanted the words of her familiar safeguard over and over.

I am Caroline. The emotions within me are my own and no one else's. These other emotions exist beyond me and are not mine. I am Caroline...Caroline... Caroline...

Her concentration snagged on a wave of hot confusion.

Caroline hesitated. It seemed there were *two* people out there who were drenched in the sort of fear she was fishing for, not just one. Both felt lost and abandoned. Both were in pain and needed comfort. One was small

and female. The child pulsed like a star. That was
Megan.

But the other? He was more like a supernova.

His confusion and pain yanked Caroline in his direction. She drew back with an inner wince but couldn't
close him out. She pushed him to the back of her soul
and followed Megan's thread of fear instead. The child's
fear painted a picture of her in Caroline's mind. She
was a spark of life huddled under a pine, crying for her
mama.

Caroline opened her eyes. "Take the Fletcher trail
east about a half mile, Sheriff. She's a few yards off the
path, on the left."

The sheriff flushed red-purple and cleared his throat.
"Thanks, ma'am."

The child's parents leaped up from Caroline's sofa
and caught her hand in theirs with simultaneous thank-
yous. Caroline flinched, gutted by the onslaught of their
gratitude and disbelief, but she forced a smile.

"Glad I could help. You can thank me best by not
mentioning me to anyone. Okay?"

They offered her money—people always did—which
she refused. Not that she couldn't use the cash. But
people who got paid for services rendered were less
anonymous and not nearly as forgettable as she needed
to be. The couple left, taking their whirlpool of emotion
with them.

But anguish lingered. The man lost out there in the
night radiated agony in all directions. He was haunted
by loneliness that was deep and old.

Caroline honed in on him again. His heart was a

black hole, a hungry cauldron. His kind of need could drain her dry. But he had no one.

She slumped back in her chair and breathed deeply until she felt like she was alone in her own skin again.

John turned from the door with a grin and ran a hand through his tousled, salt-and-pepper hair. "That was awesome. The minute the sheriff showed up at my place to ask me to come along with the search party, I told him you were the one who could find that little girl."

Caroline inhaled and exhaled. "We're not finished, yet. There's someone else out there. Can you help me find him? It'll only take a few minutes. I think he's close, but—"

Her evening bout with pain announced its arrival. A sliver of white-hot fire shot down her right thigh. She closed her teeth on a moan and reached beneath the blanket that covered her lap to rub her stump.

"Caroline," John admonished, "you didn't take your meds this evening, did you?"

"I wouldn't have been any help to those people if I had."

"Sugar, how can I help you with your pain management if you won't take the medicine I prescribe you?"

She followed the sound of his heavy footfall on the floor and the creaking door of the medicine cabinet in the bathroom. She winced again when he swore. "You haven't even touched these pills, Caroline."

"Spare me the lecture, all right? Those things make me feel like spaghetti all over, and I need all the muscle strength I can get." Another spike of pain shot through her half leg, and she nearly doubled over in her chair.

She felt John's arms around her. "Okay, hold on to me until you can swallow this medicine. And to think, Millie says I have a lousy bedside manner."

"I'll be sure to put in a good word for you next time she brings me groceries."

The burning contortions in Caroline's swollen knee joint subsided a little, but the twinge in the toes she didn't have anymore remained. Some nights it drove her mad. She sighed and laid her spinning head against John's shoulder.

"Well, while I'm here, let's have a look at you."

She gripped the blanket when he reached for it. "No time. We've got to go find that guy out there."

"In a minute." John lifted the blanket and her flannel nightie to examine her stump. His brow furrowed and he frowned at her. "As if you don't have enough pain to deal with, you have to go and do heaven knows what with what's left of your leg?"

She shoved her nightgown down to cover herself. "There was a cat. A really little, really helpless black cat."

"A cat."

"In a tree. Stuck. Okay?"

"Tell me you didn't climb a tree. It's only been six months since your surgery."

"She was very grateful when I got her down."

He shook his head. "You could've called me."

"But I'm always calling you. Besides, she doesn't like men. Smart cat, huh?"

"You know you can ask Millie and me to do anything for you. I'm not just your doctor; I'm your friend. You can talk to me about anything."

Caroline fixed her gaze on the dust bunnies in the corner of her two-room hideout. "No, I can't."

He sighed and kissed her forehead. "Okay, almost anything. Take that pill and get a good night's sleep. I'll go find the guy. He's probably a lost hiker."

"You won't find him without my help. He's…I don't know…hidden. Covered up. Something. Give me a few minutes to get dressed."

She was perfect for Grabian.

Neshi watched Caroline Bengal and her companion rumble away from the cabin. This time it might work. Grabian might live long enough. He could take his place among these humans as if he were one of them and feed in a way that was natural and harmless to his prey. And the woman, the empath, would know his needs and respond to them in a way that would ensure Meical's survival.

Neshi allowed himself a moment of self-satisfaction. If he could do *this,* literally rebuild Grabian, reconstitute and enliven human tissue that had lain dormant beneath vampire flesh for two hundred years, what else might he eventually accomplish? And not just for vampires, but for preternatural beings of all kinds. He could allow them to live in perfect symbiosis with humanity.

If Grabian survived the next few hours. Nothing must come between him and his prey tonight. Caroline

Bengal *must* take Meical home with her. He'd make sure she did.

Neshi wrapped himself in a gust of wind and followed the humans.

Storing her slalom behind her seat, Caroline shoved her foot into her ski boot and fixed her entire focus on the lost man. A rivulet of hunger, power and misery seized her. It was as if somebody's rejected god had crash-landed in her forest. No way was she walking away from this one.

"Found him," she murmured to John. "South of here."

But what could she do for him? A need like his would turn her inside out. She couldn't afford to help strangers. He could be anyone. For all she knew, he was one of the men Rivera had sent to kill her. Maybe even Burke himself.

She gripped the handles of her crutches until her hands tingled. No, no, no. Burke couldn't find her in a little one-store town in the Poconos. She had to believe that. She'd had enough practice picking up on his presence to know he wasn't around. He couldn't find her here. Not yet.

Still, just to be on the safe side, she expanded her senses to take in the surrounding woods. Lots of life out there. Lots of emotion. But the only trace of humanity she encountered was the man they were trying to rescue, and even though his life force had a peculiar vibration, it wasn't the throb of psychopathic hatred and fanaticism that made her nemesis stand out in a crowd of thousands.

Burke was just like Rivera. He couldn't hide his presence from her. No one could. He wasn't here. He hadn't found her yet.

Caroline breathed a sigh of relief and fixed her concentration on the woods ahead. She tried to hold on to the object of their search. But an anomaly of some kind kept getting in the way. She held her breath, tracing the pulsing aura to its source. It fractured and dissipated suddenly.

The anomaly was human-like but not human. Nor was it pure spirit. Spirits felt more like a mix of quicksilver and cotton candy, swift and sweet. This being was physically present and much more powerful spiritually than any spirit she'd encountered.

Caroline focused on the silent presence with her whole being, tuning out the Suburban's noisy heater and jostling, squeaking seat, until nothing existed in her world but the being who scrutinized her.

There was an absence of light in him, yet his soul lit up the cosmic river. There was no death in him, yet she couldn't feel his presence as she could a living soul. He was all intelligence and cunning. The only thing that made him seem to belong on this plane was his connection to the man she was trying to help.

What do you want with him? she asked the being.

He didn't answer her. Instead, he penetrated her shield with an ease that sent Caroline surfacing as fast as she could.

Words formed in her mind from nowhere. *If you think that's something, wait until you see what he can do.*

"Hey, are you all right?" John asked.

"Fine," she gulped.

She'd come across a lot of different entities in her time, but this—whatever he was—was as unique as the man she was trying to rescue. What was their story?

She fixed her concentration on the lost stranger again. She'd find him, help him out and that would be it. Whatever his situation was, she didn't need his baggage—or his cosmic companion.

His agony filled the night, condensing into a choking mass of despair that lay just yards away from them now. Caroline tapped John's arm and pointed. "There. See where the ground dips into a hollow?"

The doctor drove up the rise and stopped on the perimeter of a snow-filled knoll. He helped Caroline out of the Suburban, fetched her slalom and helped her put it on.

She stood in the icy stillness, feeling for her quarry. Snow fell like dandelions cast to the wind. His pain filled her with pain that penetrated her to the marrow of her bones, but she felt his life force tremble inside of him and a sense of alertness in him that startled her. Unconscious or not, on some level, he knew they'd found him.

Was he an empath, too?

He knew he was alone. He didn't know what he'd done to be abandoned like this. He wanted relief from his pain, the comfort of the human touch, a place to be safe. Who had done this to him, left him alone like this to die? No one deserved this.

She hadn't deserved it.

Caroline's head pounded in time with her racing

heart. Night, snow and trees faded, suddenly eclipsed by a pungent basement illuminated by a single naked bulb. She lay on the filthy floor, bound, gagged, bleeding and feverish. No one would come for her. Her only companions were pain, thirst and terror.

Dash's bark brought her back to the present. The dog had found something. John was already plowing after Dash through the snow. Caroline licked the beads of sweat and melting snow from her upper lip and glided along after them, stabbing her crutches into the snow and pushing herself along on her slalom.

Panic bloomed inside of her. The stranger's or hers? She couldn't tell. Their emotions merged too well, which wasn't good. She breathed deeply, fighting the stark terror that consumed her self-control, and followed John toward a motionless mound of snow at the bottom of the knoll.

Dash was already there, standing stiff-legged with her head down and her ears up. The closer Caroline got to the stranger, the more his hunger devoured her. He was *emotionally* emaciated.

She set her flashlight on the ground so that it shone on him, sat down and whipped off her slalom. John knelt beside the man with a pile of blankets they'd brought along and swept the snow off him. He felt for a pulse, then slipped a penlight out of his pocket. Drawing the man's left lower eyelid down with his thumb, he flicked the light back and forth across a pewter gray eye and returned the flashlight to his pocket.

"He's only unconscious. Probably working on a good

case of hypothermia. Wrap him up. I'll bring the car closer."

While John returned to the Suburban, Caroline covered the man with the blankets and tucked them close around him. She reached her hand underneath the covers and laid it over his heart. He was icy all over, right through his clothes. She felt an abundance of hard muscle everywhere she touched him. He was a really big guy, long and well-built but on the lean side, like he'd gone without eating for too long. His relief reached her from deep inside him. It flowed over her inner barriers as though she hadn't any.

The hunger she'd sensed in the man receded a little, and his skin began to warm. Incredible. He was nursing the warmth and energy out of her, emotionally and physically, but it wasn't the hard drain she'd feared. She made herself still inside, allowing him to draw on her strength. Another gulp of relief flowed out of him into her. Had he just thanked her?

He *had* to be an empath.

By the time the headlights of John's Suburban cut through the darkness, the stranger's temperature had risen to match hers. She watched John exit his vehicle like a bull elephant. He plowed through the snow to her, reached down with one hand to pull her up on her foot, hoisted the man over his shoulder and stood up.

"He won't need a hospital. He just needs somewhere to warm up and come to. I'll drop you off at your cabin and take him to the clinic where I can examine him. He'll probably be fine in the morning."

An impulse shot through Caroline like an electric

shock. The idea of the man going anywhere but her place was out of the question. "We have to take him to my cabin."

John halted on the way to the Suburban, turned and gaped at her. "Excuse me?"

What was she thinking? But the words popped out of her mouth as though she had no control over them. "He needs to warm up fast, doesn't he? My cabin's closer."

John blinked. "You're not making sense. What happened to your absolutely-no-strangers rule?"

Caroline clenched her hands together. She couldn't explain it, couldn't even try. The compulsion struck again. "Let's hurry it up, okay? Don't worry. You'll be there. And I've got Dash. I'll be okay."

He shook his head. "We don't know this guy. It's not safe. There's no way I'm going to—"

His face suddenly went blank, and his mouth hung open.

Caroline narrowed her eyes and looked him up and down. He seemed to have blanked out completely. A warble of energy surrounded them for a moment, and their patient's invisible companion loomed closer.

She edged closer to John. "John? John. Hey. Are you okay?"

He blinked again and suddenly seemed to remember himself. "Fine. Just fine. You're right. This man needs to go straight home with you where he'll be warm and… and safe…and I'm sure you'll be okay. Yeah, you'll be fine."

As though there were nothing left to discuss, the doctor turned and carried his near-lifeless burden to the

Suburban. Caroline stuck her foot back into her slalom, balanced on her crutches so she could fasten it, and followed him.

Her mind told her this was insane. Her instincts did, too. But inside her, the compulsion to shelter this man rode her hard. She turned and eyed the quiet forest again. His friend out there returned her gaze with a smug satisfaction that made her want to hit someone.

What had she gotten herself into this time?

Once they had reached her cabin, Caroline carried John's medical bag in for him and sat down in the armchair by her bed to watch him work on her Sleeping Beauty. Dash crept close to her and kept a wary eye on the stranger.

There was an unearthly beauty about him, except for the ruggedness in his face that hardship had made. His thick, dark gold hair curled with moisture from the melted snow. His square jaw suggested he'd be intractable in an argument.

Caroline let her gaze wander over the powerful torso and arms John revealed during his examination. The man's chest was covered with the same chestnut-golden hair that made his stubbly chin glisten in the firelight. She swallowed hard and raked her hand through her hair. "I'll go fix some coffee."

"Can't hurt," John mumbled over his stethoscope.

Caroline plucked up her crutches and, with a backward glance at the man in her bed, hobbled out of her room. What was his story? His intensity scared her to death, but she was relieved she'd rescued him. Relieved?

No, overjoyed. In fact, it was the first joy she'd felt in weeks.

Ducking behind the curtain that served as a makeshift wall between her tiny living room and her kitchenette, she made the coffee mechanically. Her focus seemed tethered to the guy. She could feel his hunger eating away at him.

When the coffee was ready, she poured two mugs. "Hey, it's ready."

John came and carried their coffee back to her bedroom. He had removed the rest of their patient's wet clothing and bundled him up to the chin in blankets. Caroline eyed the long jeans, white Oxford shirt and spotless T-shirt John had draped over the back of a chair to dry. No coat or shoes? Who dressed like that in this weather?

With a shake of her head, she curled herself up in her bedside armchair and took her coffee from John. She stared at Sleeping Beauty over her cup. There seemed to be no sunshine in him whatsoever. He was all darkness inside, darkness and misery. Poor guy.

No, no, no, she chided herself. Hadn't she learned her lesson with Rivera's son? Don't get involved on a personal level. It didn't matter if it was a seven-year-old boy traumatized by his father's secrets or an unconscious guy she'd pulled out of a snowdrift. Her empathy would always lead her right into trouble.

John put his stethoscope away and sighed. "Very strange. Very lucky for him, but strange all the same."

She cast a glance at the doctor. "What's that?"

"He exhibits symptoms of severe malnutrition, but I know he isn't starving. He's perfect."

Caroline grinned. "You can say that again."

John chuckled, stood up and drained his coffee. He took the mug to the kitchen. When he returned, he regarded his patient with a furrowed brow.

Caroline caught the snag of exasperation and indecision in her friend and shrugged. "Look, you've got your rounds to do at the hospital in less than an hour. He's comfortable where he is. Leave him here. It's okay."

John met her gaze with a scowl. "We don't know this guy."

True—and not true. If he was like her, she knew him in ways she'd never known anyone before. She eyed the man's still face. "You know I can take care of myself."

"I know you're an excellent psychologist, but I don't think you ran into many psychopaths during your internship."

"He's nothing of the sort."

"You'd know, I'm sure, given your vast experience."

She laughed. "Actually…"

"Right. But that's another tale from Caroline Bengal's adventures among the mentally infirm, right?" John buttoned up his coat and picked up his bag. "Seriously, Caroline, you'd tell me, wouldn't you, if this guy felt dangerous to you?"

In fact he felt absolutely lethal, but not because of the darkness in him. "I'll be fine. Go on now."

"Okay. Not that he's going to wake up anytime soon, I can promise you that, but swear on Dash's squeaky cow you'll call me the minute he even *looks* like he's coming to. I mean it."

She nodded. "Gotcha, Doc."

He took his leave, locking the door for her on his way out.

Caroline grabbed one of her crutches and went to the fire to add more wood. She just couldn't get warm. She fetched a blanket for herself from the closet behind her chair, sat down in her armchair again and wrapped herself up. The moments crept by, while she watched and waited for her Adonis to wake up.

His inner hunger kept gnawing at her. When she began to feel like one of Dash's rawhide chews, she leaned forward in her chair and took his hand. The physical contact made her feel like a soda straw. Unconscious or not, he sucked her emotions right out of her. Hungry, hungry.

She held his hand only long enough to realize that his skin wasn't warm anymore. What was wrong? Maybe wool blankets weren't going to cut it. She one-crutched her way back to the closet again to get her electric blanket, wincing with every step. After her romp in the snow, her muscles and joints would probably scream all night.

Dragging the electric blanket off the shelf, she returned to Sleeping Beauty, set her crutch aside and stood on her aching leg while she covered him and turned on the blanket.

Dropping herself back into her chair, she caught her

throbbing stump close to her and eyed the pain pill and glass of water, still where John had left them on the table beside her. It would be so good just to have a little relief. She took the pill quickly, settled back in her chair and gave it a few minutes to work.

The electric blanket ought to be nice and warm by now. She felt the man's hand again. If anything, he was colder. Alarm skittered along Caroline's spine. When she opened herself up to him a little, his rush of despair took her breath away. He was suffering, and she could feel his need for relief as clearly as she felt her own.

She squeezed his hand. "Looks like we're both in pain tonight. Only thing is, I can't figure out what you need unless you wake up and tell me. I—"

An image swam through her mind like a lean, dark fish, in and out of shadow, first clear, then obscure. Her heart skipped a beat.

"Hey, Sleeping Beauty, are you trying to reach me?"

Closing her eyes, she squeezed his hand again and focused on the image until it was clear in her mind. He lay on a beautiful bed in a castle chamber. She stood poised over him, ready to wake him with a kiss.

With a hiccup of laughter, Caroline dropped his hand and leaned back in her chair. "Either you're a wise guy, or that pain pill's about to zonk me good."

The image persisted. She couldn't shake it from her mind. She could almost smell the tallow of the candles burning low beside the bed he lay in. Without warning, the vision exploded, sucking her into it.

She was there, bending over to kiss him. Closer.

Closer. His lips were firm and dry and perfect. Warmth poured out of her into him. She felt him soak it up and send it rushing back into her, hotter than before. She gasped as it spread pleasure through her soul and body. Her pain became a shuddering beast that couldn't reach her. She pressed her mouth to his and let the waterfall sweep her down into an ocean of euphoria.

Drifting into a bed of cotton that felt remarkably like her own bed, Caroline imagined she felt the stranger's mouth move under hers. Delicious. Pure fantasy. She could count the kisses she'd had on one hand, and they'd never made her feel like this before.

She even thought she felt him close his arms around her and pull her closer. It felt so good to be held like that. He was definitely warm now. Long, strong fingers caressed the back of her head gently, rhythmically. It felt so real that she moaned.

The coaxing, big hand tangled in her hair, and the warmth of his body beneath her lured her into the balmy shadows.

Just before sleep claimed her, she thought she heard a raspy murmur, British, sexy and very male. "Thank you."

Chapter 2

Meical Grabian managed a smile when the girl nuzzled against his chest hair, but when she nestled her soft body closer, it raked open a hole inside of him. His unclothed flesh felt every inch of her. Her closeness dulled his appetite a little, but it wouldn't stave off the inevitable.

Something about this woman was special, something he couldn't identify. She had felt his need out there in the cold darkness, felt his very soul reaching for hers. Was that why the Alchemist had left him close enough to call to her?

The Alchemist. Meical curled his lip to snarl, but without the three-quarter-inch fangs he was used to wielding, the effect was rather pathetic. He ran his tongue over his smooth, straight teeth and hissed.

Where was his maniacal creator? He focused his bleary eyes on the confines of the cabin. No sign of the hell-bat. The great Alchemist, Benemerut Neshi himself, had abandoned him.

Something must have gone wrong, and Neshi had reckoned he wasn't worth saving. Or, perhaps, he couldn't be saved.

Best to face facts. His strength was waning like the hours of the night. Every nerve in his body told him he had less than two hours until his first dawn in two centuries. It would be his last. All he wanted was to survive long enough to see it.

And here in his arms lay his portal to the sun.

He ran his hand over the woman's shoulder. His palm tingled from the softness of her burgundy flannel shirt. He swept his hand lower, down her narrow back and over her round bottom, feeling his way downward to the thigh of one supple leg, until he came to—nothing.

The leg of her jeans was empty below her knee.

He gently palmed the joint beneath the denim. Even in her sleep, she flinched when he touched her there.

"Not that I'm going soft," he breathed into her hair.

Hunger twisted his muscles into knots, and he savored the taste of her creamy, soft ear. She moaned in her sleep. The sound filled him with need, and on sheer instinct, he kissed her mouth quickly.

A pool of energy radiated from her into him. With a growl, Meical lapped up the nutritious tease without really knowing how he did it. The girl moaned again and moved against him. He groaned, harder and hotter than he could ever remember, nearing a desperation he'd never experienced as a vampire. No, he'd never felt hunger like this before. It made him feel capable of doing anything to satisfy it.

Slow down. Slow down. He ground his teeth together, fisted his hands in agony and grappled with his self-control.

Quiet filled the room. The snapping fire and the whistling wind were the only sounds to be heard, besides the girl's soft, sighing breaths. She whimpered something in her sleep, and across the room, a growl caught Meical's attention. The dog, of course.

He sighed and focused his thoughts on the shepherd. She kept her distance but bared her teeth. His probing mind met with a barrage of canine angst and territorial zeal, along with an image of his ankle caught in her salivating jaws.

Meical grinned, in spite of his pain. *Good dog. But what you really want to do is go to sleep. I need your lady's undivided attention right now.*

For a moment the dog eyed him, then with a yawn, rolled onto her side and slept.

Meical looked at the girl in his arms. His last feed. He ought to have a really close look at her, just to commemorate the moment. She was a pretty vision to take with him, wherever he was bound.

"What do you say, sweet?" he murmured. "Send me off to my death with nothing on my mind but you."

He smoothed her ash blond bangs out of her eyes and filled both of his hands with her thick short curls. Her mouth was painfully tempting, rather pouty at present, full and ripe from his kiss. Her high cheekbones suggested integrity and character. She was probably a force to be reckoned with when she was mad. Her delicate, flyaway eyebrows made her look perpetually amused with the world, even though she'd obviously had little to laugh at lately.

Meical kissed her again, gently, savoring her waking response. It must be an automatic reaction in his prey to what he was now—whatever that was. Kiss your prey, and she wants more. Simple and straightforward.

So what had gone wrong with the Alchemist's experiment?

Meical kissed her again, and then he did what he had done on a thousand nights as a vampire. He reached for her inner being, and with a thrust of his will, took possession of her soul.

Sweet, merciful heaven, this lady was a fountain of fire. But sadness had turned her cold and still inside. He sucked in a breath between his teeth. She needed to be touched, needed to trust again, but she was afraid of losing herself.

Primal terror haunted a cavern in her soul. She kept a close guard on that place. Even now, her soul rebelled against his invasion. He shouldn't pry. The least he could do was leave her privacy intact. But he just had to know. What was she so afraid of? He struck deep.

The violence of what her attackers had done to her played itself out before him in vicious clarity. Metal baseball bats rose in the darkness and descended, over and over again. He could hear her legs shatter, hear her scream.

Suddenly, the memory grew dark and fuzzy, and then

Meical watched as though through a haze. The girl was only semiconscious now. Her attackers moved in for the kill.

Wait. She shouldn't be able to remember any of this, not in her condition. And if she couldn't remember it, there was no memory for him to see. So he shouldn't be seeing this at all.

Yet he did see it, and as her attackers closed in on her, rage shook him, and he sounded a menacing growl.

The two men spun around to look at him.

For seconds Meical forgot to breathe, while the two human faces before him contorted with mute terror. They dropped their bats and scrambled out of the cellar as fast as they could.

Meical was drawn along like a balloon on a string in their wake, as though he were chasing them. Just as he hit the top of the stairs, his strength wavered and drained away, and he couldn't hold the image in his mind.

Darkness descended, and he opened his eyes to see the rustic cabin ceiling above him.

With a curse, he slid the woman off him, weary and hurting. In his condition, there was no telling what kind of confusion he was suffering from. It hardly mattered because there was no way on God's green earth he was going to make use of this girl. He couldn't.

He would leave. Just go. He'd put this feast far behind him. Maybe he'd last long enough without sustenance.

He made an effort to get to his feet. Half an hour later, he was still trying. His strength had deserted him, and in its place he felt a fire in every muscle and nerve, as though his hunger would tear his flesh from his very bones. He'd never suffered like this as a vampire, even on the leanest nights. But dawn was coming. He could feel it in his flesh. If he could just hang on.

The girl stirred beside him. His heart pounded like a piston in his chest, and he wrapped his hand around hers. A trickle of her life force flowed into him, a pitiable tease that served only to torture him.

"Do us both a favor, baby," he gasped. "Don't wake up."

He moaned again, and as if in answer, she rolled over, laid her good leg over his thighs and wrapped her arm around him. Her soft, sleepy breath against his chest felt so soothing, as soothing as her need to be held.

A throb in his chest shut off his next breath, and he gasped, choked and writhed. Fear consumed him. He wasn't going to make it until sunrise. To come so close and die without seeing it…. He couldn't bear that.

Meical fixed his gaze on the woman's face and closed the door on his good intentions. Levering his arm underneath her, he lifted her onto him again. When her chin rested on his chest, a momentary smile touched her mouth.

He cupped her face in his hands, breathing hard. He was too weak now to reach for her mind, so he spoke to her aloud, trying to keep his voice low and gentle. "Wake up. Please?"

She fluttered her lush dark lashes. When she opened her eyes, they were too dilated for him to see what color they were. Beneath her confusion, he sensed her struggling against the compulsion he had saddled on her, yet her unleashed hunger poured over him like warm cream. Hunger for him, as though it were her natural need.

Her husky, breathless voice touched him everywhere. "Oh...you're awake..."

Awake? Meical winced. He was as hard as— "Yes. Very."

Her gaze fell to his mouth, and a sigh escaped her. Her face turned white, then red, then white again. She looked down at his bare chest. "What's happening to me?"

"It's all right." He caressed her face. She shivered all over him. "I'm the guy you saved. Do you remember? I feel what you feel, and you feel what I feel."

She nodded. "You're an empath. Like me."

If it made things easier for her, why not let her believe it? It wasn't entirely untrue. He settled for half a truth, unable to out-and-out lie to her—which bothered him. "Yes, I am. Sort of. It's okay. This is only a dream. You're safe."

They locked gazes. She seemed to revive a little because even though her eyes said she wanted him desperately, her frown said she didn't trust his words.

"No," she murmured. "I'm awake. I can tell. What's going on? What are you...what are you doing to me?"

"What's your name?"

Her gaze darted away. "Caroline."

Sweet. A name fit for a Yorkshire girl. "Just Caroline?"

She nodded. When she looked at him again, the softness had gone from her eyes, leaving only caution. It put his teeth on edge. So, it was en garde, was it?

He might have just enough strength to finesse her through this. If it came down to a tussle, it would be costly for both of them. He absolutely must not lose control. He ran his hand over the crown of her head and down her back, opening himself up to her completely. Almost without trying, he poured himself into the caress.

She gasped and jerked, but he held her. Exquisite.

"I'm Meical Grabian," he whispered. "And you, Caroline, are mine."

Her throat worked convulsively to swallow, while her eyes gleamed, then darkened. As he lowered the mantle of his power over her, the last of her resistance faded. The rush of her arousal snatched his breath away.

He kissed her mouth slowly, then deeply, and held her while she came off her ruddy hinges. Her hands opened and closed on his chest, while her body ground against his.

Meical groaned when the first flush of strength and power surged through him. For a moment, he drifted into mindless bliss. He felt no pain. Only power. By the time he realized it wasn't his arousal, but hers, that brought him relief, she was mouthing her way downward along his abdomen.

He laughed softly, shuddering over the irony of it. It was his prey's pleasure that fed him, not his own. *Oh, yesss....*

He caught her face in his hands and stilled her searching mouth. She whimpered and undulated downward, closer to her goal.

"Caroline," he whispered, "I have a better idea."

Lifting her head, she blinked her big, sleepy eyes at him, panting softly.

"Come here."

She rose and wobbled into his arms, flush-faced and beautiful. His prey. His.

While he gathered her in one arm and unzipped her jeans, he focused all his will on her. He slipped his hand inside her panties and hissed out a breath. So warm and wet. Her breaths came in soft gasps while he gently parted her with his fingers and stroked her slowly.

Tears welled up in her eyes. Meical watched them roll slowly down her cheeks. Why was she crying? She was too deep in his trance to be frightened, and by her body's response, he knew she was enjoying this. She moved for him as though she had been made for his touch.

He nuzzled her temple and reveled in the nourishing heat of her rising need. "Why are you crying?"

Her gasped answer followed every shudder of her flesh beneath his hand. "It's been so long…"

Meical grimaced. "Don't let what they did to you take away who you are."

"I'm trying."

Meical pressed his mouth against her ear. "You are strong. You are powerful. I feel it inside you. All the strength you need is there, Caroline. Inside you. You will overcome this time in your life. And when you do, you will be more beautiful and powerful than ever before, in the way all humans are when they've gone through hell and survived it."

He looked into her half-closed eyes, hoping she'd

heard every word. He couldn't let her remember much of this when she woke, but he didn't want her to forget what he'd just told her. "You'll sleep for a while after this, and when you wake, there will be no pain in your leg. I would like to do more for you, but I…I'm headed elsewhere. I think it's best you don't remember me. But I want you to remember how strong and beautiful you are, Caroline. I don't ever want you to forget it."

She nodded compliantly. Hunger shone in her eyes now. No more tears. Meical rose up on his elbow and kissed her until they both moaned. Opening himself up completely, he swallowed down her pleasure and turned it back on her. Sweet madness.

She filled her hands with his hair and kissed him feverishly while he caressed her, until with a high, keening cry, she spilled the very essence of her life force into his soul. Raw power snapped through Meical's body, through every nerve and vein. He clutched her closer to anchor himself in the fury, glutting himself in her pleasure with a hellish growl he couldn't help. For a few precious seconds, he wanted to go on existing, to drink up this beautiful human being whenever, however and wherever he pleased. Never had he felt so horribly powerful.

How could Neshi have failed? What could possibly have gone wrong? It all seemed so perfect, so easy.

When Caroline fell still, Meical basked in her afterglow as though it were his own. He closed his eyes and listened to her breathe. Her soft sighs made him want to begin again.

He drew a deep breath and stood up. He no longer felt

weak. Warmth and strength surged through him. Blood was a pale shadow by comparison. This satiation went deeper.

He righted Caroline's clothing and smoothed her hair, letting his hand linger on her face. Did she have family or friends living nearby? Someone who could help her when she needed it?

"Not that I care," he murmured, covering her with a blanket and tucking it close around her. "And that's best for you because believe me, baby, you wouldn't want me around if you knew what I am."

The dog woke again and watched him with soulful eyes while he gathered his clothing from the chair before the fire. He grinned at the shepherd. "You are one lucky dog to belong to this lady. You know that, right? Better take good care of her."

He pulled on his jeans, but zipping them up was another matter. Meical looked down at himself and whistled softly. "Neshi, my man, never let it be said that you aren't a perfectionist."

Meical grinned and zipped up his jeans—carefully— and finished dressing. Without warning, he shivered. It was a familiar feeling.

Dawn.

The sensation stole over his spine like pinpricks. Soon every soul he knew would be wrapped in the deep sleep of the vampire. But this time, the day-death would pass him by.

He went to the door of the cabin, opened it and stared at the night sky. There was a bit of light blue toward the east. He slipped out the door and fixed his gaze on it, drank it down.

There was pink. Rosy pink. Only hours ago, it would've been enough to kill him. Neshi's experiment hadn't been a complete failure.

Meical bounded into the yard and skidded to a halt in the snow. His heart thudded in his chest, while the pink became orange. Beautiful fiery red came next, but it was the gold he wanted to see, the bright, gold-white light of a new day, full in his face until it blinded him and burned its way into his memory forever. He'd take it with him wherever he was bound.

Defiant, he shot into the air. Birds in the trees took flight around him. The wild things ran for cover.

Higher. Higher. It was brighter now. So bright. Too bright. Oh, yes! Nearly there. Nearly sunrise. He let the fragile warmth engulf him, felt it all the way to his soul. His face, his head, his entire body were warm in a way he hadn't felt in two centuries.

The ball of fire and life topped the horizon and blasted away all the night, all the darkness, all the pain and isolation. Meical flung back his head and let his exultation fill the world below. "Neshi, you are a GENIUS!"

Closing his eyes, he basked in the golden glow that touched every inch of him. The sun rose higher, while he hung suspended in its light.

Voices echoed up to him from the woods far below. He ignored them. He wanted only the silence and the light, clean and pure and unending.

The voices became clearer, and the smell of human

males tainted his serenity. Meical growled and turned his head to look down. It was just a pack of hikers, laughing as they slogged along the trail that passed Caroline's cabin. They were harmless, pleasant enough fellows.

So why did he have the urge to rip their heads off?

The contentment of the moment paled as Meical hung lazily in a sunbeam and eyed their progress closer to Caroline's home. As they trudged along, their heavy, sweating bodies made crunching noises in the snow with every step they took. Even that bothered him.

Surely they weren't foolish enough to come so close to Caroline, to encroach on what was his. Never mind that he wasn't going to be around much longer. While he was still breathing, she was his to protect.

With another glance at the sun, Meical dropped out of the sky and landed soundlessly in the woods. Seconds of icy wind in his face and an easy burst of speed brought him to Caroline's porch. He slunk into a pool of shadow the sunlight couldn't reach and dissolved to watch the intruders.

As the hikers reached the cabin, one of them made the mistake of stopping to admire it. Meical scarcely felt himself move. He materialized and stepped from the shadows of the porch, into the yard. Judging by the guy's change of expression, he must look like the devil's own. The men hurried on, casting nervous glances over their shoulders at him.

Meical glared at the woods with the irksome feeling that it might spew forth a host of similar trespassers. Caroline was alone and unprotected, hurt and vulnerable.

What harm was there in lingering awhile, as long as his hunger stayed at bay? She had friends, no doubt, who would come to her soon. He would wait and see. And while he hung around, he'd see what he could learn about her—not that he cared who she was, of course, but there was no point in dying with a lot of questions disturbing his peaceful last moment.

Meical reentered the cabin without opening the door, so as not to wake her, and had a look around. There was a closet with a pair of jeans and some sweaters in it. Three single left shoes stood all in a neat line. Their companions lay discarded at the back of the closet in a pile.

Dog-eared paperbacks lined the mantel and overflowed from a small bookcase nearby. Meical ran his hand over the titles. Most of them were novels. Jane Austen seemed to be a favorite, although he spotted a number of her predecessors and contemporaries. There was some nonfiction, too, droll and dry and not particularly enticing. But a pattern began to emerge. By the time he'd looked through all her books, rummaged through all her DVDs and flipped through all her CDs, he began to realize Caroline's peculiarly limited taste in escape and entertainment. His chosen prey was a walking compendium of eighteenth-century British life.

Meical let his gaze wander to the dark beams of the ceiling above. It would be just like the Alchemist, given his twisted imagination, to think Caroline's interest in the day and age Meical had known as a human would somehow make her more conducive to what Meical needed from her.

Magazines lay strewn in front of the bookshelf. Meical knelt to thumb through the titles. *Counseling Today. The Holistic Counselor. The American Journal of Juvenile Psychology. The Child Psychologist.* There were other magazines of the same type, too many to suggest a casual interest in counseling children. It must surely be her profession, or had been.

How had Caroline ended up on the wrong side of people who were sadistic enough to bash her legs to bits and leave her to die? Who were they? And where were they? And how difficult would it be to find them and wipe them off the face of the earth?

Meical quirked a brow. It was something to consider if not for the fact that he'd probably be dead by nightfall.

He prowled the cabin for anything else that might tell him more about Caroline than her love for his moment of history and her professional interests. There was nothing, not even a photograph on the wall. Did she have no family, then? Perhaps *that* was why Neshi thought she was the perfect fatted calf. No ties meant no one cared, should something happen to her.

Well, something had. *He* had happened to her.

He watched her curl into a ball of vulnerability on the bed and realized with a mixture of regret and longing that he might be inclined to elude death a while longer.

Chapter 3

She definitely had more respect for John's meds.

Caroline's brain felt like mush, but her body told no lies. She grinned, stretched long and hard, and with a shudder of delight, curled up under the blankets of her bed, languid from head to toe.

When was the last time she'd had one of *those* kinds of dreams? About a faceless stranger, no less, a delectable man who knew just which buttons to push.

She had felt no fear. No fear of being powerless, no fear of being hurt. She'd felt only pleasure and a sense of her own sexuality she thought she'd lost forever.

The sound of her own laugh surprised her. It sounded free. Happy. Neither fettered with cynicism nor laced with an undercurrent of tears. Maybe she was finally healing inside.

Dash's ecstatic bark broke the still morning. There was only one thing that provoked that kind of joy in her dog and that was chasing her squeaky cow. But she didn't play with just anybody. Who was out there with her? Not her patient, surely.

She sat up and looked around her empty sunlit cabin. His clothes were gone. He'd really recuperated quickly. Maybe all he had needed was warmth and rest.

Caroline grabbed the closest of her crutches, surprised to find them propped up within reach instead of by the chair where she'd left them last night. She was halfway to the window when she realized she wasn't hurting this morning.

Maybe the medicine was still in her system. Even so, she'd have expected to feel more stiff and sore than usual after her romp in the snow and sleeping in a chair all night.

But she hadn't slept in the chair. She had awakened in bed. She'd been moved from the chair at some point and never even realized it. Caroline's face flushed blister hot, and she looked over her shoulder at her rumpled bedcovers.

That dream…

No way. No matter how real it had seemed, it had only been a dream. She wouldn't climb into bed with some guy she didn't know, no matter how drugged out she was. Her Adonis had obviously been nice enough to move her from the chair to the bed when he woke up. Considering the condition they had found him in last night, it was amazing he'd had the strength to do it.

She peered through the frosty glass of the window,

but all she could see was Dash dancing around someone who looked real good in jeans. Who in the world…

Rubbing the condensation off the window, Caroline looked again. It was her Adonis. And by the look of him, he'd made a stunning recovery.

She dug her cell phone out of a drawer and dialed the number John gave only to close friends and family. While she waited for John to pick up, she eyed herself in the mirror over her dresser. She looked more rested than she had in weeks. In fact, she looked really nice for someone who'd just woken up.

John answered with an absent "hello."

"Hey, there," Caroline said, "just thought I'd let you know your patient's awake."

"Any sign of fever?"

She laughed. "Not a bit. He's up and at it, in fact."

The alarm in John's voice made her wince. "I've got one more patient to see, and then I'm on my way. Maybe I'd better call Millie to come over and wait with you until I get there, so you won't be alone."

"No, I'll be okay until you get here. I've got Dash."

Dash, who was at that moment selling her soul for another bout of catch with the stranger. If Dash trusted the guy, that meant he was okay. Caroline double-checked with a quick empathic probe of the man's emotions and sensed nothing threatening in him. His soul seemed to gleam with contentment.

After John said goodbye and hung up, she went to the kitchen sink to wash her face. Moments later, having brushed her hair and dressed, Caroline donned her parka and went outside.

She told herself it was just a lingering throb from her dream that made her ache inside when she saw her Adonis. He was just so beautiful to look at.

He stood with his back to her, looking up at the sun, with the sunlight glistening on his collar-length golden hair. He was a lot bigger and beefier than he had seemed last night. Easily six-three, with a build like Mr. Hard Body. He held Dash's squeaky cow poised in one bronze hand. The dog bounced around him, electrified by the joy that emanated from him, begging him to throw it.

The elation of man and dog filled the morning, washing over Caroline in waves of pure joy. She stifled a sigh. "You sure look better than you did last night."

He turned, and her breath hung in her chest. There should be a law against a guy looking this good first thing in the morning. He had electric gray-blue eyes that crinkled with suppressed laughter and a sun-bright smile, with perfect white teeth. When he looked her up and down, Caroline felt as if he'd embraced her. His energy wrapped around her, from head to toe. Part of her froze inside; part of her wanted to dive in.

She maneuvered off the porch, propped herself on one crutch and held out her hand. "I'm Caroline."

His hand was warm and callused. The instant he touched her, a rush of teasing humor poured out of him. "Meical Grabian. Thank you for rescuing me last night."

Caroline waited for him to explain how he'd managed to end up unconscious in a snowdrift. When he didn't, she dropped his hand and turned to pet Dash. She shouldn't pry. After all, *she* didn't like questions. He probably didn't, either.

"Hey, if you need to call home, you're welcome to my phone. Your family must be pretty worried."

"There is no one I need to call."

No family or friends? He was alone, then. Just like her.

"Need a ride somewhere? John will be by as soon as he's through at the hospital."

"John?"

The edge in Grabian's voice made her look up at him. His eyes narrowed, and caution wafted from him like an arctic wind. "John is my doctor and friend. He helped me bring you in last night."

His gaze fell and he seemed to relax. "I should thank him, too, then."

"Let me fix you something to eat."

He ran a hand over his middle but shook his head. "But you should eat. You're very hungry." He looked into her eyes, straight into her soul. "Perhaps I'll rediscover my appetite in a while."

He really did have the most beautiful eyes, the kind that held secrets she wanted to be in on. The rest of the world disappeared. She didn't think. She just opened her mouth and said it. "Look, you've obviously been through something terrible. If you need to talk to someone…I'm a psychologist. My specialization is juvenile counseling, but I may be able to help you. You just have to ask."

He had a nice laugh, the sort she'd call smoky because it came from deep in his chest like a dragon's chuckle.

"Being a counselor, I'm sure you know much more about this than I do, but isn't confiding a two-way street?"

Was she transparent or something? "Right. Well. Not that I wouldn't like to spill my guts to someone and have it turn out to be the best decision I've ever made, but sometimes life doesn't work that way."

He leaned closer and his gaze slipped over her again. "I'll make you a deal. If I ask you a question you don't want to answer, you can say so. The same goes for me. Fair enough?"

As fair as could be—and they'd both part ways as clueless about each other as they were now. What a lousy way to treat the only other empath she'd ever met. But she couldn't afford more. Maybe he couldn't either. And maybe that was for the best.

Caroline patted Dash again to avoid looking at him. "Okay. Come on in. I can at least make you some coffee."

He followed her onto the porch, as silent as a cat, and reached around to open the door for her. That put him close enough for her to see the lines of strain around his eyes. He definitely didn't feel up to full strength yet.

He sat at her table and watched her while she fed Dash, made oatmeal and ate. Did he even blink? Not a word passed between them, but she rode the steady hum of his emotions, which felt like floating on her back in a heated swimming pool. Interest, benevolence, total openness and beneath it all, unmistakable attraction.

Oh, cut it out. He's just one of those people who's naturally sensual. And it's not like you can keep him.

Caroline reached for her coffee and took a sip,

probing his mind a little. She'd done it so many times with her patients. He'd never know she was there.

Smack. She ran headfirst into a wall inside him, a big reverberating muscle of power as black as night and as thick as steel. What was he hiding on the other side? She surreptitiously plumbed the ethereal haze of emotion surrounding the barrier.

Grabian groaned.

Caroline jerked her gaze up to look at him. He sat with his eyes closed and a soft smile on his face—a knowing smile. Whoa.

He opened his eyes. "Why did you stop?"

She stared at him. One second his pupils looked dilated and his irises burned fiery red, and the next, his eyes were cool gray again. It had to be a shadow in the room or something.

She smiled ruefully. "Sorry. You shouldn't have been able to feel me checking you out."

His brow rose. "Your stealth leaves something to be desired."

"Oh, yeah?" She set her coffee mug down with a laugh. "Let's see you try to sneak up on me like that. I'll bet you my shield will hold."

Now *he* was laughing.

Caroline gave him a come-hither wave of her hand. "Come on, let's see what you've got."

His smile widened. "Are you sure?"

"Yeah, I can handle it."

"You won't take it personally?"

"You're just scared, aren't ya?"

He laughed again, shaking his head. Oh, such a

smug and superior man, but oh, so gorgeous when he grinned.

Caroline mimicked his posture, crossed arms and all. "Go ahead, buster, hit me with your best shot. Come on and—"

The words hung in her throat. Grabian locked on to the center of her being so hard she had to grab the sides of her chair. That was no probe. That was an all-out delving dive, right down to her soul. And it felt really, really good.

Better than good.

"Hey…" she moaned, "…enough…"

His teeth grated, and his smile hardened. He closed his eyes and—

"Ohhhhh…"

Everything in Caroline ran like a river, bleeding into the thrust of power that surged into her, manifesting itself in her body as pure, raw pleasure. A roar in her ears swept everything away but the sound of her own labored breathing. The splash of sunshine on the floor dimmed to splotchy gray. A heartbeat away from cataclysmal ecstasy, the gray turned to black.

The next thing she knew, Grabian was picking her up off the floor. "You were saying something about your shield?"

Caroline looked up into his teasing gray eyes and waited for the three of him she was seeing to stop circling like vultures. "Not funny. That was below the belt."

His gaze slipped over her and he grinned.

She laughed. "Okay, so that's a poor choice of words, but what you just did to me was overkill."

He lifted her into her chair and gave her a friendly pat on the back. "Nothing personal, remember?"

"Yeah, right. Never mind how you did it, just tell me why."

He returned to his chair across from her and sank into it with a graceful shrug. "I wanted to give you back some of what you gave me last night."

"Hold on, I never gave you anything like *that*. All you needed last night was someone to pull you out of the weather, throw a few blankets on you and keep you warm." But the blankets hadn't warmed him. Not even the electric one.

He'd sapped her warmth from her last night, drunk it down like a thirsty man in the desert, and only then had his body warmed. She had eased his emotional emaciation, seen him go from starving to robust. But overnight? Unbelievable.

Caroline leaned forward. "You *are* an empath."

He hesitated, running his tongue over his upper lip. "I have empathic abilities."

Which wasn't the same as saying, "Yes, I am an empath," but he was probably as reluctant as she was to disclose that to anyone. "I knew it. But how did I give you what you needed? How does that work?"

"Haven't you ever met someone who drained your energy and left you feeling lifeless?"

"Lots of people, yes, but they're not empaths, and they don't do it on purpose. And they sure don't do it like that. Last night, you just…took what you needed."

"But you trusted me, didn't you? You trusted me not to take it all."

Caroline looked down at her lap with painful, reckless hope that vied with her self-preservation. He was someone like her. She could learn so much from him. And he could learn a lot from her.

But that didn't matter. As long as Rivera kept sending men like Burke after her, she was no good for anyone. She'd only get Meical killed.

"You're in such pain," he whispered.

And suddenly there was nothing in the room but that whisper. She raised her gaze to his and couldn't look away. His eyes were pewter gray again, cool and soothing. Gray mists swathed her, wrapped around her body, caressing...

"You have nothing to fear from me."

But it was fear that had kept her safe.

"You trust me completely. You know you do."

His mouth seemed close enough to kiss. She wanted that kiss so badly.

"Take what you need from me. I'm yours."

Yes, she'd take him. All of him. She'd never get enough.

Halfway into the hungry fog, Caroline's inner senses picked up a quiver of desperation coming from somewhere beyond the cabin. She came back to herself with a jolt and jerked her head around to look out the window. Two throbbing, familiar waves of hurt and confusion reached her.

"Oh, no. Not again."

* * *

Meical latched on to the slap of emotion that hit Caroline about two seconds before she plucked up one of her crutches and half hopped, half hobbled to the door. Her dog leaped up and followed her.

Caroline threw the door open. Outside stood a pair of children, shivering with cold and panting from their exertions. Relief swept over the face of the little girl when she looked up at Caroline. The child clutched her companion against her, though he was nearly as big as she was.

The little girl's gaze lit on Meical, and she took a step back and dragged the boy behind her protectively. There was no emotion on the boy's face. He stared at nothing and made a high-pitched chirping sound like a wounded bird.

Judging by the rush of adrenaline that heightened Caroline's luscious natural scent, she anticipated danger on the approach. She eyed the area beyond the cabin, although she greeted the children with the calm, controlled tone of a professional.

"Hey, Sandy. Hi, Ray. Come on in."

Meical scanned the area, too, a little bit farther than Caroline could. What had she anticipated?

Caroline drew the children into the warm cabin, closed the door and sat down on the sofa. Sandy cast wary looks at Meical, but when Caroline hugged her close, she seemed to go limp. Her little brother curled up in a ball at Caroline's feet. He looked to be about five or six, and his sister a couple of years older.

"Is it your dad?" asked Caroline.

Sandy nodded against her shoulder. "He just showed up out of nowhere this morning. Mama was downhill at the Petersons' borrowing bread so we can make cinnamon toast. Daddy…he…"

"Did he hit you?"

"I mostly dodged him. But then he swung at Ray. I had to get us out of there."

"But you couldn't go to the Petersons' because you didn't want your dad to follow you there and find your mom."

The girl nodded again.

Caroline hugged the child tight. "You did the right thing to come here. Do you think your daddy followed you?"

Meical suppressed a growl at the thought.

"I don't think so." Sandy sniffled, her eyes grew red and her thin chest rose and fell. "I think he stayed there to wait for Mama to come home."

Caroline reached into the drawer of the lamp table by the sofa and took out a cell phone. She dialed calmly, all smiles for the two children, while inside he sensed her outrage and fear for their mother.

"Hey, Sheriff, it's Caroline. Looks like Mr. Hicks has turned up again. Sandy and Ray are here with me, and they're safe, but Mrs. Hicks is due home anytime, and the kids think their dad is waiting for her to show up at their place. No, they'll be fine here until Mrs. Hicks wants them home. Yeah, better hurry. She's just downhill at the Petersons', and she's probably on her way back home by now."

She put the phone back in the drawer and lowered

herself onto the floor beside Ray. The little boy scooted closer to Caroline, peeping like a chick, put his head in her lap and his thumb in his mouth.

Caroline ran a hand over Ray's tousled, sandy-haired head. "I see Ray has turned into a bird today."

"At least it's not a robot this time," murmured Sandy. "That worried Mama sick. Coming over here to talk to you has helped him a lot, Ms. Bengal. He was okay until this morning."

Caroline nodded. "Well, Ray made a good choice. Birds can fly away from their problems, if they want to. Isn't that right, Ray?"

The boy flapped his elbows like wings.

Caroline's melodious voice nearly mesmerized Meical as much as it did the children. She was truly gifted. "When Ray feels safe, he'll be himself again. Right now, he's just hiding. The problem is, his friends can't fly with him. He's going to have to keep his feet on the ground so he can play."

Sandy slumped onto the floor and wiggled closer to Caroline. The three of them closed their eyes and sat quietly, while Caroline exuded comfort and safety that made even Meical relax. Her warmth and love filled the room like a fragrance. That was how she used her gift. She mended broken lives.

Who held *her* like that when she was frightened? The thought of another giving her comfort set his teeth on edge.

Well, the least he could do was aid Caroline's efforts with his own remedy for human fear. Meical engulfed Caroline and the children in a spell of relaxation and security. Sitting back in his chair, he watched them while it worked. Did Caroline have any idea how delectable she looked when she was sleepy?

The sound of a large vehicle lumbering to a stop outside ruined it.

Sandy Hicks sprang out of Caroline's arms and clamored to the window. "It's Dad."

Meical sighed and joined Caroline, who was trying to stand and commandeer her crutches at the same time. Her anxiety permeated the air.

"Sandy, have a seat," Meical said.

Sandy backed away from the window and hauled Ray up on the couch beside her.

Meical wrapped an arm around Caroline from behind and lifted her to her feet. He could feel her shoulder blades tremble against his chest and taste her righteous anger. "Let me take care of this for you."

She shook her head. "Mr. Hicks will punch your lights out."

"Better me than you."

A car door slammed outside and a heavy tread vibrated on the porch. Ray whimpered.

The door shook under Mr. Hicks's fist. "Sandy! Ray! I know you're in there. Get out here. Now!"

"Come on, Caroline," Meical urged. "Let me do this."

He looked down at Caroline's hands on his arm. He wasn't fooled by her shrug and offhanded tone. She was glad he was here. "Have it your way. At least John will be here to patch you up after Hicks breaks your nose."

Meical pressed his mouth closer to her ear and felt her catch her breath. "Thank you."

Before opening the front door, Meical released a tide of menace in the cretin's direction. The pounding ceased. He probed Hicks's mind. He was reconsidering making an ass of himself. In the quiet that ensued, the patter of the children's feet on the rug behind Meical sounded like sighs. He felt a featherweight touch on his right thigh and looked down. Ray stood beside him. The child wrapped one arm around Meical's leg and the other around his sister. He looked up at Meical with suddenly coherent, soulful hazel eyes. Meical reached down and chucked the boy's chin with his knuckles. With a quick smile, he opened the door.

"Good morning, Mr. Hicks," he said. He seized on the man's gaze and held it. "It's too pretty a day for this, don't you think?"

Hicks fell back a step and stared into Meical's eyes. His bulldog jaw hung slack for a moment, and he blinked. The man had mush for brains that were steeped in whiskey and not very sharp to begin with. Meical detected the scent of fresh blood beneath his clean flannel shirt.

He felt Caroline's hand on the small of his back. Warning him to be careful or urging him on?

Hicks rose up on tiptoe and looked over Meical's shoulder at Caroline. "Got yourself a boyfriend now, weirdo?"

Before he could think, Meical reached out and gripped Hicks by the throat.

Chapter 4

Meical squeezed the air out of Hicks's windpipe, enjoying the shade of purple that infused the man's lips. His quarry clutched at him with bulging eyes, then twitched nicely. When Meical realized the man's feet were swinging in the air, he laughed and lifted him higher.

A feral growl broke through his focus, somewhat louder than an enraged cat. Meical looked down. Ray squeezed closer to him and snarled up at Hicks with arms raised and fingers splayed like claws. Meical reflected. Inciting the little guy to violence would hardly impress Caroline.

He fought for control and let Caroline's angelic voice reach him. Sweet, cool water for his thirsty soul. Thirsty. Yes, he was. Terribly thirsty. Oddly, it reminded him of the blood thirst he'd known as a vampire. His soul was parched, his mouth like dry paper, his body yearning to be quenched. By her.

The wail of an ambulance sounded in the distance. Meical curled his lip and glared at the squirming human in his grip. "That would be Mrs. Hicks going to the hospital." He shook Hicks and roared, "Isn't it?"

The man gurgled, then nodded.

Caroline squeezed Meical's arm again. "Let him go, Meical."

Meical opened his hands and dropped Mr. Hicks. "If you ever come within a hundred feet of Ms. Bengal again, I'll kill you."

Hicks held one hand to his throat and struggled to his feet. "I'm gonna sue, you freak!"

Meical took a step toward him. "Wrong answer."

Hicks hightailed it to his truck, slung the door open and turned to glower at his children. "Sandy and Ray, get yourselves over here. We're going home."

The children refused to move. Hicks gave Caroline a menacing frown, but when Meical took another step toward him, he jumped into his truck, jerked the engine on and sped away, narrowly missing the sheriff's car and Suburban coming around the bend.

Meical eyed the newcomers and swore. "Caroline, you've no end of visitors this morning."

Caroline went to meet the sheriff and the owner of the Suburban. Meical watched her, suddenly weary. And this thirst…no, he definitely wasn't himself.

Maybe this was how he'd end. He'd just go out like a

fire. But not here, not where it would cause trouble for Caroline. No point in that. Where then?

Meical searched the shadowy forest beyond the cabin. Anywhere would do, as long as it was as far from people as possible. He cast a glance in Caroline's direction. She and the others wouldn't notice his exit. He took a step backward, keeping his gaze on her, even as his eyes watered and his body began to chill.

A small, warm weight wrapped around his thigh. Meical looked down to find Ray attached to him. The adoration in the boy's eyes exhilarated him, even as it filled him with squeamishness. He reached down and disentangled the child from his leg.

"Sandy, take your brother and go help Ms. Bengal tell the sheriff about your dad."

Sandy took Ray's hand and ran down to the adults gathering by the sheriff's car.

Meical's legs shook underneath him so hard he had to sit down again. He'd rest just for a moment, then go. Leaning back against a post on the porch, he let himself drift, oblivious to everything but the hum of voices and the drone of the morning turning to midday.

"You're really something, you know?"

He opened his eyes, but squinted when they burned and watered. Caroline stood looking down at him, grinning. He smiled at her and yawned. "Sorry I lost it just now. I hope I haven't made things worse."

She eased herself down beside him with a shake of her head. "I'm glad you were here. You were right. They did have to take Mrs. Hicks to the hospital. Sheriff

Crantz says that jerk worked her over really bad this time. But she won't press charges. She never does."

She looked away and waved at her departing friend, who had put the two children in his vehicle.

"That's my doctor friend John, the one who helped me with you last night. He's taking Sandy and Ray to his place on his way to check on Mrs. Hicks at the hospital. He and his wife Millie will take care of them until their mom comes home."

The Suburban left, and the forest fell still around them. He was alone. Alone with Caroline. Finally.

Meical smiled when she shouldered her way closer to him. He could still feel anxiety oozing out of her like little rivulets of blood.

Blood? His jaw throbbed and tingled. He blinked his eyes open, holding his breath, listening to his body. The ache in his gums was all too familiar—but he wasn't supposed to sprout fangs anymore.

Was that how the experiment had failed? Was he some sort of hybrid now? Not quite a vampire, but not entirely incubus yet either? Of course, nothing so profane could live.

How long did he have? Hours? Another night? Another sunrise? No, he wouldn't have the chance to savor that again.

"Meical, when you confronted Hicks a moment ago, the rage I felt in you was…it was just…. Where does all that anger come from?"

Of course, she couldn't understand his behavior. But she was his; no one threatened what belonged to him. "That's one of those questions I can't answer, Caroline."

"Hey, you don't look so good."

Meical tried to focus on her lovely face. He caught her scent on the breeze. In half a heartbeat he was so hard he had to stand up, but when he did, he swayed on his feet.

She caught his arm. Her touch unleashed a swell of lust so harsh he groaned. What was happening to him? He'd always been able to count on his self-control. His body was responding to Caroline with a will of its own. He wasn't safe for her.

Another touch of her hand, and he didn't care. He swayed toward her, his gaze fixed on her mouth, while the heat of his lust swallowed everything around him the way he wanted to swallow her, burn her, take her. He wanted to shout at her to run for her life. Instead, he reached for her wrist to tug her closer, mouth open to devour her kiss, lungs heaving, heart on fire.

At the last instant, he saw her clueless half smile dissolve, and he was so sure she saw the hunger and madness in him that he turned away with a growl, eyes closed, straining for breath. He couldn't do this. This was not what he was. Nor would he ever let himself become…this creature…

But if he didn't go now, it would be too late for Caroline. At the end, he'd try to save himself by any means he could. He'd be ravenous. She'd be utterly defenseless against him.

Turning to glare at her, he used the last of his

strength to try to take control of her mind. *You will not follow me.*

Caroline smirked. "If you'll stop trying to convince me you're an ogre, I might let you stay for lunch."

"You have no idea what you're suggesting."

"Nothing scarier than ham sandwiches."

"No. I must go. Now."

She looked so hurt. "But you can hardly walk. I can feel your need for—"

"Yes, you can feel my need." Unable to keep from touching her, he caught her arm and jerked her closer. "And I promise you, if I stay, you'll be obliged to do something about it. Is that what you want?"

Stark fear bloomed in her eyes. He hated it, but perhaps it was the only way. He let his gaze slip over her and licked his parched lips. When he looked into her eyes, he let her see all the way to his soul—the hunger, the approaching madness, the death in him that would be the death of her.

But she stood her ground. "I've seen hell before, Meical Grabian. I'm still alive. If you'll let me, I can help you."

Meical shook his head, but it only made him dizzy. He let go of Caroline and grabbed the post behind him to keep from falling. The downy heat of her attraction to him vibrated through his body and eclipsed all else for a blessed moment.

He closed his eyes, soaking her up. "I'm warning you…"

"I'll consider myself warned, then. Shut up and let me get you inside where you can rest."

She opened the door and nudged him in. Meical scarcely felt his feet move across the cabin floor. He literally fell onto the sofa. He felt a blanket cover him and Caroline's soft caress on the crown of his head. For a moment, he fought the lethargy that sought to claim him. Was it the day-death? No, it couldn't be, because there was no pain. But he couldn't hold his eyes open, just had to close them and...

Sleep? After two hundred years of never resting... to rest in the way of mortals? Impossible. But it was happening. He was falling asleep.

The bed dipped, and he felt Caroline close to him. She hummed to him in a husky alto voice. Peace encompassed Meical, and he gave in.

Heaven help her if she was within reach when he woke.

A shady glen lay just ahead. It drew Meical onward. In such a place, one could crawl into the greenery like a wild thing and never be seen. It would feel so cool to his feverish skin. It was so hot. Where had the snow gone? It felt like a summer day.

The glen opened onto a clearing, and in the clearing was a tent, and outside the tent sat a woman dressed in a simple cotton dress. She was all alone. Dark-haired and dark-skinned, beautiful in a maternal, mature way, she fixed her gaze on him and smiled, even though he had yet to emerge from the trees.

Meical turned away, intent on putting as much distance between him and any living thing as possible.

He had to go and find himself a place to die. He had to. He couldn't go on.

"Would you care for something cool to drink?"

Meical shivered, then broke into a sweat. Slowly he turned to find the woman only a few feet behind him. No mortal was that swift and silent. He narrowed his eyes and tried to discern what manner of being she was, but there was nothing familiar about her, nothing to grasp at all, nothing to identify. Cosmically speaking, she was as close to nothingness as she could be. Was she even real?

Perhaps this was part of dying. She was a hallucination. Meical rolled his eyes. He might have hallucinated something more profound than a middle-aged siren out for some quality time with Mother Nature.

But it was her very nothingness that gave her presence such a peculiar strength. Or perhaps it was the way her eyes lured him. Meical found himself following her back to her tent like a sheep to the fold. She smiled regally and motioned for him to sit in a chair opposite hers. He could have sworn the chair wasn't there a moment ago.

She slipped into the tent and returned with a glass of cold tea. Beads of condensation formed on the glass and sparkled in the sun as she placed it in his hands.

Meical looked up to search her eyes. "Thank you."

She steadied his hands while he took a sip. His sensitive taste buds picked up on a taste that reminded him of something he'd drunk before, but he couldn't be sure what it was. It tasted green, sweet and a little tangy.

"It's good," he said. "What kind of tea is it?"

She had such a low, dulcet voice. "It's an old family recipe. I would tell you the herbs I use, but that wouldn't be fair to my ancestors."

He smiled and finished the entire glass without taking a breath. It made him feel invigorated and relaxed at the same time. Handing the glass back to her, he watched her set it aside on a table that seemed to have appeared out of nowhere. No, it had been there. He just hadn't noticed it until now.

Meical sat back in his chair, surprised by the subtle contentment that flowed through him. "Good stuff, your tea."

She sat down across from him, resting her arms on the armrests as though the chair were a throne, and regarded him with a small smile.

Meical thought he'd seen the height of exotic beauty in Queen Freya's countenance. But this lady, in spite of her years, was more beautiful than his vampire queen. He liked to see older women wear their hair long. She had the hair for it, too, thick and as black as a raven's wing. Her tawny almond-shaped eyes gave him the impression that she could take in the entirety of the clearing without shifting her gaze from his face. Eyes that missed nothing.

Momentarily wary of this hospitable lady, Meical pushed himself out of his chair. "Thank you. Have a good day."

He sounded like a bloody human.

"Are you going so soon?" she asked.

He turned and sat down again, uncomfortable with her disappointment. "I have little time."

"People are in such a rush these days." She looked away. "They used to call on me long ago. You wouldn't know it to see me now. These days, I am forgotten, except for a loyal few."

All of which was entirely too surreal to be borne, and none of which had a thing to do with him. But what could he say? *So sorry, but look at the time. I have to go off and die now.*

She spoke as though she were in her dotage. She didn't seem elderly, by any means. The sunlight slipped out from behind a cloud and cast the lady in a halo. The radiance suited her, even with a tent for a backdrop.

"*You* know how it feels to forget and to be forgotten." Her gaze returned to his, seeming exquisitely feline all of a sudden. "But in your case, I believe, *you've forgotten yourself.* You, Meical, have abandoned the man you were meant to be."

Maybe he had, but he wasn't going to share that with a stranger, no matter how good her tea tasted. "So, you're camping out here all by yourself, are you?"

She hesitated, eyeing him closely. "I came to help an old friend with a difficult situation. And I think I know, now, how I can help him the most. I am here to visit his brother as well. I knew them both long ago, way before your time on this earth."

She leaned forward and lowered her voice to a near whisper, as though to impart a secret. "I've already been in contact with his brother, but we're keeping my presence here a secret from him. I want to see what he's been up to, before I let him know I'm here."

"Have you found out yet?" he asked, although he didn't know why he should.

"Yes. He has been working long and hard to accomplish a great feat and he has invested all his hope in it. Many fear him because of it; others regard him as evil. But I have come to understand what he is attempting and know his noble heart well enough to see that it is a worthy goal he seeks to achieve."

Meical shifted in his chair, trying to string together some meaning from her words. It wasn't as though he hadn't been listening; in fact, the sleepier he became, the more he hung on her every word. "You sound sure of him."

Her gaze slipped over Meical, assessing and calculating. "I begin to see the good in what he has done, even as we speak. He can, I believe, be trusted with still greater things. I have plans for him and his brother. You would agree, I'm sure, how vital it is to be needed."

That hit too close to home—and this conversation was becoming ever more unreal by the minute. But he was so sleepy he couldn't pull together a suitable response. Meical rubbed his eyes, feeling as if he could drift away on the breeze.

What a good joke, to find Death was a woodland mater with a penchant for herbal tea. He'd laugh if he weren't so sleepy. He could think of worse things than crawling into a cot in the Grim Reaper's tent and falling asleep forever to birdsong.

But she wasn't Death. She couldn't be. Not with eyes like that. Not with a smile like that. But she *was* immortal. He could feel it in her presence. Who was she?

Perhaps he'd simply ask her. He opened his mouth to do so, but was momentarily distracted by a small cat that emerged from the tent and wrapped itself around the woman's feet. It was as ebony-black and soft as its mistress's hair.

"You're not alone after all," Meical observed.

"This is one of many. She brings me information about people I want to know more about. She recently visited a mutual acquaintance of ours, a charming person with great courage and a selfless heart."

Among the few people in Meical's world now, only Caroline fit that description. But, of course, this lady couldn't possibly know Caroline. None of this could even be real.

"Speaking of information," he strove to say, "who are you?"

"I can't tell you that. It might get back to my friend."

"I'm not likely to spoil your surprise. I'm not going to be around much longer."

The winsome light in her eyes dulled. "It's a mistake to leave such a beautiful place, don't you think? You have loved ones who will miss you. *She* will miss you terribly."

She? Caroline? Of course Caroline. No one else mattered. But this woman couldn't possibly know about her. Meical couldn't keep his eyes open another minute.

The warm sun and the cool breeze felt so good. He let the downy sunlit fog surround him.

"I'll only hurt her if I stay, and she's been hurt enough. Leaving is the best choice. I don't have the right to love her."

"Love is both the birthplace and the battleground of our sweetest choices. I promise you, Meical, it is strong enough to survive. And so is she. The question is, are you?"

That was the last thing he heard before he nodded off.

Chapter 5

How could anybody affect her this way in so short a time? It was infatuation. That was all.

Caroline cuddled Dash closer, where the two of them lay in front of the fire. She cast a glance at Meical, still asleep on the sofa. He hadn't moved in hours.

John had dropped by to check on him after lunch. He said his vital signs were okay—not wonderful, but okay. That was hours ago. It was well past sundown now, and still Meical hadn't even rolled over in his sleep.

His hands jerked suddenly, then curled into fists. A hoarse moan escaped him. Caroline sat up and scooted close to check on him. He seemed okay. Just dreaming.

She took his hand in hers, and her world turned upside down. She felt darkness everywhere and heard deafening noises. Cannons boomed so close she thought her skull would split. Waves of icy fear and hot rage poured through her, and the darkness lifted. She looked up at the smoke-shrouded sky through blood-smeared eyes, prostrate on a battleground in the dark of night, up to her ears in a pool of blood. The death wails of men and horses rose around her. The stench of gore and death clung to the back of her throat.

Caroline snatched back her hand and stared at Meical in horror. Empath or no empath, his dream seemed as real as memory. But how could it be? The soldiers she had seen wore the uniforms of British infantry—from the time of the Napoleonic Wars.

She took his hand again, raised her shields and let the dream swallow her.

Two ethereal forms filled her vision. One bent close, a woman with red eyes.

"We'll take this one, Ellory. Oh, yes. I must have him."

"No, Aloisia. Pass him by. Let us leave this place."

"But he won't survive. I think that's a shame. He's so young and beautiful."

"Indeed, madam. With a face like that, he was made for a heavenly choir—not a siren's bed. Slake yourself with me, but let the boy be."

Her cool fingers felt delicious to Caroline's pounding forehead. Her hand came away bloodied, but she sucked the blood from her fingers. "Mmm. Perfect. Tell me, sweet one, would you like me to make your pain go away and take you far from this dreadful place? You will be safe with me. But, of course, there is a cost. Ellory, you will carry him for me. We'll take him home with us. By tomorrow night he will be mine."

Powerful arms lifted her, and Caroline and Meical jerked simultaneously as the ground fell away beneath them. Darkness fell over her vision. The next images blasted through her mind, starkly vivid, but so disconnected that she couldn't follow them.

Pleasure and blood, death and rebirth, the sensation of leaving something behind and beginning anew...a sudden release burned its way through her body like a bolt of lightning, and she and Meical gasped together.

When Caroline opened her eyes, she was lying flat on her back, staring up at her ceiling, and Dash was whining and licking her face. Her entire body tingled as though every muscle had fallen asleep and was now waking up with a vengeance.

What had she just witnessed in that dream of Meical's? She had felt it as though she were one with him. Was it his death? Had he died that way in a past life?

No. Not death. She clasped a shaky hand over her eyes. It had felt more like a rebirth.

Dash growled at the door. The growl ended in an anxious whine. Intruder.

Caroline listened with her entire being. The stranger was male. He was alone. But he wasn't Burke. Beyond that, all she could sense about him was...

She focused. A shiver ran through her as she connected with a wall of raw power, and at the heart of him, a gaping emptiness that terrified her. Clutching at her crutches, she got to her feet and dug her can of Mace out of her dresser drawer.

Dash circled the room and whined like she was trying to find a place to hide. That wasn't like her. Normally she'd be tearing the door down to get to whoever was out there.

Caroline's upper lip beaded with perspiration. She locked both hands around the Mace can and waited. Dash began to howl as if a hundred sirens split the silence. The nameless wave of power advanced onto the porch like a tsunami and slammed against Caroline's shield so hard that she staggered backward. The rap on her door made her thoughts scatter.

Don't open the door, she told herself. *It's the last thing you want to do.*

Yet she found herself setting aside the Mace and walking to the door. She watched her hand grasp the doorknob, turn it and pull the door open. Wide open.

Dash retreated behind the sofa and fell utterly silent.

Black eyes flashed at Caroline from the half light of her porch lamp. The man's ebony hair fell in waves around his face and shoulders. With skin the color of café au lait, he was the most exotic person she'd ever seen. He would have been stunning if not for the hint of cruelty in his provocative smile. Like Meical, he wore no coat. Just a black turtleneck and jeans.

His voice was soft and deep, as mesmerizing as his eyes. "I've come for Meical."

The bolt of energy Caroline had sensed a moment ago evaporated suddenly. All he exuded now was a paradoxical mixture of aloof benevolence and a disinclination to be crossed. She couldn't quite place his accent. Middle Eastern, maybe?

Her mind cleared, and she closed the door until it was only ajar. For all she knew, this man was the reason Meical had ended up in a snowdrift. "How did you know he was here?"

"I followed him."

She longed for her can of Mace. "Why would you do that?"

His smile widened. He clasped his hands in front of him and said as though she were a child, "I am his physician and an old friend of his family. He's been in my care for some time."

But Meical said he had no one. No family. No friends. "What's your name?"

"Benemerut Neshi."

"Well, when he wakes up, Dr. Neshi, I'll tell him you came by. If he wants to see you, he'll contact you."

She pushed the door closed. It caught on something. She looked down. Neshi's black boot. It was dry, with no hint of mud or snow. That was weird. He was weird. This whole thing was weird.

Caroline met his gaze. "Don't mess with me, mister."

There was as much beauty as harshness in his grin, but when his grin faded, there was only resolve. "Meical needs me."

Who could look into that face, into those eyes, and say no? She opened the door and stood aside, eyeing the can of Mace that was way beyond her reach.

Neshi pushed past her and bent over the sofa. His hair partially concealed his face, but she thought she saw his mouth move. He placed one hand over Meical's heart and the other at Meical's temple. That was all. No stethoscope, penlight, tongue depressor, etc. No doctor stuff at all.

Caroline approached the bed. "He's been like this all day."

"When he wakes…"

"What?"

He straightened and met her gaze, eyes glinting in a way that sent another shiver up her spine. "He'll need nourishment."

She shrugged away her uneasiness. "I have a freezer full of Lean Cuisines on the back porch. I'll find something he'll like. Where did you say your clinic is?"

Neshi went to the fire and warmed his hands. Immaculate hands, large like Meical's, only darker. "I didn't say."

He said it with such finality that Caroline got the idea she wasn't to ask him again. "And you're his family's physician?"

"They put him in my care to avoid having to commit him."

Commit him? Caroline opened her mouth to scoff at Neshi, but all she could think of was the enormous strength and out-of-control rage she'd witnessed in Meical when he'd attacked Hicks.

She sank down to sit beside Meical and took his hand. Extending one crutch to fork the blanket up from the hearthrug, she spread it over him. If he had turned out to be alone, really and truly, she could have helped him. But family ties meant connections, and connections meant she could be found.

Yet her compassion—and every inch of her body— screamed, *Do it. Help him. Take him. Claim him.*

What was she thinking? She absolutely would not, could not get involved. She rubbed her temples, feeling dazed. The fire's heat reached her, hotter than it should be.

Trust him. You want to. You need to. Give in.

The glow from the flickering flames danced in Meical's golden hair, and his pale skin took on a swarthy copper look. His luscious mouth parted. In repose, he looked so sensitive. So in need. A weakness stole through her, bringing thoughts that made her face burn.

She hadn't thought of making love to anyone since Rivera's men had attacked her. Loving someone was a haven she'd never know again. It wasn't fair to Meical to pin her attraction on him. She couldn't follow through, and he obviously had enough of his own concerns.

She rose and sat down in her armchair to put some distance between them. "Tell me what he's been through, Doctor. What caused his problems?"

"Meical has lived with one foot in darkness and one foot in light, and between the two, he feels constantly called to return to something old and long ago." Neshi leaned against the mantel and ran a finger over her paperbacks. "He remains caught there, somewhere in his past. His grasp on the here and now is such that it was only a matter of time before he suffered a breakdown. He's emotionally unpredictable and subject to…an unusual psychosis."

Unusual psychosis? She'd helped patients through everything in the book. How unusual could it be? There was something Neshi wasn't telling her.

"Come on, you know as well as I do he's suffering from posttraumatic stress disorder. He has all the symptoms. And don't talk to me about his grasp on reality because that's more a matter of being oversensitive to emotion than a mental imbalance. He's trying to escape something, yes, but PTSD doesn't just happen out of the blue. Meical has been through a crisis of some kind. What happened to him?"

"I think it would disturb Meical for me to discuss that with you. He's done things, you see, things he's not proud of."

Like nearly kill people? Would he have killed Mr. Hicks if she hadn't been there to stop him? Caroline sighed. "Has he tried group therapy? I've seen it alleviate some of the struggle with PTSD."

Neshi shook his head. "He doesn't play well with others."

That didn't surprise her. Caroline looked down at Meical again. She could help him. She knew she could. Trauma was her specialty. Not to mention the fact that she understood Meical's response to whatever he'd been through. He was an empath. Empaths were, by their very nature, emotionally sensitive and reality-challenged.

But there were a hundred reasons why volunteering her services would be a stupid mistake. Burke was only one. The best reason of all was Meical himself. She didn't need to encourage herself in his direction. To say that she was unsure of her ability to maintain her objectivity where he was concerned would be an understatement.

If she took his case, she'd have to keep their relationship professional.

She looked up to find Neshi regarding her with unveiled mockery as though he could read her mind. The fire's golden flames turned his face to a bronze mask, making him seem like an inscrutable ancient god.

Neshi shoved his hands into his pockets. "I was his last chance. He hasn't responded to any of my treatments. But I can't have him wandering off unattended. He could hurt someone. I suppose he'll have to be incarcerated after all."

Caroline had seen how much Meical enjoyed the sunshine that morning when they were first getting acquainted. Being locked up would strangle him. He'd be a sponge in an asylum, with no way to shield himself from the emotions all around him.

"I can assure you, Dr. Neshi, if you institutionalize this man, he'll die inside. He needs to heal from the inside out. That takes a lot of trust and sharing on his part, and a lot of time and patience on yours."

"Forgive me, but the severity of Meical's emotional unrest requires a practitioner trained in psychology, not feel-good remedies and warm fuzzies."

Caroline felt a rush of professionalism she'd forgotten she had and embraced it like a long-lost friend. That was her only haven now, and nothing should ever change the way she addressed a colleague. "I'm a psychologist and a certified counselor. Trauma cases are my specialization. I was working on my Ph.D. in juvenile psychiatry last year when…something interrupted my plans. I still practice when I can. I…" She sighed. What was she getting herself into? "…I can probably help him."

Neshi crossed his arms and looked her over like a backstreet bully sizing up a new recruit. Caroline fought off the urge to squirm under his dark and assessing gaze, squared her shoulders and scowled back at him.

"You're offering to take him as your patient?" he asked.

Stupid, stupid, no, no, no, don't do it. "I am."

"What is your name?"

"Caroline."

"Caroline what?"

"You don't need to know that."

"Do you live alone?"

"What does that have to do with anything?"

He cleared his throat, all smug machismo. "Meical's particular psychosis will stress the boundaries you're accustomed to between you and your patients, specifically because you are *female*."

What did he take her for, a coward? How dare he question her ability? She glared at him. "It's just a leg I'm missing, not my common sense and professional ethics. Believe me, I can handle him."

Even though her shield hadn't held against his probe that morning. Even though he'd lain her flat on the floor with the force of his inner energy alone and probably hadn't half tried. Even though his probe had been the most erotic experience she'd ever had. No matter what, she couldn't let Neshi think she couldn't deal with a patient.

The doctor pursed his lips and smiled in a way that gave her the feeling she'd just been played by a master manipulator. "Very well. I'll inform his family. How much do you charge for your services?"

"I'll let you know when I'm finished with him. When I do, I'll expect to be paid in cash. No receipt. I'll start when he's feeling well enough."

The familiar grumble of John's Suburban pulling up outside eased the tension in Caroline's chest. At the doctor's knock, Dash sprang up, tail wagging. Caroline felt like she could have done the same. She admitted John, who took one look at Neshi, then at Meical and then at her.

Caroline nodded. "This is Dr. Benemerut Neshi, Meical's physician and personal watchdog."

If Neshi felt disparaged by her dig, he didn't show it. He stepped forward and offered John his hand. "Pleasure."

"This is Dr. John Calvin," supplied Caroline.

John shook Neshi's hand with a wry grin. "Glad to know Meical isn't all alone in the world like we thought."

"Thank you for taking care of him," Neshi returned.

John gave Meical a cursory examination and checked his pulse. "Got any Gatorade, Caroline?"

"Only the orange kind," she replied. "It sucks."

"Darlin', he'll be too thirsty to care."

"Yes," put in Neshi. "Dehydration is to be expected after what he's been through these past few days."

How could he even have noticed Meical was dehydrated? He hadn't done a thing for him since his arrival, and what little he *had* done didn't constitute much of an examination. Something about Neshi just wasn't right. Caroline went to fetch the Gatorade, but kept her eye on him. She couldn't penetrate his emotions. His barriers reminded her of that big, black wall she'd come up against in Meical earlier.

A groan from the sofa hastened her. When Neshi and John propped Meical into a sitting position between them, she touched Meical's icy cheek, held the glass of Gatorade to his lips and spoke his name.

His pewter-gray eyes jerked open. His gaze lit on her and his eyes darkened. Hunger flooded out of him, hunger for everything inside her. He growled deep in his chest, clutched her face with both hands and dragged her mouth down to his.

He heard Caroline scream inside herself. He could taste her fear and outrage. But that was only part of her response. She moaned against his mouth, even as she tried to push away, showering them both with orange Gatorade when she let go of the glass she held.

No escape. He couldn't afford to give her one. If he was dying, so be it, but he wasn't going to die suffering like this. He had never spared his prey before.

And Caroline was his.

John tried to haul her off him. Neshi intervened before Meical swatted the good doctor. The red-faced human was under a trance before his backside hit the chair the vampire shoved him into.

Caroline's dog paced and growled. Meical shot her a withering look. No time for patience. She retreated to the corner, but whined incessantly. Wrapping his shaking arms around Caroline, he kissed her until her inner screams were silent and her moans grew plaintive. Deep inside, she wanted him, but still she resisted.

He reached into her very soul and found the thread of thought she clung to. *Caroline, just let go and let me in.*

She jerked in his arms, and her hands closed into fists, but she didn't hit him. She just pushed against him, even while she locked her mouth on his and deepened her kiss.

Get out of my head. Now. Nobody touches me like this. Nobody. Let me go.

I'm going to die if I don't make love to you.

I'm sure there are plenty of women that line will work on, but not me. Let me go.

Caroline...please...I don't have time to argue...

The warmth of her arousal turned to ice. She recoiled from him, mentally and physically. When she lifted her mouth from his and their gazes locked, her eyes were the dull black of an entranced human, but underneath the shadow, Meical saw the fire inside her.

There. That was what she was made of, this woman he wanted to feast on.

Her thoughts scalded him inside. *I won't let you hurt me. No one will hurt me again. Not you. Not anyone.*

I swear I won't hurt you.

Meical caressed her face with both hands and pushed her toward an abyss of complete compulsion. He watched her fight, felt her grapple for her control. She was so strong she almost surfaced from beneath his power, but he opened up to her and let her feel exactly how devastating his hunger for her was. He made it her hunger. He'd make it hers all night long.

She gasped and arched against him, eyes wide, mouth open in a perfect little "oh." Between one breath and the next, he exploited her sudden weakness and dragged her under.

"Well done," Neshi said from across the room. "She'll wake to think you're completely insane and be smitten with all sorts of professional pity on your behalf— exactly according to plan."

Meical snorted. "What plan? I'm dying."

Neshi examined John's staring eyes. "Not *yet,* you aren't, but you're not helping yourself by trying to survive on foreplay. You never settled for tidbits as a vampire, did you?"

"Don't tell me you were watching us while we—"

"You are the test specimen, Grabian, and she is my lab." Dragging John Calvin out of the chair, Neshi lifted the doctor onto his shoulder. "Feed properly, and I may require less observation in the future."

Neshi opened the door without touching it. The soft, cold night wind blew in, sweetened by the scent of pine. Outside, the plopping noises of snow falling from trees in the yard dented the quiet night.

"Neshi," Meical called.

The vampire turned, his eyes agleam with hunger.

"Don't damage her friend. She depends on him."

"He won't know what hit him. I'll leave him on his own front porch, and I'll even end the evening with some professional chitchat."

"What about his car?"

"He'll believe I've given him a ride home. He'll come for his vehicle tomorrow."

Meical fixed his gaze on him. "All things considered... I should thank you for giving me back the sun."

Neshi's smile turned his blood cold. "Thank me if you live, Grabian."

Neshi disappeared into the night, and the door clicked shut behind him.

If he lived.

Meical shifted Caroline in his arms and looked at her. Her eyes were dilated and velvet black with arousal. His mouth watered. Pulling her close, he floated to his feet, deposited her in a chair and knelt in front of her.

"Caroline, can you hear me?"

She blinked at him and nodded with a half smile.

"I want you to put aside all your inhibitions. Do you understand? There are no obstacles between us."

"No obstacles."

"Good. When I let you wake, I want you to do the first thing you feel like doing. Don't think. Don't question. Just act on your very first impulse."

"Yes. Oh, yes."

His heart pounded. "You can wake up now."

She blinked again and stared at him. Her half-choking gasp and scarlet face told him she'd remembered what had just happened, but without her inhibitions to stop

her, she was as good as his. He readied himself to take
her in his arms and love her as she'd never been loved
before, to feed until he was utterly satiated, to glory in
her arousal, to—

He hardly saw her hand move. She'd slapped him
twice before he recovered from his surprise. Then all
he could see was her dainty finger at the end of his nose
and her eyes aglitter with rage.

"Never—ever—invade me like that again!" she
yelled.

She bounced out of her chair, hopping on her one
foot, and shoved him backward onto his back. Hands
on hips, she balanced there and glared down at him.

"Understand this, Meical Grabian. You are my
patient. I am your doctor. You will show me respect."

Her hands plucked nimbly at the buttons of her
blouse. Meical watched, mesmerized. No inhibitions.
None. "Yes, Caroline. Of course."

She whipped off her blouse and plopped down beside
him. "I won't have any of this sneaking in and out of
my mind like that anymore. Got that?"

His "Yes, Caroline" was swallowed by her kiss. She
filled her hands with his hair and pulled, nibbling his
lower lip until he wanted out of his jeans.

With a groan he rolled her over and kissed her mouth.
"Whatever you want from me, it's yours. Anything. Just
tell me."

"I want you to make love to me."

"Yes."

"I want you to…"

He paused in his kisses and looked down at her. "Yes?"

Her eyes glinted and narrowed. "I'm not afraid of you."

He fought to keep a straight face. "Evidently."

"But I should be."

"Should you?" he whispered. He bent and kissed her cheek, clinging desperately to the last vestiges of control that enabled him to parody a harmless human. "I won't hurt you."

"You…I…"

"Yes, that just about sums it up."

"Wait."

Meical hung in breathless despair, dangling from that one word. No. Not yet. Not when he was so close.

Caroline was coming out of her trance.

Breathing hard, Meical shook his head against her soft shoulder and scraped his fisted hands on the floor. He couldn't bring himself to back off, so he remained as he was, poised over her, and waited.

The silence in the room stung his ears.

"Look at me, Meical."

When he did, he saw no recrimination in her eyes, but her face was as white as the snow outside. "What are you?"

Chapter 6

Meical smoothed her hair out of her eyes. "I'm someone who needs your healing. Someone who needs *you*. Right now."

Her brow rose. "You *are* an empath, right? Like me?"

"Actually, I'm nothing like you. And considering what you've been through, I'm the last person on earth you should think of as your friend." Meical hardened his heart. "But I need you."

Her lower lip trembled, and her hands fell away from his face. Her eyes were dull again, but not from any preternatural trance of his. He could feel her struggling to hold on to who she was. "Look, if you've got a clinical addiction to sex, *this* isn't going to help. Get off me, and we'll talk."

An addiction. That was a tempting, easy lie. But he couldn't lie to Caroline. He just couldn't. "There's no way I can explain it to you. And since it doesn't matter whether you believe me or not, I—"

"It matters to me." She scowled. "I'm a psychologist. I want to understand your problem, okay? Is it like a need for emotional contact that can only be resolved through intercourse? Is it a compulsion? What?"

Meical caught the scent of desperation on her skin, mixed with that of her arousal. The combination stoked his hunger and pushed him closer to the edge. He let his gaze wander over her and watched the rapid rise and fall of her breasts beneath her shirt. He heard her breath catch in her throat and her heartbeat leap into a charge.

He met her gaze again. "It's nourishment, plain and simple. I need to feed. On you. On your pleasure."

The skeptical arch of her brow and her calm, nonjudgmental tone told him how hard she was clinging to the solace of her professional jurisdiction, all the safe, sane, familiar things that people used to combat the unexplainable. But that wouldn't see her through this. No. There was another way.

He bent and took her succulent earlobe in his mouth and teased it with his tongue. Her feeble protest ended in a soft moan. Her arousal flared, shoring up his flagging strength. When he was sure his blow would be swift and clean, he took her mouth in his again and plunged her into sleep so deep she wouldn't be able to come out of it without his help. Her sudden whimper tore out his heart.

But he had no heart. Best remember that.

Meical gave her a moment to drift off, then rose and carried her to the bed. He laid her down and undressed her gently, aching over the beauty of every cream-and-ivory inch of her that he unveiled. All the while, he struggled for a way to make the night sweet for her. He wanted it to be unforgettable, a truly healing experience. He wanted to give her something more precious to her than the pleasure he knew he could give her.

He took off his clothing, slipped into bed beside her and drew the covers over both of them. Pulling her into his embrace, he ignored his body's immediate reaction and took strength from the sleep-veiled undercurrent of desire that throbbed inside of her.

Somewhere in her mind, surely, there lay a conception of what Caroline wanted lovemaking to be, a fantasy she craved. If he couldn't find it, he would invent it. Strengthened by her closeness, he delved into her imagination with care. Where did she keep her secrets? Her prizes. Her joys and dreams.

He found a haven deep inside her where she'd tucked away a thousand images. All from books. Books, books and more books. His gaze rose to her paperbacks on the mantel and in the bookcase.

It would be so terrifyingly simple. If the Regency was what she longed for, he could give her this and more. He could create a dream out of her imaginings, endow it with the authenticity of someone born in that age and salt it with her favorite heroes and heroines. And when he'd wrapped her in the solace of her dream, he'd make his loving part of it.

Meical grimaced. Incubus, for sure.

But Caroline must believe she was the one in power; he must, in every respect, appear to be the powerless one. That was the only tonic for her fear of intimacy. Meical lifted her onto him and conjured the dream with care.

She'd always been here in this room. Hadn't she? No past. No future. The present was a thousand miles away from her.

Caroline breathed in the fragrances of heliotrope and roses and opened her eyes. She blinked in the sunlight that filtered in through an open window on her right. The light was so bright that it made a haze of everything. As in a dream.

She stood in the middle of a room she'd seen a thousand times in her dreams. But it was so real this time. Old oriental rugs on the hardwood floors. Beamed ceiling. The Chippendale furnishings, the reading nook at the window, the portraits of people whose faces she recognized from her nighttime wanderings.

All so real this time. She shivered, then broke out in a sweat, trembling while her body throbbed. Her breasts tingled, and an ache charged into her loins that made her slick and warm between her legs. She gasped in the hushed, golden room and wrapped her arms around herself.

No…those were his arms…embracing her…

Caroline turned around and stepped back. Meical stood there. Her questions were halfway out of her mouth when the butterflies rampaging inside her cut them off.

Gorgeous man. She drew a fluttery breath, looking him over without a thought for what he might think. His golden hair curled over the open collar of his loose, flowing white shirt. He wore the tight-fitting breeches and Wellington boots of a British gentleman. Perfect.

He indicated the room with a wave of his hand. "How did you do this?"

Uneasiness turned her butterflies to razor blades. "I was just about to ask *you* that."

His gray eyes gleamed. "I've done nothing. It's you."

"I…I'm dreaming…"

He took a step closer to her. "You've brought me here to be in your dream?"

She took another look around. "No, I…"

"Then what am I doing here?"

She ran a hand through her hair and tugged at her bangs. "Just let me think. I've dreamed about this room before."

He lifted a hand to touch the white satin ribbon on the bodice of her nightgown. "It seems real."

It did. The huge four-poster bed in the corner seemed real. The voluminous old-fashioned linen nightgown she wore seemed real. The fire in Meical's gray eyes seemed real.

"But it isn't," she murmured. "See, this is just a reaction I'm having to…"

His gaze rose and swallowed hers. "To?"

To him. To her attraction to him. After weeks of

subjugating her desires, of hiding from her need to reach out, her natural attraction to Meical was bringing all of it up and out of her subconscious in the form of a lucid dream.

Meical took another step closer to her. Caroline's mouth went dry when she caught the scent of his cologne. It was an old scent, green, masculine, earthy and totally Meical. He looked so perfect. So big and beautiful and right for this dream.

She smiled. "Look at you. You look wonderful. I did good."

His eyes twinkled, and he motioned her toward a full-length mirror. "No, sweet. Look at *you*."

Pleased, Caroline walked to the mirror. No hobbling or limping, of course. In her dreams she always had both her legs.

She stood before the mirror and turned this way and that, admiring her nightgown. It fell in yards around her, all the way to the floor. Her bare feet peeked out from beneath its hem, identical twins, pink, healthy and whole.

Meical joined her. "You're a powerful dreamer."

"It's always like this, except this time it feels real."

She bent and touched the perfect toes, wiggled them, laughed, stomped her foot and pirouetted in circles until she giggled from dizziness. Meical laughed and caught her just before the world turned upside down. He set her on her feet and took a step back.

Caroline locked her gaze on his. Unafraid. Empowered. Aroused. She hadn't a care. She felt it in the marrow of her bones. This was *her world*. Here she was safe. Here she was free. Here she had nothing to lose. She'd made it up. And now she had made Meical part of it.

She'd probably wake up in a moment or two and struggle to remember these things for her dream journal. Back to reality, with her fear, pain and one good leg. But not yet.

Caroline looked Meical up and down again, as boldly as she pleased, and watched his body respond beneath the close-fitting pants he wore. A shock of excitement licked over her erogenous zones and made her face burn. She didn't know how to put it into words, this thing she wanted. She'd shunned the very thought of it for so long.

Meical looked pretty clueless. He just stood there looking around with a smile that was pleasant and unknowing. It made her want him more.

He ran his hand over the bed curtains and laughed softly. "Empaths have vivid dreams, to be sure."

She reached up and touched his smooth cheek. "I want to find out how vivid."

He looked confused for a moment, then smiled slowly and pressed her hand to his chest. Caroline felt his heart pounding under his soft white shirt.

"You did say," he cautioned, "that this isn't what I need. It's possible it isn't what you need either."

She moved closer to him, wanting to see what he felt like in her arms. It had been so long since she'd held anyone. "Yes, but nothing's real here. It's all make-believe. I probably won't remember half of it."

He bent his head toward hers, drawing her closer.

His arms felt so sure and strong. Closer. Closer. "No, no. Anything worth doing…" His mouth was a breath away from hers. "…is worth making memorable."

Caroline rose up on her tiptoes and kissed him. He closed his hands over hers and pulled her arms down to her sides. Catching the ribbon at the collar of her nightgown between his thumb and forefinger, he slowly pulled it loose from its petite bow and eased the garment off her shoulders. He bent to kiss her throat as he slid the nightgown down to her waist.

Caroline drew a shuddering breath.

"Don't be frightened, Caroline," he whispered in her ear. "You're in control here. I'm just a part of the background."

He sank gracefully to his knees before her. With a soft exclamation, he took her breast in his mouth, first one and then the other. He rolled the flat of his tongue over her nipple and caught her close when she bucked away from him.

"Meical…" she breathed, closing her eyes, "…how can this not be real?"

"It isn't. That is one thing you must not question."

His big hands circled her hips and tugged the nightgown down to her knees. Wrapping one arm around her, he lifted her, drew it away and looked at her as though he had put her on a plate and was sharpening the cutlery.

"Caroline, you are so beautiful." He looked up at her. "Not that you need me to tell you that. You surely know it's so."

Tears burned her eyes, as real as anything else here.

Beautiful, yes—on the inside, as a person, as a whole person inside. But physically? How long had it been since she'd let herself feel beautiful in that way? She had allowed all thoughts of her physical beauty to slip away in her trauma and rage.

She wanted it back, everything she'd felt about herself before the attack.

Caroline swept a hand through Meical's hair. She'd wanted to do that from the moment she met him. "You can't make me feel beautiful, you know. I have to do that for myself."

"But I can help, can I not?"

He stood up and leaned close to her face to lick a tear from her cheek and rolled it around in his exquisite mouth as though it were sugar.

"There are sweeter things to make you cry, Caroline," he whispered. He drew his shirt off, keeping his gaze fixed on her. "I think we both know why you brought me here. Tell me what you want me to do."

Caroline watched, mesmerized, as he dropped his shirt on the floor. When he reached for the broad black belt he wore, she could scarcely breathe. He unfastened it slowly and slid it out with a whirring sound. His fingers closed over the button fly of his breeches. By the time he was unclothed, her breath came in gasps, and she shook all over. He was so big and beautiful.

Meical caught her hand and drew her into a kiss that was no more than a tease. She moaned, wanting to devour him. He backed them into the bed and drew her down on top of him.

Yes, this was exactly what she wanted, what she had

wanted the moment she pulled him out of the snow. Ears roaring, head spinning, drugged by arousal, Caroline kissed him again and then knelt between his knees. She just wanted to look at him, take in his long, muscular body with her gaze. A field of riches. All hers.

Meical reached over his head and clasped the headboard with both hands. His voice was as hypnotic as the dose of adrenaline running rampant in her bloodstream. "You have nothing to fear. You're the one in control. You cannot be hurt. You may do as you please. I will do only what you tell me to do. And if you're frightened, we'll stop."

Whoa. Meical seemed considerably less clueless suddenly. Was she really in control?

A schism opened beneath Caroline. The sunshine dimmed a little and the colors in the room faded. The room itself seemed to tremble as though it might crumble and blow away.

Caroline reached out quickly and flattened her hand on Meical's taut abdomen, like reaching for a lifesaver, and the room became bright and colorful again.

No darkness. No pain. No fear.

She slid her fingers downward, following a line of chestnut hair down to his shaft. Her need intensified with the smooth, soft feel of him in her hands, hardness beneath smoothness, heat and throbbing life that made her long to have him inside her.

"I think my imagination got carried away," she whispered, running both her hands up, then down. "You're very well endowed for a dream."

Meical laughed softly, but the laugh ended in a grunt

in the back of his throat. She closed one hand over the head of his erection and with the other hand sought the sensitive place beneath his scrotum. She watched his mouth part and listened to his breath come faster. He liked that. Yes, he did. How awesome to feel this power, the power to please and not be afraid.

She bent and nuzzled that hidden spot she'd found underneath, and he gasped her name. She ran her tongue across his belly, nipping as she went, until she crouched above him and looked him in the eyes. He ground his teeth together. A flood of heat poured out of him, as tangible as the taste of him on her tongue. His hunger wove around her, embraced and welcomed her.

Mindless with need, Caroline held her breath as she climbed up his body and sheathed him inside of her, dying from the pleasure of it. She moved slowly at first.

"Tell me what you want," he murmured.

"Push."

He lifted her with his hips.

"Oh, yes," she moaned.

Caroline caught his arms and held on. He hardened deliciously when she bore down on him, pushing her closer to release. Tears sprang to her eyes when Meical changed his rhythm, undulating between slow, deep thrusts to circling his hips beneath her. Meical locked an arm beneath her good leg and lifted, opening her more so he could stroke her in front.

"Come out of that silent, dark place you've been keeping yourself, Caroline Bengal. Let me hear you."

As though made to order, a half cry broke from deep

inside Caroline's soul, followed by a litany of moans she couldn't hold back. No more silence inside her now. She couldn't stop crying. The first flutter shot through her core, draining the strength from her arms and legs. Her lungs heaved for air. The enormity of what waited, just beyond the precipice, overwhelmed her. She felt it sweep upward inside her, spilling into his body and back into hers again, his ecstasy feeding her own.

Meical caught her hips and thrust hard, holding her down on him while she sobbed and bucked in the onslaught of their combined hunger. She peaked again and felt him turn to concrete inside her. Seconds later he gasped and moved beneath her like an ocean wave, filling her with the creamy warmth she longed for.

He drew her down to him and held her close, slowing his movements until she lay limp. She was sure she'd never move again. No strength. No muscles or bones. Just flesh, joined to his, warm and wet and safe in his arms. He ran his hand down her wet back, murmuring something sweet about sleeping late.

And sleep she did.

Chapter 7

Talisen approached Ellory from behind just as the moon slipped behind a cloud, and a light rain began to turn the sand underfoot to mush. In the distance, somewhere down shore from the deserted beach on which they waited, the inhabitants of sleepy Camden were going to bed.

And some of Ellory's fledglings were just beginning their night's hunt.

Talisen rose up on tiptoes and kissed his cheek. "Don't give up. Maybe he'll show up this time."

He shook his head. "Three nights in a row and still he hasn't shown. We made our request clear. Everyone knows we're looking for Meical."

"But we'll wait anyway. We won't give up on finding him."

Ellory drew her around from behind him and pulled her close. "Assuming there's anything left of him to find."

The pain Ellory exuded made Talisen wince. His emotions traveled like water drops on a wire, straight to her soul. She shook her head and kissed him again quickly. "If Meical was gone, wouldn't you feel it? And if he was beyond saving, this vampire we've been waiting on wouldn't put the word out that he knows where Meical is. Whoever it is we're waiting on, he—"

A wave of energy filled the night chill with a momentary heat, bathing the damp air with a scent Talisen couldn't place. She gasped in the rush of power.

Ellory tightened his arms around her. "Don't be afraid."

"That's no hapless wanderer," she breathed. "He feels—"

"Like an Ancient, yes. And he's just announced himself without a bit of fear for his safety. He's strong, this one."

Talisen probed with all her senses, as she had learned to do in her first few weeks as a revenant. "I can't find him. Can't get a fix on him."

"Don't bother trying. He's sizing us up," Ellory added with a snort. "Typical of his generation."

She followed his gaze as he eyed the woodland behind them, the boiling clouds above and the rising ocean beyond. The wind fell still, and then everything else did, too.

Suddenly, Ellory flew backward out of her arms and

hit the sand about six feet away. An arm materialized from out of the dark to clasp her around the waist, and a hand caught her under the chin. The Ancient's touch was gentle, but the fever in his skin stung her. It was the fever of severe hunger.

She swallowed her scream and fixed her eyes on Ellory, who'd picked himself up and now stood with his exquisite mouth gaping at whoever had hold of her. He recovered his composure in a heartbeat and gave her a reassuring, if pained, look.

"Don't move, Talisen."

She drew a ragged breath. "Not planning on it."

She heard the sharp intake of breath from her assailant. He pressed his nose into her hair, and his chest expanded against her shoulder blades as though he were filling his lungs with her scent. A sigh, ending in a moan, filled her ears, made its way into her mind, into her very veins…

"Talisen," murmured Ellory. "Stay with me."

She shook off the lethargy that crowded out her awareness and nodded at him. *Maybe you'd better do that dissolving thing to me you're so good at.*

Ellory drew at his lip with his teeth. *But you hate it.*

Turning to sand and slipping through his fingers is a lot better than being sucked dry.

He shook his head. *It's too risky. He's volatile. And… well…*

What?

He knows you're a revenant.

Great. Everybody hates revenants. At his age, he's bound to hate them more.

Ellory winced. *Actually, at his age, he's more likely to feel exactly the opposite and think you're my plaything.*

Talisen frowned at him. *You're not making me feel better.*

The Ancient nuzzled her neck with his stubbly chin.

Ellory, do it.

It could backfire on us. I could end up spending the rest of the night sifting bits and pieces of you out of this beach.

I'll take my chances on being Humpty Dumpty. Get me out of this. Now.

Not like that.

All right. What's your plan?

Keep your focus on me. He can mesmerize you, so if he speaks to you, don't answer him.

Ellory?

Yes, love?

I'm scared.

I know.

Ellory sidestepped in a half circle with his hands upturned in a gesture of peace, but Talisen took heart in the raw steel she heard in his voice. "The delicacy you're holding in your arms is mine, blood and body. Release her."

The husky, youthful voice that answered Ellory shattered Talisen's idea that she was in the grip of an old codger. He sounded like he was barely twenty. "You did good work on this one. Revenants make such a sweet feast. Human blood and that of our kind, all in one fountain…"

The depth of his appreciation, backed by the raw power he exuded, was enough to make Talisen's head pound. *Ellory…*

Ellory stepped closer. The bite in his voice bore a promise of retribution. "She isn't chattel. She's my mate. Let her go."

The scent on the stranger's skin flowered on the breeze again, clouding Talisen's thoughts. Such an old aroma, so provocative. What was it? Patchouli? It was oddly familiar. Who did it remind her of?

Ellory's voice broke through her musing. *Stop thinking about him. He's trying to draw you in. Your only protection is our unity. Resist him.*

He smells really good.

Talisen…please…

But not as good as you do.

She grinned, caught the arm that held her and gave it a good shove—not that it made a difference—but it got her point across. "Look, Wonder Boy, let me make this clear without the flowery language you're used to. I'm spoken for. If you don't let me go in the next six seconds, Ellory's going to do his best to rip your guts out. If he doesn't manage it before you kill him, I will. Between the two of us, you're not going to have a nice evening. So why don't you stop wearing out your welcome and tell us what you know about Meical Grabian's whereabouts?"

She braced herself for the possible ramifications of

her bluff. Ellory seemed frozen. He gaped at her as though she'd just sealed their fate.

The vampire behind her was silent. That could mean he was going to break her neck, or it could mean he was considering making a show of patronizing mercy by letting her go.

What she wasn't prepared for was his laughter. It echoed off the woods and the waves and cliffs. He was laughing at *her*. In spite of her relief that he was capable of genuine amusement, it made her want to pull his arm hair out.

"In all my three thousand years of night," he said, "never have I been spoken to in this way. Certainly not by a revenant."

Three thousand years? Talisen felt the first bloom of panic in her chest. This Ancient was as powerful as the Alchemist.

She caught another whiff of his signature scent, a dizzying mix of cool night breezes on thirsty desert sand, green rushes, musk, cypress, frankincense and... blood. He'd feasted very recently, but apparently, it hadn't been nearly enough to satisfy an appetite as old as his.

She fidgeted again.

Ellory edged closer. "Our revenants turn out a bit more modern than what you're used to. She is, however, the sun in my sky. Let her go."

The vampire ran his hand through Talisen's hair, and her fear turned dull and distant, like her thoughts. Dark velvet softness dragged her down to a place she didn't belong.

Talisen. Ellory's voice jerked her back to the surface. She felt his love surround her, laden with a vampire's stark possessiveness.

The Ancient behind her laughed again, except this time he was inside her mind. Had she done that to herself by speaking to him? Ellory had warned her.

He gives your leash a cosmic snap, he taunted, *and you're his again. I say again, he did very good work on you.*

Unexpectedly, Talisen was free. She swayed into Ellory's arms. He caught her close, held her until she thought her ribs would mesh and then steadied her on her feet.

Talisen turned to face the stranger. A world-weary soul returned her gaze, a soul as dark as the Alchemist's and as dulcet as Freya's, a soul steeped in the madness of hunger.

He was an inch taller than she was, no more. Lithe and sinewy, with glossy, black curls that fell to his shoulder, he looked like a prince from another time and place. Just as his scent seemed familiar to her, so did his swarthy beauty and the intelligence in his gaze, the square jaw, the exotic mouth, the black-brown eyes that held an eternity of history, wisdom, life and death.

"I am hunting the one you call the Alchemist," he murmured.

"Whatever business you have with Neshi is your own," Ellory returned. "Do you or do you not have news of our friend?"

"He has been ill-used by Benemerut, but he's alive."

Who dared to address the Alchemist by his first name? Not even Freya, the queen.

The Ancient lifted his chin, his eyes full of the kind of rage that revenge makes friends with. "Benemerut has done our kind a disservice we will rue for ages. I am the only one who can stop him."

"Great," said Talisen. "We'll help each other."

"I need no one's help, sweetmeat. I am here because I wish to confirm what I have heard."

"Which is?"

"I am told, she who calls herself your queen will applaud anyone's efforts to rid you of Benemerut."

Ellory took another step closer, head-and-shoulders taller than the ancient vampire. His voice was breathy with menace. "You speak of Freya Bloodmoon, midget. She *is* our queen."

The Ancient fixed his gaze on Ellory, nostrils flaring, eyes glowing red with vehemence. His voice was as smooth as before, but his words came out in clipped, sharply enunciated English that barely masked an older tongue. "Queens I have known. *True* queens. In my time, our kind was not ruled by the children of our race." He gave Talisen a stern glance. "And though our revenants were beloved by us, they understood their place."

She stared daggers at him. "Spare us the history lesson. Just tell us where to find Meical."

He turned his back on them and paced along the shore a few feet. For a moment she thought they were wasting their time. He stretched out his hand and the waves at his feet churned and boiled and rose to form a swan that licked his palm and flapped its wings before disintegrating with a splash.

"We're born from a crimson sea," the Ancient said hoarsely, "and long before we perish in the same way, we watch the world we know dip beneath the waves, drift out of sight and go under. We grapple to begin again, to forestall the inevitable, by seeking our salvation in the gaze of someone who is new to this world…someone with soft eyes full of trust and hunger strong enough to forge a new world…"

Ellory cleared his throat. "You do have some idea about where Meical is being kept, don't you? Or else you wouldn't be here."

The Ancient nodded. "Benemerut is not without talent. He clothes your friend's whereabouts well. I am only certain of the general area. Benemerut himself is invisible to me, as yet."

Ellory nodded. "That's Neshi. If he doesn't want to be found, he won't be. And if he's hiding Meical, it will be next to impossible to find him."

"No, sooner or later, I will find them, although I doubt that will improve your friend's chance of survival. And so, I have come to offer you my condolences and inform you of his eventual demise, as a courtesy to you."

Ellory shook his head. "Meical doesn't deserve to die. Let's pool what we know. If we work together, we can—"

Talisen caught his arm. *Hold on. He has an agenda and we don't know what it is. We shouldn't volunteer any information until we at least know his name.*

"My name, sweetmeat," the Ancient spoke up, having picked up on her thoughts, "is Badru. Millennia ago, you would both be on your knees right now, begging for a sip of my blood."

Talisen snorted. "Change happens. Get over it."

"For the duration of your stay," Ellory warned, "if your needs are extreme, satisfy them in the neutral zone that borders my domain. Keep clear of my inn. And under no circumstances will you approach those in my household."

"Be at peace. I am no threat to your children." Badru bowed his head and shuffled from one foot to the other. For a moment he looked as young and vulnerable as one of their fledglings. "You are wise to fear the insanity in me. It will claim me, just as it has claimed Benemerut. Just as it will claim us all. Your friend Grabian will not have to endure that horror. I hope that gives you some comfort."

"Stop talking about Meical like he's already dead," snapped Talisen. "If you get to Neshi before we do, you can set Meical free. You can save him. You're powerful enough to do that."

When Badru met her gaze, there was no malice in his eyes, but neither was there sympathy. He'd show no mercy. The deadly resolve in his gaze made her skin prickle with warning.

"If I find your friend before you do," he murmured, "you have my word, I *will* free him. But you will not see him again."

In a heartbeat, he vanished, leaving Ellory and Talisen stunned by the implication of his words.

Ellory's mouth parted and his words came in a rush. "He knows Meical is a victim. He's trying to be fair. That warning is the closest thing to a reprieve Meical is going to get."

"But it doesn't make sense. Why kill Meical? What's he done to deserve that?"

"It's a sanctioned kill. There will be no survivors."

"Sanctioned by whom?"

"Considering how many enemies the Alchemist has, it could be anyone. We can only be sure of one thing: If Meical is still with Neshi when Badru finds them, he won't survive."

She wrapped her arms around him. "Then we'll find them before Badru does."

Meical tried not to stare at Caroline's bedroom door while waiting for her to wake up. Dr. Calvin and the Hicks children had stopped by to visit, but he could scarcely follow their chitchat. His entire being seemed tuned to Caroline.

Last night he had kept her fast asleep while he washed the lovemaking off them both. She surfaced once while he was dressing her for bed and smiled at him like a sleepy child, then fell asleep again nestled against him. Even his second sunrise that morning couldn't match the thrill of the trusting, pretty smile she'd given him in that moment.

Fool that he was.

He'd come to a discovery about himself in the watch hours of the night, holding Caroline while she slept. He wanted to live, if only for a few weeks. He wanted all the power Neshi's dark experiment could afford him, all of which he'd put to use for Caroline's sake.

Not that he'd hang around. He'd leave before she realized he'd told her the truth last night, that he was a danger to her. He wouldn't wait until she had to ask him to go. He wouldn't put her through that, knowing how tenderhearted she was.

This morning, he could hardly wait for her to wake up. Yet he dreaded it, too. She'd wake to her reality, pain and haunted past.

"Your friend Neshi is brilliant," John Calvin spewed. "Most fascinating young man I've had the pleasure of meeting. We need more doctors like him."

Of course Calvin had no recollection of the events of last night. Neshi had seen to that, just as Meical had done with Caroline. She would remember nothing but the dream.

"Tell me, Dr. Calvin," he asked, "how much do you know about Caroline?"

Calvin hesitated. That was as it should be. He was a true friend to Caroline and could be trusted with her secrets.

"Hey, you two," Calvin said to the children, "I'm sure Ms. Bengal won't mind if you get the toys out and play with them."

The children went to a cardboard box in the corner and opened it. The box was labeled "Manipulatives" in orange crayon. Out came an assortment of playthings, families of little dolls, plastic soldiers, modeling clay and a dozen toy vehicles.

It seemed such a simple thing, yet so ingenious, that

Caroline could make use of the language of childhood
to help her young patients with their problems. What
had she called it? Play therapy.

Her world was so different from his. It had never
mattered to him before, the abyss that existed between
him and humanity. The only common ground he could
hope to find with Caroline would be in her dreams.

Calvin lowered his voice. "I can tell you what I know,
and I can tell you what I think. Which do you want
first?"

"Let's start with what you know."

"She showed up at my clinic one day," Calvin began,
"in a lot of pain. She'd run out of her prescription. She
wouldn't let me send for her records. She wouldn't tell
me who her surgeon was or even where she'd had her
surgery. I wanted to start over on all her tests, so I'd have
my own reference point for what she needed, but she
wouldn't go for that either. So, I just picked up where her
last doctor left off. It didn't take Millie and me long to
realize she was hiding from someone. We keep an eye
on her as best we can. She's the closest thing to a child
we've ever had."

Meical touched Calvin's mind briefly to confirm
that he wasn't holding back anything. "And she's never
discussed what happened to her?"

"I don't think it's all come back to her yet. I hope
it never does. But even if it does, I don't think she'll
risk putting us in danger by talking about it. Based on
what I've managed to put together, she was attacked
about eight months ago. She was doing her psychiatry
internship at the time, and the attack had something to

do with an emergency case she was called in on, late one night. As for the severity of what she went through, the surgical procedures she needed to salvage her legs were bad enough that the shock alone would have killed most people."

Meical fixed his gaze on the sunlight glistening through the window, recalling what he'd seen when he'd delved into Caroline's memory of her attack. Whether he lived a day or a thousand days, this was a score he wanted to settle before he left this world. By the time he was done, there wouldn't be enough left of her enemies to bury.

Perhaps John knew who it was who had reached Caroline that night, in time to frighten her two assailants away. "How *did* she survive it, John?"

"She calls it a miracle. They were closing in on her, and she thought they were going to finish her off, but they turned around and hightailed it out of that basement. She blacked out, and the next thing she knew, she was waking up in a hospital."

Meical remembered from Caroline's recollection how the two men had run for their lives. They had looked straight through him—at whom? The only person he'd seen in that room, besides them, was Caroline. Of course, considering he'd been half-dead from hunger himself when he'd gleaned that memory from Caroline's mind, there was no telling what he'd failed to notice.

"Physically speaking," John went on, "she's been a fast healer, but emotionally? It takes a normal person a long time to come out of a trauma like hers, let alone someone who's special like she is."

"Empaths are very special, yes."

"Caroline has blown my mind so many times, I don't rule out anything anymore." Calvin's gaze softened and he looked at the Hicks children. "Before she started working with that little guy over there, he wouldn't speak a word. He just made noises. But the two of them came up with a game, a language actually, using nondisruptive sounds and some hand signals. Mrs. Hicks and Sandy have been able to really interact with Ray for the first time in his life. Caroline says when he feels safe enough, something will click for him and he'll start really talking."

She knew this, of course, because she could speak to one's heart and mind the way only empaths could. There was nothing a person like Caroline couldn't accomplish. Perhaps even with him.

Meical caught the sound of the bed creaking beyond Caroline's door. He tuned out everything around him and listened to the swish of the sheets against Caroline's skin as she sat up. The sound raised a fire in him that went straight to his groin. There came the sigh of her yawn, followed by the scrape of her crutches as she dragged them to her and stood, and the soft shuffle of her small bare foot on the wood floor. When she opened her bedroom door, the crisp soapy scent of her pajamas reached him, and he clenched his teeth.

John grinned at her. "'G' morning, sleepyhead. Hungry? Millie sent me over with breakfast, along with a coat and some clean clothes for Meical."

Meical sensed Caroline's glance in his direction as

she sat down beside him and set her crutches aside, but he kept his gaze fixed on the children. She might be a bit embarrassed after her "dream" and the least he could do was not ogle. The better to preserve his lie, of course, to say nothing of her modesty.

The husky contentment in her voice was most gratifying. "Just coffee for now, Doc."

Meical made an illicit probe of her emotional state. Her heartbeat was swift, her spirits serene, but she was irked by his silence. Meical smiled inwardly. Oh, yes. She was all curiosity this morning. Perfect.

The soft undertone of intimacy in Caroline's voice drew at his heart. "Meical, I haven't seen you eat since we found you. Have some of Millie's oatmeal."

Meical looked up and smiled at her. "Last night I helped myself to your pantry."

Her face became rosy, and he caught the scent of Caroline's sudden rush of arousal over his choice of words. Her breathless half smile made her mouth intolerably tempting. The longer he regarded her, the deeper her blush, until he felt a flush of warmth pour out of her, and she looked down at her plate.

"Well, that was last night," she said. "It's a brand-new day."

She got up, hobbled into the kitchen and returned with a bowl and spoon. Pulling a casserole dish closer, she opened it up and scooped a cup or two of the oatmeal into the bowl and set it in front of him. "Eat."

Meical smiled again. "I'd better not."

A small, hesitant voice filled the silence. "My mom says oatmeal's real good for you, Mr. Grabian."

He thought at first it was Sandy who'd spoken, but when he looked, he found Ray looking up at him like an owlet.

Caroline's exuberance flooded his being. She, John and Sandy beamed at him as though he were a ruddy saint. Hope shone in their faces, the hope that he wouldn't waste this opportunity to coax Ray a little further out of his shell. He returned their gazes, inwardly aghast that he, of all people, should be someone who made Ray feel safe.

Meical crossed one leg over the other and regarded the little guy with as gentle a smile as he was able to manage. "I'm sure your mother is right. Mothers always are. But I'm not sure I'm supposed to eat oatmeal."

"You probably just don't know how to make it taste right," the boy said sagely. He came to the table, squeezing close to Meical and reached for ingredients. "First, you put in the butter. Never put your milk in first."

Meical eased his arm around the boy's waist. "Okay. Why?"

"'Cause cold milk keeps the butter from melting."

"Good point."

Of course, the idea of refusing to eat the sticky mess was out of the question. He'd eat it, and he'd act like he liked it even if it killed him. After all, it wasn't as if he could actually taste any of it. He'd just slip away in an hour or so and rid himself of the noxious mush. But for Caroline's sake, he would do this.

While Ray reached for the sugar bowl, Meical lifted him onto his lap. He'd never held a child before. Ray was light and small and warm, covered in a mixture of scents. Mostly life and youth and crayons, the syrup he'd eaten on his pancakes and the milk mustache on his upper lip. A tiny pink lip that looked like it belonged to an infant. It hurt to feel the boy's utter defenselessness.

"That's enough sugar," Sandy said in a big sister voice.

"No, it's not," argued Ray. He heaped half the contents of the sugar bowl onto Meical's oatmeal. "It's gotta taste good if he's gonna like it."

Caroline covered her laugh with a cough. Meical glanced at her. The admiration in her eyes left his heart in pieces. It seemed criminal to let her feel that way about him, and yet it felt so good.

"There you go," said Ray. He sat back against Meical's chest. "You can eat it now. It'll taste real good."

Meical nodded grandly and reached for his spoon, ready to make a to-do out of Ray's culinary accomplishment. Before he could scoop up a little dab to taste, Ray giggled and grabbed the spoon out of his hand.

Ladling up a glob, most of which dripped down the front of Meical's shirt, the boy held the spoonful of oatmeal up to Meical's mouth, making circling motions with it while he recited, "Buzzy, buzzy, buzzy bee, open up your mouth for me."

Meical complied and opened his mouth, braced himself to swallow the tasteless toxin, and closed his eyes in complete surrender.

The first thing that startled him was the sweetness. Then there came the taste of the milk and butter, and the undertone of grain. It took him back to his mother's kitchen hearth where the two of them shared a bowl of barley porridge for breakfast every morning. Freddie was hard at work on his studies with Father. Father was working on his next sermon. The girls were playing on the floor with the kitchen cat's latest brood.

Meical was there, if only in spirit, in that golden, safe place, enjoying the treasured company of his mother, the one person who had ever understood him.

"Well?" asked Ray.

Meical squished the bite of oatmeal against the roof of his mouth to get every nuance of taste. Stunning. What had Neshi done to him? He swallowed the bite, murmuring "Delicious" before Ray poked another into his mouth and patted Meical's lips with his soft little hand.

Meical waited for the nausea to set in, made ready to counter it with his very will to keep from ruining this moment for Caroline. Instead of nausea, he felt a strange rumbling in his stomach. It was sharp and vaguely familiar. Rather like hunger, but…

"Your stomach's growling," Ray said with a squeal. "Miss Bengal's right. You *are* hungry."

Meical took the spoon from Ray and took another bite. Maybe he'd pay for it later, but for now, he wanted it. All of it. It was as though he'd never eaten. Well, he hadn't. Not like this. Not in two centuries.

And the more he ate, the better it tasted. The growling

ceased and a feeling of contentment settled into his belly. A nice full feeling, rather like when he'd been all vampire and had a decent slaking.

Meical set the spoon down in his empty bowl and lifted his gaze to Caroline's. "I think I'd like some more."

Chapter 8

Tracking one's prey meant figuring out their particular mixture of preconditioning and habit.

Usually Burke found his targets predisposed toward behavior that was easy to follow and therefore easy to infiltrate. Routine was always their downfall. It opened up pathways into their personal lives—invitations to become a new friend, a regular face at their favorite pub, an innocent bystander in the background of their lives.

Burke sat at the table in his roadside motel room, sifting through the intel he'd gathered since he'd accepted the job of killing Caroline Olek—or Caroline Bengal, as she preferred to call herself.

In the months since he'd been on her trail, she'd taught him just how exceptional her survival skills were.

She never made mistakes. She never left a dent in her surroundings. She left no paper trails, paid no bills, received no mail and owned nothing. She had no habits. She maintained no predictable behavior whatsoever.

The flawless prey.

He turned to the copy of a newspaper clipping his associates had faxed to him. *Missing Child Found by Anonymous Psychic,* the headline read. After skimming the first paragraph, he reached for the phone and dialed his contact in Rivera's organization.

"Burke here. I have a lead. Pennsylvania."

After hanging up, he thumbed through the file Rivera's people had sent him. Most of this he'd already seen. The transcripts from Rivera's trial were nothing to him. Water under the bridge. Caroline hadn't even been there. The list of all her old contacts was useless as well. She'd cut her ties with all of these people in her naive notion that she could stay safe as long as she stayed hidden. Her hospital records? He'd already memorized the nature, seriousness and location of the injuries she had sustained from the attack by Rivera's men.

Burke curled his lip. Where was the art in bludgeoning someone to death? The fools Rivera had sent after Caroline had no feeling for sportsmanship. They had no reverence for life. The sanctity of the kill was squandered on them. To make their failure worse, they'd concocted a lie about some kind of demon who'd chased them away from the scene before they'd finished with Caroline.

Fear was the real weapon. Fear was foreplay. His bullet was just the parting kiss.

But it would take a great deal to make Caroline afraid. He pulled his photograph of her out of the pile of papers on the table and studied her pretty, trusting face. He'd flushed her out of her hiding places again and again, but this time he wanted her to stand her ground and meet him on her own terms.

When her Adonis finally discovered his appetite, he gave new meaning to the idea of being eaten out of house and home. Meical left no survivors in her fridge or pantry. For some reason he found the box of Count Chocula cereal especially funny.

For as long as she lived, Caroline would never forget the sight of Ray perched on Meical's shoulders, hysterical with laughter, waiting to see what Meical would eat next. Meical was still scavenging when John left.

She drew the line at asparagus and jelly sandwiches.

"Meical, stop now unless you want it all to come back up again," she cautioned, trying to drag him out of her kitchen nook, with Ray bobbing on his shoulders like a parrot. "Come on. You can walk it all off on the way to the Hickses' place."

Meical relinquished the asparagus and set Ray on his feet.

The boy grinned up at him. "Don't worry, Mr. Grabian, there's more food at our house."

While Sandy helped Ray into his coat, Caroline strapped on her ski boot and got her slalom out of the closet. She felt Meical watching her. The man made her feel like a magnet this morning, with everything in him pouring out, rushing in her direction. After the dream she'd had about him last night, it wasn't exactly smart to indulge herself, but she loved the feel of his vibrations. He felt just like a Jacuzzi.

They left her cabin and trudged through the snow along the path that led to the Hickses' trailer. Caroline appreciated the fact that Meical didn't hang back and try to help her along on her slalom. He seemed to know she didn't need that or want that kind of help from him.

So what *did* she want from him? More than she dared to consider, with a psychopath on her trail and a dismal future on the run.

As she scooted along on her slalom behind the three of them, with Dash running circles around them all, she couldn't take her eyes off him. She admired his interaction with Ray—along with the graceful way he maneuvered through trees and snow. And his fine set of shoulders. And his articulated derriere. And the deep, gravelly sound of his voice. And his—

He stopped short as though she'd just spoken to him and turned to smile at her. He looked as though he'd just won the lottery. What was that about?

Caroline coasted down a little dip in the path, breathing in the morning air and the jubilance of the children. Maybe this whole arrangement of counseling Meical was going to be as good for her as it was for him. As long as she kept it quiet and didn't draw attention to herself, no problem.

She came to a sliding stop beside Meical and only vaguely noticed that the children had run on ahead with Dash, because the gleam in Meical's eyes was just about all she could take in at the moment. He had looked at her like that last night in her dream.

She felt a hot blush coming on and turned her head away to look up at the trees and the crystalline blue of the cloudless sky.

Pushing past him, she dug her poles in and shoved herself along. She was way too in tune with him this morning. She needed to pull in a little, put the brakes on. She could actually feel him looking her over, knew exactly where his gaze was wandering…a slow, meticulous and deliciously lusty gaze.

She smiled. Guess it was his turn to eyeball *her*.

But where was it headed, all this checking each other out? She didn't have the wherewithal for a relationship. She couldn't begin to contemplate intimacy. And even if she could, it would be the most stupid mistake she could make right now. It could get Meical killed if Burke found her again. And he would.

Well, why shouldn't she just enjoy the moment? She swallowed hard, feeling Meical's gaze linger on her behind. The wave of desire that emanated from him made her feel weak in the knee.

Time for some conversation. Definitely. "Hey, Meical, has anyone ever told you that you have a way with kids?"

He laughed. "Not once."

"Well, you do. I'm not a bit surprised at how Ray is opening up to you. He sees you as a safety zone."

Meical was quiet for a moment. Caroline listened with her whole being. But a door closed between them. He could be so silent, and not just on the inside. The whole time they'd been walking, she hadn't heard him as much as snap a twig underfoot.

"Does he really?" Meical asked.

The door opened a bit, and a pall of darkness slipped out of him to nip at her heels. Darkness. Sadness. Loss.

"Yes, and why shouldn't he? You're big and strong, you exude a reassuring sense of being in control of everything in your environment and you defended us all from Mr. Hicks like a real hero."

She eased herself around a fallen log and waited for him to open the door a little wider. The forest hadn't felt cold this morning until now.

"As long as you're pleased," he murmured. "It doesn't matter why."

What did he think he was, some kind of curse? She wanted to ask him that very thing but knew better. Keep it light. He was sensitive. If he was feeling defensive, challenging him was only going to drive him back into his own hole. It was remarkable how like Ray he was, in fact.

She laughed. "You could be handy to have around."

"But do you dare keep me?"

"I can handle you, Mr. Grabian." She glanced over her shoulder and gave him her best don't-mess-with-me look just to drive the point home. "Just watch me."

His amusement with her response was as genuine as the warning in his eyes. Caroline's next verbal parry, which would have been sassy enough to cover up the sudden chill she felt, was preempted by their arrival at the Hickses' trailer. The children ran inside with Dash, and Caroline sat down on the front steps to take off her slalom.

Meical retreated to the picnic table under an elm. She glanced up just as the sun emerged from behind a cloud and cast him in gold. Beautiful.

Except for the sudden wince that crossed Meical's face. His jaw tightened as though he'd just cut himself with a knife and was trying not to let on that it hurt. He scooted farther down on the bench, into the shade of the elm. Sensitivity to sunlight could be a psychosomatic ailment brought on by posttraumatic stress.

"Are you okay?" she asked him.

The door between them slammed shut. Not that it mattered, because there was enough fear and self-doubt etched on his face to tell her that something had just happened that he hadn't expected.

But when he lifted his gaze to hers, the only trace of emotion she saw was a come-no-closer warning. "I'm fine."

Caroline backed off, giving him a placating smile and went inside to help the children gather the things they wanted to take with them to the Calvins'. Once inside, she watched Meical from the window.

He rubbed his arm, where the sun had touched him a moment ago, and covered his face with his hands.

Meical forced out a sigh and watched the sun glisten on the snow in the yard—light that he had borne painlessly only a few hours ago.

Was he reverting? Was this one day all he would have? Or was it like Neshi said, and he was just having a difficult transition?

He didn't have himself under control. That much was certain. For that reason alone he shouldn't risk remaining here with Caroline. It would be easy to disappear from her life, right now, while her focus was fixed on the children.

Meical's heart ached to think how hurt she would be to find him gone. She really needed someone. But it was better to leave now than risk becoming a monster in her eyes.

He stood up and edged backward toward a trail, keeping his gaze on the trailer. He focused on her thoughts, her scent, her serenity.

A movement in the underbrush behind him made him turn. He narrowed his eyes and searched the shadows there. A pair of feline eyes glowed for a moment, and a small black cat sauntered out of the greenery to study him. The golden charm on its collar twinkled in the sunlight.

A whisper of a presence bloomed on the breeze, very close to him, then dissipated, leaving behind a voiceless plea. *Stay.*

Who was this lady who had the power to reach him, asleep or awake, the power to hide herself even from Neshi?

Whoever she was, he could no more resist her plea than he could resist the call of Caroline's blood and pleasure.

Four hours into the evening and not a twinge. Not even an ache. She must be healing, really and truly. Caroline sat back in the warm bath water and let her gaze wander over her candlelit bathroom. Beyond the door, Meical's rhythmic footfall made him sound like a guardsman on duty. She heard his footfall pause, as though he were listening, as though he could see exactly what she saw in her mind.

It had been that way all day between them. They were in perfect syncopation. How awesome to experience that with someone. They'd gotten the Hicks kids settled over at the Calvins' place, and John had given Meical the key to their other extra cabin so he'd have a place to hang his hat for however long he needed it. The cabin was just a stone's throw up the trail from Caroline's, and Millie had supplied Meical with clean towels and sheets, a couple of blankets, a sack of groceries and a spare set of John's scrubs to sleep in.

On the surface, Meical had been appreciative and charming, but underneath, Caroline could feel the aching restlessness that drove him. It was eating at him, that hunger she'd felt in him from the start. And then there was that horrendous dream he'd had—or past-life memory?

She needed to get to the bottom of his psychosis. Tomorrow she'd begin her sessions with him.

Low murmurs reached her ears. Meical and Neshi? Funny. She hadn't heard Neshi arrive. Dash, who'd been asleep on the rug beside the tub, lifted her head and whined plaintively.

"Yeah, you didn't hear him come in either, did you?" Caroline whispered.

And Dash never missed anything.

Caroline pulled the plug to let the water out of the

tub, grasped the safety rail and levered herself onto her foot. Balancing, she pulled the towel off the shelf close at hand and wrapped it around herself. She'd scarcely dressed when the voices stopped, and Meical resumed his pacing. Neshi seemed to have gone.

Meical's footfall became more agitated, and when she tried to discern the nature of his agitation, she felt the door close between them. That wasn't the first time he'd done that today.

Exasperating man.

She joined him in the living room.

"Had a good bath?" he asked.

Caroline studied his face before she answered. He still didn't look like he felt well. His eyes were as big and bright as a full moon next to the pallor of his skin, and so very intense.

"I sure did. Was that Dr. Neshi I heard you talking to?"

Meical pulled a chair up to the fire for her, and when she sat down to towel dry her hair, he sat down at her feet. "Yes. We had a talk about my progress. He seems to think you can fix all my problems, if I let you."

She hung her head to one side and admired the ripple of muscle under his borrowed turtleneck as he scooted closer to the fire. He was so deliciously strong.

"So, are you going to let me?"

"I am. And I will perform to all your expectations."

Expectations? That sounded like a guy who'd been put through the psychiatric mill more than once. "I have no expectations. We'll just talk and share. Okay?"

He eyed her with a mixture of good humor and sheer

lust that turned her to jelly. "It takes two to 'share' anything."

Uh-oh. Here it came. Classic bargaining approach. Well, if negotiation made him feel comfortable enough to open up to her, fine. Whatever it took.

"Okay. We'll start tomorrow morning. Ten o'clock?"

"Will you let me play with your toys?"

Caroline grinned. "You smarmy thing. How can you say that with a straight face?"

He gave her a pretend hurt look. "I want you to see how genuinely cooperative I am."

"Do you think play therapy will help you?"

"You never know. Just give me the right toy and—"

"Oh, go away." She pointed at the door. "Shoo."

Instead, he rose and caught her hand in his, and turning it palm upward, kissed it as gracefully as Mr. Knightley himself.

"I'm not ready to turn in yet. How about you?"

"You look pretty tired to me."

"I'm fine." He perused the books that lined her mantel. "I have just the thing. I'll read to you. That'll put you right out of the picture before either of us turn into pumpkins."

She laughed and settled back in her chair, more enamored than she could admit with the idea of listening to Meical's smooth, deep, polished voice. It would be almost as good as listening to someone out of a book by—

"Jane Austen," he said, running his hand over the

creased spines of her collection. "This will do the trick. We'll be yawning our heads off in no time."

"For your information," she countered, "I don't find Jane Austen boring in the least."

"Obviously. You must have everything she wrote, by the look of it. But this—" he held up her dog-eared copy of *Pride and Prejudice* "—is your favorite. You're a Mr. Darcy fan, I bet."

"Who isn't?"

He settled down again on the rug, and Dash edged closer and rested her chin on his thigh. He gave her a sideway glance and cleared his throat, opening the book to the beginning.

"What *is* Mr. Darcy's secret? Besides the fact that he's filthy rich and has good taste in clothing?"

"He's hot," Caroline murmured, watching the firelight glisten in Meical's hair.

Meical snorted. "That's what my mother and my sisters thought, too. They were absolutely prostrate over Darcy."

Caroline grinned at him. "So, naturally, being a discerning reader, you wanted to know why and you read the book yourself."

He waved a hand as though to banish the thought. "I went fishing to escape the inevitable."

"Oh, good grief, Meical."

"They insisted I read it anyway."

"Good for them."

"All to enlighten me about what a catch Darcy was. When I refused, they told me, 'You will like it, Meical.

There are soldiers in it.' So I read it, and nary a battle was to be found."

"Was, too. What about all that verbal swordplay going on between Elizabeth and Darcy? *That's* battle."

"But Darcy, being an idiot, failed to realize that it takes more than wealth and a wardrobe to match wits with a woman like Elizabeth Bennet." He gave her a wicked grin. "What Darcy should have done is bring out his heavy artillery."

She couldn't resist. "His heavy artillery?"

"The three-part plan for initiating courtship."

"Oh, I have to know."

"One: he should have shown Elizabeth's mother he's a decent fellow by attempting to make conversation she could prosper from socially, because that was what she really wanted. Two: he should have shown Elizabeth's father he had some sense by showing an interest in the way Mr. Bennet ran his estate. Three: the first chance he had, he should have strolled in the garden with Miss Bennet—*her garden,* not his—and when the moment presented itself, he should have kissed her until her head spun."

Caroline laughed. "Please, tell me you're not speaking from experience."

"It's not all my own wisdom. What else do soldiers talk about from one moment to the next, when they know it might be their last conversation?"

Judging by the way Meical avoided her gaze, set the book aside and suddenly got very busy tending the fire, he hadn't meant to say that. If he'd been in combat recently, that could explain his traumatic dream about soldiers from long ago. Maybe he identified with those men and saw their cause against Napoleon, a tyrant, as his cause. Or wanted to.

"So, you're a soldier?"

He said with his back to her, "Long ago."

His tone warned her it was not open for discussion, which meant, of course, they'd eventually have to discuss it. But not now. Right now, he was trying to get comfortable with her.

Meical sat back and picked up the book again. "May it please you, then, madam, I will read."

It was such a simple, sweet thing for Meical to do for her. Somehow he had known how much she would enjoy this. The language of that day seemed to roll off his tongue. And even when he paused to make fun of Mr. Darcy, he gave the character such life when he read, it was as though Mr. Darcy were there in the flesh. She put her head back, closed her eyes and enjoyed her favorite book as she had never enjoyed it before.

The night seemed to fly by. It was nearly one o'clock before she noticed his voice had grown more lulling. Her eyes grew heavy and she felt like she was drifting with each word, on the sound of his beautiful voice.

"Sweet dreams."

She opened her eyes to find him leaning over her chair. "Oh. Sorry. Are you going?"

"Yes. Good night. I've had an enjoyable evening."

She smiled up at him, feeling warm and relaxed and full of affection. "I did, too. Thank you. I really enjoyed this."

"We'll make a habit of it."

"Did we get to the dance scene?"

His eyes glinted strangely. "Let's save it for later."

She nodded and looked around for her crutches.

"Allow me."

He picked her up and carried her into her bedroom. There was electricity in his touch. Or else that was her infatuation talking to her libido. It plunged her into the closeness they'd shared in her dream last night, the intimacy, the pleasure…

In her sleepy, bemused, aroused state, Caroline didn't even think twice. The words tumbled out of her mouth before she could keep from saying them. "Just so you know, Meical Grabian, Mr. Darcy can't hold a candle to you."

For five seconds after she'd said the words, she regretted them. Then she saw the beaming grin he gave in response, the appreciation in his eyes. The glint. The gleam. The need.

Caroline held her breath while Meical laid her down on her bed—very slowly—and remained poised over her for a moment. His gaze settled on her mouth.

He was going to kiss her. She could see it coming. But was it the right thing to do? For either of them? Dreaming about him was bad enough, but this? *This was real.* If she kissed him once, she'd be kissing him all night long. But she wanted that kiss so much. She wanted him. Caught between confusion and anticipation, with her safe self-identity teetering and her safeguards trembling, Caroline closed her eyes in breathless expectation…

"Sleep well, Caroline."

She opened her eyes to find that Meical was already halfway to the door. "Oh. Okay. Right. Good night."

Dumb, she chided herself. His body language was enough to tell her she'd just exposed them both to something neither of them was ready for. The moment he was out of sight, she covered her face with her hands. She wouldn't make that mistake again.

Chapter 9

After centuries of rooting out Benemerut's lairs, Badru could practically find them by scent. He had found them all, though always after his quarry had flown. This time was no different. Just before sunrise, he discovered the catacomb beneath a stretch of Maine's rocky coastline, where the so-called Alchemist had committed his latest atrocity.

With practiced stamina he defied the deep sleep, while searching the underground corridors for Benemerut's inner sanctum, his sleeping chamber. It was almost mid-morning when he came upon the room. Only a narrow bed in the center of the chamber remained.

Upon the bed lay a note.

Benemerut had never left anything behind before. Badru read the note without picking it up.

Badru,
I am close to perfecting my research. If all goes well, life among humans can soon belong to our kind again. I have the perfect subjects for my experiment. They're young and strong and beautiful. The union they will forge will bear out all of my work. Give me time.
Benemerut.

Badru sighed. "Benemerut, you haven't been paying attention. After all these years, you still underestimate me."

He held his palms poised above the note and murmured the arcane words. The text began to glow like flames and disintegrated the paper upon which they'd been written, leaving behind an orb of energy, like a tiny blood-red star, that floated just under his hands.

Bracing himself, Badru turned his palms up and murmured the final words of the spell. The orb sliced through him, icy-hot, burning into him the very essence of Benemerut's emotional state at the moment he'd written the note. When the heat dissipated, he possessed a copy of Benemerut's signature vibration, his soul's thumbprint, so perfect that he would know it anywhere.

It took him by surprise, how familiar Benemerut's essence felt to him. Surely, eternal night had changed them both, yet he recognized echoes of the man Benemerut had been, when he had been the one man Badru looked up to.

But on the night he had needed Benemerut most, he had had no advice, no answers and no help to give.

It was only right that he should be the one to end Benemerut's existence. Before his own end came, he would leave behind no stain on the memory of the most promising young physician Cairo had ever known. That was what Benemerut the man would want, even though Benemerut the vampire was lost to reason. All evidence of Benemerut's shame must be obliterated, especially the creature Grabian.

With his strength exhausted, he succumbed at last to the weariness of the deep sleep and sank onto the bed. His heart began to shut down for the day, and his mind dulled, yet the vibration of Benemerut's being remained with him, like a fire in his soul.

Miles from everything and everyone. Safe and warm. The sound of the gentle rain outside was all she heard.

Rain?

Caroline opened her eyes to find herself in one of her favorite dreams. Nighttime in a dark, gothic mansion, an old ruin of a castle that was given a facelift in the eighteenth century.

She grinned at the tapestries that adorned the gray stone walls in hues of rich burgundy and gold and green. They depicted scenes of private gardens ripe for romantic trysts, vignettes brought to life by the light of the torches on the walls.

"You've outdone yourself, I do believe."

When Meical stepped out of a corner beyond the

light of the fire, Caroline couldn't help but stare. He was dressed like a commoner this time, in a rough woolen shirt that hung loose and open. His pants were rough-woven, too, dark brown like his boots, and they fit him perfectly—everywhere.

Caroline gulped down her next breath. What kind of spell was she weaving for herself now? The thought of her last dream with Meical made her face burn, but she couldn't get the memory out of her mind. The feel of him…

She sat up in the big canopy bed and drew her legs up close to her. "We seem to be making a habit of this."

Devilish humor shone in his eyes. "I can't say I'm sorry about it."

"Well, I'm not so sure it's a good idea. I have to be professional with you when I wake up. And even though this is just a dream, you're way too gorgeous for your own safety, and that last dream left me with some very realistic feelings."

He laughed and then bowed. "I'm honored. Or at least I would be, if this were real and I knew anything about it."

Yet it was there in his eyes, even now. A knowing look.

The thunder boomed outside and lightning danced into the room, casting a glint in Meical's eye, but not the gleam of romance.

A shiver skittered up Caroline's spine. She felt out of control and vulnerable here in the middle of a lucid dream with a man who was half-mad and very angry inside. And hungry. He was so hungry.

On instinct, she got out of the bed. "Let's explore."

"Sure, Caroline."

She went to the wardrobe. It was empty. "I seemed not to have dreamed up any clothing for myself. That's not fair. You're wearing clothes."

"I like what you're wearing."

She turned slowly from the wardrobe and leveled her gaze on him. "I don't usually dream for two, okay? I don't know why I'm…dreaming like this…"

He looked down at himself as though he hadn't heard her. "You seem to have cast me in the role of a—"

"Rogue," she gulped.

He smiled. "That's a quaint word for it."

Great. That was all she needed. Meical the Gothic bad boy. What was she doing to herself?

"Well, let's see how far my imagination has gotten carried away this time."

With a sigh of exasperation, Caroline marched to the door of the chamber. It opened on its own accord before she reached for the latch. That had never happened in her dreams before.

Beyond was a larger room, with a fireplace that took up one whole wall and a fire that burned so high and bright that it could have been consuming a small hut.

She had never dreamed about this large chamber before. Maybe if she kept pushing the confines of her imagination, she'd wake herself up. Lucid dreams were like that. Once you were aware that you were dreaming, you could change the dream.

She took one or two tentative steps into the big room. Looking over her shoulder, she found Meical following close behind, with his hands behind his back and a smile on his face.

There. There was that knowing look in his eyes again.

The big chamber was warm and bright and beautiful, with more tapestries and rugs and bits of armor on the walls. The swords gleamed in the firelight.

"Sweet," she murmured.

"Lots of toys."

She followed his gaze to the swords. "You like those, huh?"

"Apparently you do, too, or they wouldn't be here." He looked down at her and smiled. "A girl after my own heart."

He pushed past her to stride across the room, took a rapier off the wall and tested its weight in his hand. "Lovely."

He was so beautiful. Caroline's face flushed hot again. She wished he really *was* here, rather than being a tease from her subconscious. She chuckled, and he glanced her way.

"Do I look that ridiculous?" he asked, grinning.

She shook her head. "No, you look phenomenal. Like you belong here."

He quirked a brow at her. "Really? I look like I belong in your dreams?"

"Um…here in this…" she waved a hand around at the room, "…this kind of…whatever."

"Ah. Well, whatever you've cut me out to be while I'm here, Caroline, I like it."

He sliced the air with the sword a couple of times

and then settled into what looked like some kind of drill or exercise, a series of movements that seemed way too authentic for anything she could come up with in a dream. She must have stored a lot more info from her reading than she realized, because he looked like he knew what he was doing.

Caroline leaned against the wall and watched him. When was the last time Meical Grabian had had any fun? She had an impish urge to indulge his enjoyment of this place. Why shouldn't she?

An idea formed in her mind. It was pure nonsense, but who cared? It wasn't like any of this was real.

Caroline turned and eyed the row of swords above her head. She reached for one that looked like Meical's. The instant her hand closed over the hilt, it felt right and real and familiar to her.

"Cool," she murmured. "I can do this. Amazing."

She eyed her golden-haired opponent, who was making a show of himself on the other side of the room, hitched up the folds of her voluminous nightie and approached him.

"If you want to play, Meical, let's do it right."

She amazed herself by giving him a perfect salute. She raised her blade to her nose and snapped it down with a flick that made a satisfying whooshing sound.

Meical's eyes widened for a second, and then he emitted a low, dastardly, thrilling laugh. "You're on. What shall we play for?"

Caroline followed him into the center of the room where they had more room. "Just to win, I guess."

He shook his head. "Come on, we have to have a bet."

She watched him shove his hand in the pocket of his breeches, wiggle his fingers around and dig out a leather lace. He looked at it and smiled. "Accommodating of you."

"Yes, well, the human mind is a remarkable thing. What's it for?"

He winked at her, set his sword aside on a nearby table and used the tether to tie his hair back in a ponytail. Plucking up his weapon, he started toward her with a gleam in his eye.

Caroline lifted a hand to hold him off. "Wait. How will we know who wins?"

He laughed again, with relish convincing enough to give her a chill. "I suspect we'll know when the moment comes."

"Whoa. I don't want to hurt you."

Meical turned his head aside and coughed loudly. When he looked at her again, his eyes were twinkling with laughter. "I don't think that's possible, is it? I mean, if all this is merely a dream, what's the worst thing that can happen? If you feel pain, won't you just wake up?"

It was funny that Meical thought the worst thing that could happen was that she would wake up.

But of course, that was just her putting words in his mouth. All of this was her doing, all of it her, talking to…herself? To her fears? It was all symbolic of larger issues, and she was actually about to battle something inside her on a psychological level, and whatever it represented, she had put it in the guise of Meical and turned the whole thing into some kind of enticing competition between the two of them.

Why swords?

Well, she could have a field day with that one, but Meical was getting impatient, as if he didn't have time to waste while she sorted out her psychological wherewithal.

"All right," she said, "if I win, I want…"

It came to her as though someone whispered it in her ear. What she wanted was Meical. In her life. For real.

These dreams were just her unconscious mind's attempt to invent a safe place for her to admit this to herself. They gave her a buffer zone where she could feel it was okay to really, really want this man, regardless of what she'd been through and what she might face in the future.

Not that it could happen.

"You know what you want, Caroline?" he asked her.

He was as serious as death suddenly. His gaze probed hers until she had to look at the floor, his booted feet, his exquisite legs.

"Yes, I know. But…"

"It's only a dream," he murmured. "It's all right to want anything here. Isn't it?"

Caroline raised her blade and struck an en garde position. "Maybe I'll keep it a secret until I win."

He gave a half bow and then assumed a deadly pose

of his own, as if he'd run her through if she gave him half a chance.

"You haven't said what *you* want, if you win," she said. "Not that you will because that would mean you were in charge of this dream, and because that's impossible—"

"You, Caroline. I want you."

Good grief, he was terrifying. Her voice came out in a squeak. "That's kind of redundant, don't you think? You had me in the last dream."

He smiled like a satyr. "No, dear heart, *you* had *me*."

"Okay, but if I don't want to go through with it—"

"I expect no quarter. I give none." He pointed his sword in the direction of the bedchamber. "If you're not ready to see this through, you'd best quit dreaming."

There was so much more to his words than a mere taunt.

Dream though it was, the very thought of what she could be getting herself into was enough to make her want to claw her way back to wakefulness, but nothing seemed as important as facing up to Meical's challenge.

Deep down inside her, in a place beyond fear, the risk itself felt sublime to her, and Meical's taunt boiled deliciously in her blood. The psychological diatribes with which she armed herself by day were far from her now. In her hand she held the only weapon she needed here. Could she wield it?

There was only one way to find out.

Caroline squared her shoulders. "Don't let the

nightgown fool you, buster. If I had the nerve to dream all this up, I'm sure I equipped myself to handle you just fine."

Meical grinned. "That's my girl."

"I'm not your girl until you win." She snapped her sword in the air again and circled him. "So don't get cocky."

He began to circle, too. "No verbal swordplay for us, eh?"

Caroline studied Meical's face. He was perspiring, pale and sharp-eye, as though he were focusing all his will and concentration on one thing and it cost him his strength.

The jar and clang of Meical's sword connecting with hers ended her perusal of him. "No quarter. Remember?"

"You look exhausted," she said. "Don't make this too easy, or all our fun will be over too soon."

His only reply was a quick, half smile. Then he lunged, and all Caroline could do was react from pure instinct that came from heaven knows where.

For the next few moments, their swords did all the talking. The sound of it echoed off the walls, fit for an Errol Flynn movie. Once, Caroline let her guard down and narrowly escaped a nip from Meical's sword.

"Keep your eyes on mine," he rasped, "and stop watching my sword hand."

"Are you giving me advice in the middle of my dream, you cheeky thing?" she shot back at him.

She laughed and parried another of his thrusts,

turning his sword aside, which brought them shoulder to shoulder.

With a low growl, Meical bent and kissed her swiftly.

"Cheater!" she half squealed, and shoved him back.

"This will end the way you want it to end, Caroline. Just remember that."

"Then you're going to need bandages, buddy."

He was so fast. He seemed everywhere. But she found she could anticipate his moves, as though they were dancing, as though she'd been fencing with him all her life. They seemed perfectly matched in every way.

After a few minutes, however, the sword began to feel heavy in her hand and the room a lot warmer. Meical looked more tired than she did. What was that about? Why should either of them feel tired in a dream?

Needing a rest, she maneuvered to get the table between them for a moment. She thought she'd just duck and roll, but Meical planted his boot on the hem of her nightgown, and with a rip, she almost rolled right out of it.

"Time out," she said, trying to straighten her nightgown.

He smiled and withdrew for a moment, panting and pacing.

"How much longer are you good for," she asked, "just out of curiosity."

"Not tired, are you?" he shot back.

"Aren't you?"

He smiled, but it was a hard, resolute smile. "No quarter."

She got her nightie untwisted and came out from behind the table. "Fine, then."

Meical closed the distance between them in two strides, and they were at it again.

Either he'd been taking it easy on her before, or else, Caroline's skills were waning with the night. She barely managed to keep up with him, let alone stay ahead of him. He worked her backward, foot by foot, into the wall. When she couldn't go any farther, she tried making a fast slide to the left, but he blocked her and beat her back.

She parried three swift lunges, feeling the weight of his blow all the way to her molars.

With a feint and another lunge, he speared the sleeve of her nightgown to the wall. They eyed each other, breathing hard.

"Surrender," he whispered.

Caroline made a pretense of considering it, while she caught her breath and watched Meical let his guard down. When he seemed to relax a moment, she leaped away, and with a rip, left her empty sleeve on his sword.

Meical laughed and sent the sleeve flying with a flick of his wrist. "I see you intend to fight until I've stripped you naked. Good. It'll save me the trouble."

She darted away and kicked the table over when he charged after her. He leaped it as though he had springs in his feet, rolled and came to his feet, all in one move, just in time to corner her again.

She lunged and tried to get around him; he parried and forced her back and back and back until she again had the wall behind her and nowhere to go.

Caroline elbowed him in the ribs, shouldered him to push him back and whipped her sword around, certain she was about to leave a mark on him somewhere.

But he caught her by the wrist, nudged her into the wall once more and disarmed her in two seconds, all with ease that told her he could have done it at any moment he wanted to and had only been playing with her.

Caroline stared up into Meical's brilliant gray eyes, watching his mouth descend. He kissed her deeply, but oh so gently, while the damp heat of their bodies wrapped her up like a blanket and drained away the last of her strength.

Teasing her lower lip with his teeth, he parted his mouth from hers slowly. "I say again…surrender."

"Okay, but…what if I don't want to…you know…"

"But you do want to. Otherwise, I wouldn't have won. You just haven't made up your mind yet."

She hated the logic in this dream Meical. "Will you take a rain check?"

"No."

"How about an alternate prize? Name whatever you want."

"Hmm. Let me think."

While he was "thinking," he nuzzled her neck, nipping her from her earlobe to her shoulder. Caroline slipped precariously closer to surrender by the time he lifted his head and said, "Fine. Tell me what you wanted if you had won this little scrap, and I'll let you off."

She shook her head, mute with need from the memory of his lovemaking in the last dream. It rushed through her mind and body in full color, sensation, sound and life, eclipsing everything but this moment here and now.

Meical kissed her cheek. It was a chaste, butterfly kiss, and yet it lingered. "It appears you're in a dilemma, then."

"P-part of me sure is," she gasped.

He laughed softly, tossed his sword aside and swung her up in his arms. He turned and started toward the fireplace, where the table still lay on its side.

"Hey, Meical, aren't you going the...wrong way?"

Her voice left her as the table jerked upward into the air and landed right side up all on its own.

She hadn't done that. She knew she hadn't. It would never have occurred to her.

When he laid her down on it, she murmured, "Hey, I'm not sure about this."

His mouth found hers. Once. Twice. A third kiss. "Liar, liar, pants on fire..."

And as he said it, the fire in the hearth behind them sprang up, hot and insatiable, like the hunger she saw in his eyes. Her skin prickled from head to toe when he bent to kiss his way along her quivering abdomen. She could feel his hard mouth through the muslin nightgown, demanding, devouring...

Let go. Let go. Let go. The words sang in her mind, voiceless, ravenous. *Let him in. Trust him. Make it real.*

But making Meical a part of her life for real meant endangering his life.

Rivera.

Caroline caught Meical by the hair and yanked his head up to make him look at her. "I changed my mind. I don't want this."

He drew back and regarded her, mouth parted, face strained. "I see."

He was so gorgeous, even as exhausted as he looked right now. She wanted him so much. She wanted his love, his admiration, his protection.

Tears stung her eyes. "It's just that this all seems—to be getting out of hand…"

Meical turned his head aside, and Caroline felt a tremor pass through him. He gathered her up and set her on her feet. By the time her head quit twirling like a top from sitting up too fast, he was on the other side of the room, retrieving their swords and replacing them on the wall.

He said over his shoulder, "The alternative is still an option. Tell me what you would have claimed as your prize, if you'd won, and then let us call a halt to this dream of yours."

If she told him, it wasn't as if he'd really know. She'd probably wake up the instant she said it.

"Okay," she answered, "I'll tell you what I wanted."

He turned from the swords on the wall and looked at her. "What you *want*," he corrected. But there was no smile, no laughter in his eyes now.

"I wanted all of this." She gestured at the room,

because her voice deserted her. Her throat ached with longing. "You and me. Like this. In my real life."

Meical wet his lips with his tongue and took a step or two closer, but stopped, ran his hand through his hair, turned and paced away, paced back, then turned once more to face her. "Say that again, Caroline. Please."

She hurled the words at him. "What did you expect me to wish for? Two healthy legs?"

The room began to dim; the walls fluttered like paper in the wind.

"I didn't expect anything," he returned softly. "Please. Say it again."

Tears clouded Caroline's vision, and longing all but closed her throat before she got the words out. "I want this with you for real, Meical Grabian. For real. But it can't be like that. Not really. I can't let it happen."

The floor turned to colorless gelatin underfoot, and Caroline slipped downward into the shadowy lake of sleep.

It can be real, if you want it to be.

Whether those words were an echo of her unspoken desires, or a plea from her dreamed-up Meical, it didn't matter. None of this was real. None of it could be.

Burke was the only reality in her world.

Chapter 10

"Thank you for giving me some of your time today, Mr. and Mrs. Feinstein."

"What did you say your name was?" asked Mr. Feinstein, holding the door open for him.

He smiled at the couple as he entered their apartment. "Burke. I'm very grateful for your help in locating my old friend Caroline."

Mrs. Feinstein led the way to a living room, and Burke took the armchair she offered him. The couple sat down on a sofa across from him. They regarded him with caution because this situation involved their child. People were always careful about their children.

The Feinsteins's little darling had brought them some momentary fame in the local news a couple of days ago, when they told how she'd gotten lost during their family vacation and was then rescued by a psychic.

For effect, Burke took a memo pad out of his coat pocket. "I don't suppose you have the lady's address, do you?"

Feinstein shook his head. "It was dark and we were pretty upset about Megan. We didn't notice. It was just a cabin out in the woods. No house number. But a local doctor seemed to be a friend of hers, and the sheriff certainly knew her. You could contact one of them."

Burke made a note of it. "The reporter you talked to didn't seem to know the actual name of the town she lives in."

"We didn't want that information released. The young lady doesn't want anyone to know where she is."

He ignored Mr. Feinstein and met Mrs. Feinstein's gaze with a hopeful smile. "If I show you a photograph of her, could you tell me if she's the lady who found Megan?"

He didn't wait for Mrs. Feinstein to agree. He took his wallet from his back pocket and slipped Caroline's picture out of it. "I'm afraid this is an old photograph. It's all I have."

That much was true. He'd located the picture in a student newsletter that spotlighted the contributions of psychology grad students attending UTEP. With a little legwork, he'd tracked down the student who'd taken the picture.

Burke looked at the picture every day. He liked to paper clip it to his visor in the car while he drove from one stop to the next along Caroline's trail. She was always a step ahead of him, and this time, she'd managed to elude him completely.

None of his prey had ever done that before. She was very special. He'd make her death swift and painless, out of deference to her ingenuity.

The Feinsteins leaned forward and looked at the photograph. Burke waited patiently.

"Like I said, it was nighttime," said Mr. Feinstein. "I'm not sure this is the same girl. The cabin was dark inside. She wouldn't let anyone turn on a light. And her hair wasn't the same. It was short and curly and a different color."

Caroline had changed her hair color three times since she'd been running from him. Burke resisted the urge to ask them what color her hair was now. He hoped it was red. She would look gorgeous with red hair.

"The main difference," said Mrs. Feinstein, "is that the lady who helped us was…well…missing a leg."

Burke nodded sadly. "Yes, I heard about the accident. This photo was taken before that. I can't tell you how badly I've wanted to be with her and give her my support."

Accident… More like fiasco. Rivera's men had bungled the job, and Caroline had suffered because of it. A true hunter would not have allowed that. Although, having come to know something of his prey's personality, he suspected Caroline was the kind who enjoyed taunting her pursuer. She was clever and beautiful and brave, just the kind of woman a real warrior might be tempted to play with before completing his job.

Hopefully she wouldn't tempt him too much.

He wasn't made of stone after all, and he had his principles—unlike the idiots Rivera had sent to kill her.

When Burke caught up with her, he would give her a chance to outsmart him. He'd even let her beg for mercy. That was something he never did. It was demeaning to both the hunter and the hunted. But for her, he would set aside his usual scruples. That was the sort of urge she brought out in a man. She made him willing to lay aside his code. She had no equal. In all his days of hunting, he'd never come across such a match for his skill.

"So, would you say the lady who helped you is the same young woman in this picture?" he prodded the couple.

Mr. Feinstein opened his mouth to speak, but his wife touched his arm, and he said nothing. Her eyes narrowed as she returned Burke's gaze. "I don't think you ever mentioned how you got to know this friend of yours you're looking for."

Mrs. Feinstein's conscience had apparently made a sudden recovery. But it was a little too late. Burke smiled guilelessly and tucked the photograph back into his wallet and returned his wallet to his back pocket. "A mutual friend introduced us, and we've tried to stay in touch ever since."

Mrs. Feinstein folded her arms across her chest. "The girl who helped us was pretty specific. She didn't want anyone to know about her. We only agreed to give the reporter our story because Megan already told a friend of hers at school, and that friend is the daughter of one of the newspaper's assistant editors. But we were very adamant that the young woman's name and location be withheld."

"That was very admirable of you," he said blandly. He stood up and shook Mr. Feinstein's hand. "I've overstayed my welcome. Thank you so much for your time. I'll keep looking for Caroline. Maybe I'll get lucky one of these days."

Once Burke was back in his car, he dialed his contact. "Tell Mr. Rivera I've found her. Not yet. Is your team in place? Just watch her father's house. That's all. The first move is mine. I don't want any accidents. Olek is of no use to me if he's dead."

How did she expect to deal with Meical's problems objectively if she couldn't look at him without imagining him naked?

This morning even the scent of him lingered with her. The memory of Meical above her, the light in his eyes, his kiss, his tenderness, his need, left her breathless.

But today she would set aside her infatuation, and when he arrived for his therapy session, she would treat him like her patient. Period. Her methods would work for him. They always worked. Everything was going to be fine—as long as she didn't think about what a good kisser he was.

Meical showed up at her door at ten, and although she went weak in the knees at the sight of him, she managed to pull it together. They stretched out on the floor in front of the fire, she handed him a tablet of drawing paper and dumped a box of new crayons in front of him, ignoring his soft smile while he watched her line the crayons in a neat row within his reach.

She took out her notebook and her green polka-dot mechanical pencil with the dragon eraser top on it and turned to him with a look of compassionate professionalism.

"I need you to help me finish a story," she said. "I'm going to start it, and you take it from there. Okay?"

He propped his cheek on his fist and regarded the crayons and paper tablet. "Are you serious?"

"Humor me."

"If I trust you enough to answer these questions, I expect you to show me equal trust and answer mine." He met her gaze with glinting eyes. "Understood?"

Caroline sighed. Meical was not the kind of man to relinquish his control in any situation. He was apt to see his cooperation as a concession on his part. He'd naturally want something in return. The difficulty was finding a way to give Meical what he wanted without jeopardizing her secrets.

"Okay," she said, "whatever subject we discuss about you, we'll discuss about me, too."

She could sense that her answer was unacceptable. Meical sighed and reached for a crayon. Caroline fixed her gaze on his choice. He went for red. That was what she'd expected. Red for anger. Next it would be black. Betrayal. Sadness. If she were right, that is.

"Once upon a time, there was a little boy named Meical Grabian," she began.

He shot her another are-you-serious look.

She smiled and went on talking. "What Meical wanted more than anything was...what?"

Meical abandoned the red crayon in favor of the black one and drew a rectangular shape on his paper. "His father's books. That is, he wanted his father to share them with him."

The rectangle he drew began to take shape. He went for the red crayon to make what looked like a doorknob. A door. She watched him take up the black crayon again. A door at the top of a stairway, and it all looked larger than life, as it would to a small boy. Good. This was just what he needed.

She prompted, "Meical liked his father's books because..."

"They were important to his father. But his father shared his books with someone else." The black crayon snapped in two. "Sorry."

"No problem. I have plenty. The books were valuable?"

"More than anything else. No. Actually, there was something else his father valued more. The one he shared them with."

"And Meical the boy dealt with that by..."

"Making himself content in the kitchen with his mom and three sisters. We had a good time every night down there without the two of them."

His shift from third person came earlier than Caroline expected. There was an old-fashioned lilt in his accent that hadn't been there a moment ago. It was almost as though he were reliving the memory. This was better than she'd hoped for.

"I love parties," she prompted again.

"We roasted chestnuts and sang and told stories."

He picked up the red crayon to add a glow of light under the door. And then he added red to all the shadows. His movements were quick and harsh and hard.

"And?" she murmured.

"It was fine until they came downstairs from their studies."

"And the fun stopped?"

He snorted. "Entertainment must always be the sort that improves one's moral fiber, or else it's idleness, and you know what they say about that."

"'Idle hands are the devil's workshop,'" Caroline quoted.

"Precisely. So, we always had to be virtuous." He broke the red crayon, too, but kept coloring with ferocious stripes of red. "Frivolity was not the good Vicar Bowman's cup of tea."

"Bowman? So you were named—"

"Meical Grabian Bowman."

But he didn't use his last name? Classic rebellion. To be such a complex man, Meical's problems were straightforward. In fact…almost too easy. She gave herself a moment to probe his emotions. He seemed to be on the up-and-up—except for a hint of a hidden agenda that she couldn't get to. Mostly there was lots of guilt inside him.

Just to be sure what direction they were headed, she made an exploratory remark. "Your father was proud of you."

"Not at all. I was a ne'er-do-well." He tossed the red

crayon aside and picked up the black again. "So, when Father lost him…"

"Whom did Father lose?"

"My brother Freddie. The good vicar's son."

"You were his son, too."

"Only by blood."

Caroline eyed the picture he'd drawn. "Where does that door lead to?"

"Father's study."

"Where his books were?"

"And where he and Freddie spent hours sermonizing. Freddie was bound for the church. Father was preparing him for a brilliant career saving souls."

"What career did Freddie want?"

Meical looked up with an expression of surprise. "He wanted precisely what Father wanted, of course. That was Freddie."

She smiled. "But not Meical."

He shook his head and rolled onto his back. "And that was the beginning of the end of Meical the boy."

She watched his chest rise and fall with the intensity of his emotions. To give him privacy, she withdrew to the kitchen.

His childhood was definitely part of his problems, but Neshi said it was a recent trauma that had put Meical into his current instability. If she could discover what had happened to him, she'd know how far into this anger cycle he was, and whether it was apt to turn inward or outward. That was crucial because Meical could go either way.

She rejoined him and settled down in the floor beside him.

He gave her an unsettled look. "You're brilliant, you know. I've never told anyone that rubbish before."

She shrugged. "It's what I do."

He reached for the picture he'd drawn and looked at it. "I was eighteen when Freddie died. Pneumonia. We were all grieved, but my father lost himself over it. He wanted me to take Freddie's place."

"In other words, he wanted you to be Freddie."

He nodded, pursing his lips. "I wasn't cut out for the pulpit. I'm too hotheaded. And not the least bit quick-witted."

She put a hand on his and waited until he looked up at her. "You were—and are—precisely who and how you need to be. And no one has the right to expect you to be untrue to yourself."

His jaw twitched and he looked away swiftly. "You'd have gotten along very well with my mother, Caroline."

"I'm glad you think so. Let's talk about friends."

She watched the smile play across his face. "That would be Ellory Benedikt and his family. And Talisen his—um—wife. Fine girl. She keeps them all straight." He cleared his throat softly. "There's nothing I wouldn't do for them."

Caroline noted the thread of longing that ebbed from Meical as he said it. "When was the last time you visited them?"

She felt him recoil. He seemed momentarily unreachable.

"Before," he murmured. "Before this."

That was the first reference to his breakdown she'd heard from him yet. Caroline proceeded gently. "Meical, do you know what happened to you?"

"Yes."

"You understand why you have the emotional problems you have?"

"Completely."

"Dr. Neshi explained things to you?"

"Thoroughly. He made it clear that things may not turn out well for me."

So much for Neshi's bedside manner. "But it will. That's what we're doing right now, you and I. We're going to see that you come out of this feeling fine."

He fixed his gaze on hers, but there was no light or life in his eyes. "Thank you."

Caroline tried to latch on to his emotions, but they trickled through her fingers before she could make them out. He found a straggling thread on the hem of her jeans and plucked it off, then covered her ankle with his big bronze hand. He had such a warm, gentle touch.

Caroline sighed and tried to recapture her train of thought. "Why not go visit Ellory and his family this week?"

Slowly, softly, he said, "I can't. We're out of touch with one another."

"I'll help you find them."

She looked down at her notebook and scribbled a note to herself. When she looked up again, Meical had risen to kneel in front of her. She hadn't heard him move. She met his gaze and felt as though she were falling headfirst into his eyes.

"My turn," he said in a hushed voice.

She smiled, raising her inner shields as fast as she could. "I had a happy, normal childhood, was probably way too spoiled, had a lot of good school friends while growing up and that's all there is·to tell. We're not talking about my secrets, so put that thought out of your mind."

"I know your secrets already. All of them. If I name just one, maybe you'll see you can trust me."

Caroline regarded him in silence. He was an empath of remarkable skill, but could he really deduce things she didn't want to share with anyone? He suddenly seemed less charming.

She folded her arms across her chest and frowned. "Be my guest."

"Your last name."

"What about it?"

"It isn't Bengal. That's just your alias."

Her heart catapulted into her throat. Nobody knew that.

"You chose that for your alias because the Bengal tiger is powerful, beautiful and stealthy—everything you've wanted to be since they hurt you. The tiger can camouflage herself, so she can't be found unless she wishes to confront her enemies or pursue her prey. And no one dares to trespass on her. Believe me, Caroline, *that* is something I understand very well. I can help you. Let me."

She'd seen what he could do when he confronted

Hicks. She could believe he was quite capable of protecting himself. Maybe even her. But a drunken bully like Hicks was nothing compared to a psychopath like Burke.

It was time to retake control of the situation before it derailed all the good their session had done. "I notice, Meical, that you seem to think very little of yourself. I'm wondering why, because offering to help me with my problems isn't the sort of thing a bad guy would do."

He slumped back on his haunches, giving her breathing room, but his eyes were razor sharp. "I'm not safe for your kind."

"My kind of what? Explain, please."

He ran his tongue over his front teeth and shrugged. "People in general."

So, his use of the words "your kind" meant the rest of the human race, as though he weren't a part of it. "So, you're saying that you're a threat to humanity?"

"Where you're concerned, in fact, I'm nothing less than a monster."

"No, where I'm concerned, you're a nice man who just offered to help me. You can't have it both ways. Either you're a good, safe man to be around and you believe that about yourself, or you believe you're dangerous and I should respond accordingly by not trusting you. Do you see what you've done to yourself? You've accepted someone else's definition of what kind of person you are, and yet it's so hurtful to you that you've begun to think of yourself as a being separate from the rest of the human race."

Meical burst out laughing, and because it surprised

her so, Caroline laughed, too. She had just speared him to the heart of his psychosis and he laughed? And it wasn't a nervous, evasive laugh, or a laugh of ridicule, but a genuine laugh of real amusement.

Still chuckling, he said, "If you knew how right you are, tigress, you wouldn't let me get this close to you."

"Okay, then," she said without a grain of emotion in her voice, "that brings us right back around to where we were a minute ago. I am your doctor. You are my patient. The end."

She went to the kitchen again to let him stew. If her logic worked, he'd fabricate an exception to his delusion of being an all-powerful dangerous being in order to obtain the state of friendship with her that he believed he wanted. And that was what she was waiting for—a crack in his punitive self-image that she could chip away at.

She reached a couple of cups down to pour them some of the coffee she'd made. When she turned around, Meical was standing there. He was much too quick and quiet on his feet.

He folded his arms and smiled at her with relish that was deliciously disturbing. "You have no choice but to trust me."

Good, good, good. He'd come up with his exception after all, a justification for suspending his negative thoughts about himself and a reason of his own for why he was worthy of her trust and friendship. Perfect.

"And why is that?" she asked.

"Because I'm the only one who can protect you from the men who tortured you and left you for dead."

The odds that Meical had read about her attack in a newspaper were slim to nada. The story hadn't even made it past the local papers at home, and it seemed doubtful he'd been in the Las Cruces area when she'd been attacked. No. He'd picked the details of her experience out of her mind, just like her chosen alias.

"Stop helping yourself to my thoughts, Meical."

"Answer my questions and I won't have to. What will you lose by trusting me?"

He looked so calm and formidably strong. But what could Meical possibly know about predators like Burke?

"It's *you* who could lose," she murmured.

He lifted her hand to his lips. "I'm resilient."

She shook her head, suddenly overwhelmed by the soothing prospect of leaning on someone. To share her burden, if only for a while. To find solace with someone without fearing the risk she was laying at his door. The idea brought tears to her eyes.

"I could get you killed. I can't live with that."

His gentle smile beguiled her. "If I swear I won't let them kill me, that you can rely on my strength and protection, free of guilt and worry for my life, and that I won't desert you when things get rough, will you tell me what I want to know?"

When tears trickled down her cheeks, he drew her close and just held her. Caroline closed her eyes and abandoned herself to the comfort of being held. It felt so good, she wouldn't let herself question how she could bear his embrace, when only days ago she would have freaked to allow any man to stand this close to her in a space as small as her kitchen nook.

This ease she felt around him had to be because of the dreams. Of course. They would naturally have an impact on her comfort zone around him. Her heart pounded. Did she really dare let Meical into the hell her life had become?

She let him lead her to the couch and pull her down beside him, but when he eased his arm around her, her initial reaction was to pull away.

"Sheathe your claws, tigress," he murmured. "I'm unarmed."

Caroline looked up into his eyes and saw strength she hoped she wasn't just imagining. His gaze dulled her uneasiness as though she'd downed a half bottle of very good wine. "I'm not going to mention names or places."

"That's okay. I know from talking to John that what happened to you had something to do with an emergency case."

She thought she'd just rattle it all off without stopping to think. But when her words didn't come, she realized it was going to be harder to talk about what had led up to that night than she'd realized.

"It was my mentor's case, a nearly catatonic nine-year-old John Doe who was picked up by the police wandering along the highway one night. I used fairy tales to reach him. I changed the plot to build a scenario I believed fit his situation and watched for a response from him. 'Jack and the Beanstalk' was the one he clicked with. So I called him Jack. I told the story over and over again with a variety of outcomes. When I ended the story with Jack coming home to find his mother gone, the patient began correcting my improvisation of the story, and from that I was able to piece together a mental picture of the nightmare he'd been living with before he was found."

Meical took her hand and held it. "I take it his giant was worse than the one in the fairy tale."

"I'll say. He turned out to be the boy's father, in fact. And I think…he had Jack's mother killed, and somehow Jack found out about it."

Meical sighed and swore under his breath.

"Jack blamed himself for not being able to protect her."

"You took your suspicions to the police, didn't you? And that's why Jack's evil giant came after you."

Tears burned Caroline's eyes and she wiped them away with her sleeve. She rested her head on his chest and closed her eyes. This closeness to another human filled her being until all she wanted was to sit there and soak it up.

"I cashed in everything I had and hired a P.I. to investigate. She managed to uncover evidence of his ties to a local drug dealer who had been indicted a month before. The police didn't get him for murdering his wife, but at least they got him. He went to prison, and I thought everything was going to be all right."

"Until he sent his men after you."

And she had dreaded nightfall ever since. But Meical—and the dreams—had made her feel safe and whole again. Even now, she wanted to curl up closer to him and stay there, even though he couldn't really protect her from the nighttime, and she couldn't protect him from Burke.

He kissed the top of her head. His voice was soft and low and deep, as though he were talking to a child. "Dr. Calvin told me that someone saved you that night. Do you remember anything about that?"

"It was probably a hallucination. I'm not even sure if I was conscious."

It could have been a shadow on the wall, and the red hazy light she'd seen was probably a result of her concussion. Caroline clenched her hands together in her lap. "The P.I. I hired, the policemen who were sent to guard my house—even my mentor—they were murdered."

"That was to make you feel powerless."

"It worked. I had to draw the line when my…when someone I loved began to get death threats. I accepted an invitation from a colleague to live with her for a while and see if we could help me overcome my trauma and get my physical strength back."

Meical pulled the coverlet off the back of the sofa and wrapped it around her. "You couldn't be sure of your ability to survive until you got yourself under control."

"Exactly. When nothing my therapist tried seemed to work, I decided the best thing to do was to go back to the place it had happened and just…face it." She closed her eyes, hating the feeling of defeat. It rode her hard, every moment of every day. "I threw up before I got as far as the front steps."

"The only thing that matters is that you're still alive."

"Only because I've stayed one step ahead of the man who's after me. He's a professional. He takes his job personally. It's like matching wits with a psychopath every day of your life."

Meical ran a finger over her cheek, and when she looked up to meet his gaze, he murmured, "If he catches up with you here, your sweet face will be the last thing he sees in this world."

She smiled up at him. "Who's going to protect *you?*"

He grinned. "You really don't have to worry about that."

Caroline rested her head against his shoulder and closed her eyes again. The protectiveness she sensed inside him made her feel that her life and safety were sacrosanct to someone besides herself.

"Caroline, I know it wasn't easy to trust me with this. I want to give you something in return."

She turned her face up to Meical's and looked right into his eyes. They smoldered now, as intense as they'd been in the dream last night. Her face flushed hot with the memory of the pleasure he'd given her, and the memory ignited her need. Just like magic. Meical's magic. Her gaze fell to his mouth, so close to hers.

His voice burned through her like a fire. "I don't want you to ever be afraid of anything again."

She felt it happening, felt the surge of his energy wrap around her shield like a wall of fire and granite. Caroline drew back. "What are you doing? Stop that."

·

He drew her closer, gentle but inescapable, and pressed deeper into her being. She felt all her walls dissolve, leaving behind only a trickle of its fragile energy.

Meical soaked it up, mingled it with his own, and before her inner eyes, rebuilt her shield for her. The barrier that surrounded her now was more powerful than any she could ever have created.

"That," he whispered, "is a proper shield."

Chapter 11

"I know what it is you've come here for. You want information about the Ancient who's hunting the Alchemist."

Talisen suppressed a shiver over Freya's choice of words. Neshi was so often the hunter; it was scary to think there was someone powerful enough to turn him into one of the hunted.

"That's right," she answered. "We need to know who he is and what his connection is to Neshi."

"We need your help to find Meical," added Ellory, "and we need it now."

The raven-haired queen, as smooth-faced as a girl, leaned back in her desk chair and regarded Ellory with mild annoyance.

"Badru is more powerful than any other Ancient I

have encountered. His business with Neshi predates my own. And since Neshi's end is what I desire above all else, I will be glad to see Badru succeed where others have failed. But of this I am certain: There is a strong bond between them."

"A bond?" Ellory murmured. "Is Neshi bound to Badru?"

"Whatever the nature of their connection, it's as old as they are. It runs deep. All that interests me is that Badru has sworn to find Neshi and spare him nothing. So, before you ask me to hinder his efforts, spare us all."

Ellory curled his fingers around the arm of his chair until the wood made splintering sounds. Freya gave him a chiding smile. She looked almost maternal—for which Talisen was grateful. Ellory's show of temper did not bode well for him.

"These are grave times we find ourselves in," said Freya. "Let us be mindful of the fact that if he wished, Badru could take the entirety of this demesne from me with a curl of his fist. Until he moves on, we must avoid provoking him."

"Did you sanction this kill?" demanded Ellory.

Freya arched a brow at him. "You know well, that's a standing order with me."

"Do you realize Badru plans to destroy Meical, too? He'll be deemed guilty by association because of whatever Neshi has done to him. So, in sanctioning Neshi's destruction, you've sanctioned Meical's as well. He is your subject, Freya, your own sister's creation, to whom you swore your protection."

Sorrow shone in the vampire queen's sapphire eyes. "That is…unfortunate."

"*Unfortunate?* Freya, you're oath-bound to protect Meical. You can't hold yourself above honor. Meical has a right to your mercy. As his queen, if not as his creator's very kin, you owe him rescue and asylum."

Freya pushed herself up from her chair and nearly floated across her sitting room. Her shoulders rose and fell with a heavy sigh. "You understand better than anyone that our turning is not always a matter of choice. So it was with me, when Neshi turned me long ago."

"That doesn't take away from the fact," Talisen argued, "that Neshi saved us all from Dylan, and if not for him, you wouldn't be here."

The queen's gaze lit upon her, red-hot for a moment, and in the next, icy with old hatred. "His merciful gesture was but salt in an old wound. I have never minced words with him. He knows I will waste no opportunity to rid our world of him. If Badru can do this, I will deny him nothing, and neither will any of those in my demesne. I will spare no one who fails to yield to my decision on this."

Ellory rose slowly, drawing Talisen from her chair with a gentle tug on her hand. He fixed a hot gaze on Freya, and even though his tone was respectful, Talisen felt territorial rage eating through his composure like acid. "I won't stand by and watch my best friend be destroyed by that Cupid-faced leech. We'll find Meical without your help."

"Stop coddling her, you stupid nit." Neshi strode out of a dark corner of Meical's cabin. "You've been feeding her psychological dribble for a week. You have her eating out of your hand. Why do you hesitate to take it further than that?"

Meical turned his back on his creator and stared out his open front door at the night beyond his cabin. "It's my business how I spend my time with her. Our sessions make her feel like she's not wasting her gifts. It pleases her. Where's the harm?"

"How long do you think you can keep up this charade in her dreams? You lose half the strength you gain trying to maintain the illusion. Make it real to her, Grabian. She must come to accept you in her waking hours."

He eyed the moon and breathed in the fragrances of the night. They called to his deepest impulses. He could hardly wait for Caroline to fall asleep. She shared herself with him more generously each night, and in return, he made her dreamscape more lavish than the night before.

But Neshi was right. As long as he spent his energy fueling Caroline's dreams, he would never obtain his full power. But her trust was too precious to risk, even for the sake of the truth.

Tonight he'd take her dancing at a ball. Dancing—yes, that was something no one else could give back to her. He'd populate the ballroom with every fictional character she loved and see that they swarmed around her, eager to bask in her company and answer her questions about their make-believe lives. Caroline would be happy in the midst of her imaginings tonight.

He cast a glance over his shoulder at Neshi. "As long as I have time to take it easy on her, I'm not going to rush her."

The vampire sat down and propped his booted feet on the table. "But do you have time? You know as well as I do, you aren't stable yet. Far from it. You're still in transition."

No sense in trying to lie. Last night he'd left Caroline completely spent, but he…he had scarcely begun to feed. He'd hardly been able to get through their therapy session today without kissing her.

He closed his eyes and flung his senses in her direction. He saw her in his mind. She looked so soft and sweet in the baby blue flannel shirt she was wearing tonight. Just that shirt and nothing else beneath…

"Can you tell me how you're managing," the vampire prodded, "or must I see for myself?"

Meical said in the most casual voice he could manage with the ache in his groin, "The vampiric symptoms come and go. Mostly I'm a little sensitive to the sunlight, a bit sleepy at midday, and…I can't seem to…"

"Spit it out, Grabian."

He turned and eyed Neshi, then the floor, then the ceiling, then Neshi again. "I can't get enough of her."

Neshi smiled slowly. "And this is a problem?"

Meical rolled his eyes. "There are limits to what she can handle—or did you take that into account when you turned me into a stag in rut?"

"So, expand your menu."

Meical turned away again and leaned in the doorway. "No."

"When you were a vampire, weren't there nights when your hunger necessitated feeding on more than one human?"

"She's different from other prey."

There was a moment of silence, and then Neshi's deep preternatural laughter echoed around the cabin. "By Ra, boy, you've fallen in love with her."

Meical scowled. "What do you know of love, you blood-sucking carcass?"

"After three millennia, more than you can comprehend. Tell me about your sensitivity to the sun."

"I'm more comfortable in the shade. The sun hurts my eyes."

"Does your flesh burn?"

"Do I look like I'm going up in flames?"

"Stop dodging my questions. Does the sun cause you pain?"

Meical hesitated. "A little."

"Well, if a 'little' becomes a lot, you must tell me. What about human food? Any problems there?"

Meical sat down at the table and shrugged. "It doesn't agree with me as well as it did at first. Today I…"

"Couldn't keep it down. Is that it?"

Meical nodded. He hadn't been able to tolerate anything in his stomach, and yet he'd been hungrier than ever. For Caroline.

Neshi rapped his knuckles on the table, his face inscrutable as he regarded Meical. Abruptly he rose and came around to Meical's side of the table. Before Meical could protest, the vampire wrapped him in a compulsion so deep he scarcely remembered to breathe.

He heard Neshi's voice as though it came from the

depths of the sea. "You're craving blood. Why didn't you tell me?"

Meical opened his mouth to answer, but the words wouldn't come. His heart began to pound hard, and the ache in his loins throbbed until he groaned. His body, his very soul, told him that Caroline was now asleep. "It's time for me to go to her."

"Answer my question. Is it getting harder for you to resist drinking from her?"

Meical sighed. "I wanted to drink from her last night."

The vampire snapped his fingers in Meical's face, and his awareness returned to him fully. "Listen to me, Grabian, and listen carefully. If you drink blood before you get through your transition, you'll revert to vampirism and be dead in twenty-four hours."

Meical stared up at Neshi, half in denial, half in disbelief. "Are you saying this process you've put me through is *that fragile?*"

"Only during this time of transition." Neshi's gaze shifted away from his. "Among my past subjects, those who reverted to drinking blood before they got through their transition went mad. They were raving animals. I couldn't have that. So I altered my formula and incantations to be sure no subject survived to cause trouble if they reverted to vampirism. If you can get through this difficult time, you'll become a full incubus and blood will no longer tempt you."

Meical ran his tongue over the roof of his parched mouth. Even now the thirst burned in his veins just as it had when he was a vampire. He had known moments, while loving Caroline, when he was half-mad with his hunger for her pleasure and his thirst for her blood. How could he resist it? How could he survive it?

How could she?

"Neshi," he murmured, "if something goes wrong, you can rectify it, can't you? That is, if I make a mistake…"

Neshi's black-brown eyes glinted with impatience. "There may come a moment when I can't help you. You're not the only one for whom time is running out. I suggest you do your best to survive, Meical."

Never had Neshi used his given name. Meical studied his creator's face, made an attempt to penetrate the shield with which Neshi hid his emotions, but it was futile.

A pull on his very soul drew his focus away from all but Caroline. It was a sweet pain he'd grown accustomed to when she fell asleep every night. She had just entered the REM state. She was ripe for dreaming.

His hunger spurred him, and he shot to his feet and pushed past Neshi. "Got to go."

The door slammed in his face before he reached it. He spun around to face Neshi, ready to tear the vampire apart.

The Alchemist lifted a warning finger. "You've come far. You have only a little way to go before you're fully changed. Don't ruin it for yourself. Use all the willpower you can. Don't drink from her. Do whatever you must to keep from doing so. The only balm for your blood thirst is her loving. It will soothe you through this time, if you will bring it into the light of day so that you can nourish yourself more completely. That is your one hope of survival."

The ire drained out of Meical, leaving only resignation to the weary vigil over his hunger. "I'm not sure of my control."

Neshi's expression softened with the first sign of sympathy Meical had ever seen in him. "Incubi are not creatures of restraint. Their appetites are inexhaustible. And yet you are by nature a giver now, not a taker. You're no longer a source of harm to her but pleasure. Remember that."

Olek stepped into his dark house and flipped on the hall light. Twelve years worth of Caroline's school pictures smiled back at him from the wall. Those were the days when all he'd had to do to make her feel safe was hold her in his lap. And what he couldn't fix, her mother could.

Even after losing Midge, he and Caroline had done all right together. Her problems had seemed so small and easy then…

"A very bright and beautiful girl, your daughter."

Olek's breath deserted him as a man in a ski mask came out of the dark of the living room. He spun on his heels and fumbled with the doorknob. He tried to elbow the intruder, but the guy slammed him against the door and held him there.

Olek managed to catch his breath enough to spit out, "I'm not telling you where she is. You may as well kill me now."

He felt his opponent's gloved hand rip his sleeve.

The man's breath smelled like mint. "That won't be necessary, and that's fortunate for both of us, because I dislike unnecessary violence. It always causes me problems in the long run."

The odor of alcohol reached Olek's nostrils, followed by the icy swab of a drenched cotton ball along the inside of his trapped arm. "It doesn't matter what you do to me. I'm not going to tell you anything."

"I'm not even going to ask. You see, I already have a pretty good idea where Caroline is. But I want to make it as painless as possible for her. She'll put up a lot less resistance if she knows I have you, Mr. Olek."

There was the sting of the needle, and then the whole world went fuzzy. *Caroline.*

Burke bent close and whispered, "I give you my word, Mr. Olek. I'll make it a clean kill."

"I can't believe it."

Caroline laughed and shook her head as she surveyed the occupants of the ballroom. She and Meical had just entered, having been announced like royalty. They'd arrived by carriage, drawn by four perfectly matched black horses.

This was only a dream, all of it, but the reality and detail of it kept superimposing themselves on her senses. She seemed to be here, really and truly, in an imagined eighteenth-century gala of her own device, under the same roof with Jane Austen's heroes and heroines, their families, friends and foes. It was as though her unconscious mind had dumped them sprawling out of the pages of each book she hoarded on her bookshelves.

Meical, dressed in his ballroom best, leaned close and murmured, "See anyone you know?"

She turned and grinned up at him. "It's amazing. I recognize everyone here because they all look exactly how I imagined them. Look, there's Mrs. Bennet herself."

"One needn't look to know she's here," Meical groused. "You surely heard her the moment we set foot in the room."

"Do you think she'll cause a scene and embarrass Elizabeth and Mr. Darcy?"

He shrugged, smiling. "I think that's up to you. I'm just your escort for the evening—one who's about to be replaced by the look of that rambunctious bunch headed our way. Is that your Mr. Darcy? You could've imagined him a little shorter and less good-looking, for my sake."

Before Caroline could respond, the tall, dark and handsome hero of *Pride and Prejudice* bowed and requested the pleasure of a dance with her. Meical bowed and gave her a nudge from behind and away she went to partner the divine Mr. Darcy in a country dance that was just beginning. Never mind that she didn't know the first thing about this dance they were about to do. As the orchestra began, the steps just seemed to come to her.

Incredible what the unconscious mind could supply when needed. And in a lucid dream like this, one had only to want something and it happened. She was in complete control here.

She danced with Mr. Knightley next, and then there

followed a boggling procession of gentlemen, some of whom she only vaguely recalled from her reading.

It didn't seem to matter that she couldn't place them, for they were only too pleased to tell her exactly who they were and what novel they came from, and would even quote her the scene in which they made their debut in the story to which they belonged.

Between dances there was an opportunity to chat with all her favorite heroines. She even took a stroll in the fragrant, twilit garden with Elizabeth Bennet and all of her sisters. She took some punch with the Dashwoods and eavesdropped here and there to find bits and pieces of dialogue in progress, as though she were in the midst of a living recitation.

And all the while, whenever she needed something, Meical was at her elbow, quiet and unassuming, constantly attentive, and oh so perfect for the atmosphere. In fact, he was the epitome of what her imagination had conspired to reproduce in this dream. No one, not even Mr. Darcy, seemed as handsome, as elegant or as appealing to her as Meical did.

He spoke little and only to her. He asked but one thing of her, and that was to allow him the last dance of the evening. But when the time came for him to claim his dance, the dream changed.

Gone were the people, including the orchestra. Yet the music played more sweetly than it had all night. The chatter turned to silence, the happy chaos to peace. It was as though someone had deigned that she and Meical should be the only two people on earth. And no country dances or reels or anything of the sort would do. For the two of them, it had to be a waltz.

He swept her into the dance as though they were one person.

"You're good at this," she said, looking up into his twinkling gray eyes. "You're really good."

He laughed softly. "I doubt I'd be able to hold my own for long if this were real."

If this were real…

The words made her wistful. "I could live here, you know."

Meical laughed. "No, thank you. It's too exhausting."

"No, really. I'm always wishing I could have been born two hundred years ago."

He shifted his gaze away from hers as they danced into a little pocket of darkness at the far end of the deserted ballroom. "You wouldn't like the squalor. Or the cruelty. Or the ignorance. And certainly not the violence. There is a difference, you know, between fact and fiction."

She studied his face, even though focusing so hard made her yawn. Under the light of the moonbeams that seeped through the curtains at this end of the huge room, his face looked pale. He looked weary, in fact. He was so serious all of a sudden.

The music abruptly became muffled, and Meical swayed on his feet a little.

Caroline caught his arm. "Whoa. Are you all right?"

"Too much wine," he murmured with a shaky chuckle.

"You really should dream up a less irresistible vintage. I swear, your Mr. Knightley and Colonel Brandon made fixtures of themselves at the punch bowl. Sots, both of them."

Caroline laughed. "Let's sit down. Come on."

Taking his hand, she led him to one of the couches that lined the walls. Meical sank onto the couch.

Caroline looked around them at the darkened, empty ballroom. Her contentment bled away in the eerie shadows. "Okay, all the people can come back now. I promised Mr. Collins I'd listen to him go on and on about Rosings."

When the ballroom failed to fill with people again, she held her breath and looked more closely around her. The wallpaper had begun to lose details of pattern and color. Not only was the orchestra gone, but the very chairs in which the musicians had sat were nowhere to be seen.

The ceiling was fuzzy gray, the floor yawned and the windows seemed ever more like the swaying curtains that hung in them, filmy and in constant sickly motion.

Caroline swallowed, feeling almost bereft. "Wow. Maybe I'm waking up."

"Or perhaps you wanted to be all alone with me."

She smiled at him, until she felt the heat of his glinting eyes. Yes, he looked almost feverish. "You look awful. Maybe we've overstayed our welcome here in dreamland."

"I'm sure you have it in you to give us a decent ride

home." He stood up and pulled her to her feet. "Come on. I think it's this way."

And as the words left his mouth, while Caroline was watching the floor and walls disappear around them, she suddenly found herself with him in their carriage again, speeding away across the moors, which seemed to be losing their color and shape with every imaginary mile they traveled.

She looked out the window at the miles of nighttime beyond them. There was a spicy, musky scent on the wind. She grinned. "Hey, it smells like you out here."

"Imagine that."

The carriage sped onto a stone bridge that stretched across an endless sea. The sky above seemed endless, too. There were two full moons to shine down on them, as if one wasn't enough. The bridge didn't end. It went on and on like a gray velvet ribbon until it disappeared into nothingness.

Caroline looked up to catch a glance at their driver, but there wasn't one. The driver's seat was deserted. The horses were there one moment, and in the next, the carriage was hurtling along on its own. Next the stars disappeared, and then the sea vanished. Only the bridge remained, stretching into nothing.

Caroline drew back into the stable confines of the carriage feeling dizzy and hot. "I feel...really weird..."

Meical smiled, wolfishly. "That's because you're sitting too far away from me."

And just like that, Caroline somehow wound up sitting beside him. Meical shifted like smoke. He was suddenly on his knees before her, and the carriage settled into a gentle, rhythmic, rocking motion.

Caroline couldn't take her gaze off him, even when her heart began to pound with the realization that this dream was both more real and more unreal than any she had had to date.

He placed his hands on either side of her on the seat and teased her mouth with a kiss. That kiss washed away everything in the world but his closeness and the motion of the carriage.

Caroline flattened her hand on his chest. "I want to know where we're going."

"You mean you want to know where I'm taking you." He kissed her neck. A soft groan sounded in his throat. "Don't be frightened. I won't hurt you. You know, by now, I want only to please you."

His mouth closed over hers again, and lethargy overtook her, leaving her limp all over, but oh so aware. The carriage pounded on. No one ahead or behind them. No one at all on that long, dark road. Caroline shivered. Here she was, awake in a dream.

Trapped.

What kind of mind game was she playing with herself? What was her subconscious doing to her now?

She laughed tightly. "I'm really doing a number on myself this time."

Meical eased her lacy skirts up to her waist. Where had her underthings gone? She had nothing on under her petticoats.

"You're just a symptom of my overwrought mind," she gulped.

He nudged her knees apart and moved himself against her damp crotch. He was so hard and ready, and felt so good.

Caroline arched against him, wanting to wrap her legs around his big body and… "Oh, I should just let you go."

"No," he whispered, touching her with his hand. "You mustn't do that, love."

"But I feel like I'm losing control."

"Yield to me, Caroline. I'll make you glad you did."

He slowed his caress until she ground her teeth together. An eddy of pleasure fluttered and teased her, a preface to an orgasm so intense she thought she might die. Tears sprang into her eyes as she felt herself slipping closer to the inevitable.

The ultimate loss of control.

After what she'd been through, it seemed impossible that she would dream about being at any man's mercy like this and not be terrified of it. Instead, it made her want him more.

"I love touching you," he whispered. "I crave your pleasure, Caroline, night and day. I must have it. I *will* have it." He slipped his fingers inside of her, thrusting gently while he circled her clitoris with his thumb.

For seconds Caroline shivered and gasped at his touch, while he whispered feverish things to her. His words were enough to send her over the edge. She drifted in a pool of satiation until he lifted her legs over his shoulders and penetrated her. He thrust in perfect rhythm with the rocking carriage.

Caroline clung to him, utterly open to him now, sensitive to his every move. The climax he'd just given her was nothing compared to what was building inside of her now. His hushed voice echoed in her mind like a thousand whispers. He was inescapable. *You are mine. I am yours. Give me your pleasure. Give it all to me, and I will give it back to you, sweeter and deeper than you have ever imagined.*

A ringing in her ears rose above the rush of the wind outside the carriage. The ringing grew louder. What was it, that sound? It was so familiar, but so out of place. Her awareness sharpened as it grew more insistent.

That was her phone ringing.

The entire world, all but the pleasure of Meical's lovemaking, unraveled before her eyes like a tapestry on a moldering wall. She opened her eyes wide and for a breath of a moment saw Meical above her in the firelight as he thrust into her, deep and hard.

"Let it ring," he whispered. He moved more swiftly. "You will not wake. Come on, Caroline…please…you're so close…"

Terror and pleasure ran together. Both poured out of her in a scream. Just as she climaxed, Meical's gaze swallowed her and darkness consumed everything.

Chapter 12

He'd been so deep into loving her that he hadn't felt
it all slipping out of his control, until he sensed her
waking.

The phone stopped ringing, but the damage was done.
Meical fought to keep Caroline unconscious while he got
her back into her nightshirt and tucked her into bed. He
needed much more from her. He barely had the strength
to keep her under, much less make her forget what she'd
seen in the brief moment when she'd awakened. He
managed to thrust her into a fitful sleep, confident that
on some level, his tigress knew exactly what he'd done
and wanted to punch his face in for it.

She deserved the chance to do precisely that.

Meical dropped himself into Caroline's armchair,
released her from his control and braced himself.

She came awake, battling her covers. "Meical!"

"I'm here, Caroline," he murmured.

She sat up and stared at him, breathless and pale and beautiful. He knew the moment she realized what he'd done, what he'd been doing all along. Her cheeks turned crimson and her perfect mouth parted. Her soft, half-gasped sigh went through him like a spear. He wanted to hold her so badly.

Her voice came out in an icy whisper, full of so much pain that he wished he could die, then and there. "That wasn't the first time, was it? It's been you, every time. Every dream."

He rested his elbows on the armrests of the chair and nodded. "From first to last, yes."

Tears slipped down her cheeks, glittering in the firelight. She wrapped her arms around herself. "Just so you could have sex with me?"

"Did I once make you feel that way?" He leaned forward in his chair, barely able to resist reaching for her. "I love you. I need you. And I know you need me, too. *That's* what the dreams were about."

She shook her head. "It doesn't matter how good it felt, how fun it was or how much I enjoyed it. You did it without giving me a choice. That wasn't just selfish, that was criminal." She ground her teeth together, her eyes afire. "You used me."

"I used *your dreams*," he countered. "And I accept with my whole heart the consequences that will come of it, but don't ask me to apologize. When I think of how happy, safe and loved you felt, I know I'll never regret a moment of it because that's exactly what you did for me, the first time you touched me."

She folded up in a ball and cried. Meical would have happily gone up in flames. He rose and pulled the blanket closer around her. She kicked it away.

"Caroline—"

"I never want to see you again!"

Meical stood looking at her a moment, cut to pieces by the sound of her sobs. A warm, wet muzzle nudged the palm of his hand, and he looked down to find Dash beside him. He picked her up and deposited her on the bed, and she curled up close to Caroline.

He turned and walked to the door, but paused to look back at her. "The dreams were only fantasies, Caroline, but what we shared when we were together was real. And you did say, though it was only in a dream, that you wished I could be yours for real."

She stopped crying. Was she listening?

"I can only hope that you meant it," he murmured, "because that's all I'm taking with me, besides the memory of loving you. I know in my own heart, even if you choose not to believe it, that our love was real. There's no way I could conjure love like that, not even to save my life. I didn't have to. It's all inside you. You're running over with it, enough for a man to feast on for the rest of his days. You just needed a safe place to rediscover it. When you did, you made me feel more alive than I've ever felt. And for that I thank you with all my heart."

The sound of the door closing behind Meical wrung a half moan from Caroline. She let his words wash over her. Her heart ached to believe him.

He'd shown her from the start how easy it was for him to slip past her defenses and pull down her shield. Now he'd shown her how easily he could invade her dreams. Her body.

His actions said he was a monster. But the feelings behind those actions, the emotions that rose from the very heart of him——what did they say about him?

She'd been probing his emotions while he talked to her. What lay beneath all his words was love. Real and timeless. Unchanging and certain. As powerful as he was. All for her. That's what hurt the most. His love was real, but instead of waiting for her to trust and accept him on her own terms, he'd manipulated her into sharing herself with him.

Why? What possible justification could he offer for taking her like that, when all she had needed was his patience?

She would never know.

Tears burned her eyes again. She found her nearest crutch and went to the fireplace. Sinking down on the floor where they had lain together, she closed her eyes and gathered every tendril of emotion that remained in the room.

What they had shared, even in such a short time, was so strong. The walls throbbed with residual passion, anguish, devotion and hunger, more powerful to her inner senses than the mingled scents of flesh and pleasure. But it was the embers left after those flames had gone that she wanted now, glowing all night long and forever in her heart. They were enough to start a lifetime of fires. Caroline found the warmth of Meical's love and wrapped it around her like a blanket.

Grabian was an idiot. Neshi bobbed in the ceiling's shadows above Caroline, invisible to her, and listened to her litany of woe over the fool. Shifting his focus, he tracked Meical's progress through the woods. He wouldn't last the night. The only thing he could do for Grabian now was end his suffering before it began.

Neshi ground his fangs together. To come so close to realizing everything he'd worked for!

A nebulous vibration of energy caught his attention. It was close, faint, but certainly not weak. Definitely human. He held his breath, tracing its origin. Caroline Bengal?

His heart skipped a beat, and he froze, as the realization dawned on him slowly. He'd labored over the reformation of Meical's body, as he had done before with his other subjects, monitoring the enlivening of each of Meical's functions—except for one.

He had wasted no effort in that quarter, of course, for it was known by all their kind, restoring that particular ability lay beyond the realm of magic, medicine and all the wisdom of the ages. It simply wasn't possible.

Yet here before him, hidden and unknown as yet, was the quickening proof that his herbs and magic had worked a cosmic miracle even he had not anticipated.

Neshi closed his eyes. What in the name of Ra had he done?

He shot upward through the ceiling of Caroline's cabin and into the night sky, materializing as he rocketed higher, faster and faster until the wind made his eyes blur with tears.

High above, he halted his ascent and floated into a cloud, allowing the gusty, rain-soaked air to buffet him in circles while he thought.

If he told Grabian…

But the fool was poised to leap in the wrong direction, and he might consider this an even bigger reason to end it all as quickly as possible. He couldn't be trusted with the knowledge.

He'd grant Grabian a boon. He'd give him a chance to make a wrong decision and survive it. Hopefully Grabian would come to his senses and make the choice to live. Let Grabian choose his own path, but by the blood of Osiris, Neshi wouldn't let him forfeit his existence easily.

He took a moment to monitor Grabian and satisfied himself that his runaway creation was not yet at death's door, and then, closing his eyes, called to those he needed to help set his plan in motion. He had his response in seconds, wrapped in a dulcet kiss of thought that made him smile.

Now, for the other. Looking down at the world below him, Neshi sifted through the thousands of heartbeats that rose to him on the night wind. Where in that mishmash of human life could he find a suitable underling for the task at hand, a human who would elicit the correct response from Grabian? There really was only one that would do. And in fact, he would do splendidly. Neshi had only to locate him.

His searching inner eye reached as far as a tiny halo

of light on the side of the highway beyond him. Toby's Bar and Grill. He grinned. Naturally.

In the mass of human life that seethed beneath that roof, amid the sweat and perfume and the clanging music, the one he sought sat soaking his witless brain in alcohol. Neshi estimated it would take fifteen minutes to lay claim to that ill-gotten wretch's life. Less, if he gave no heed to the cretin's discomfort. Grabian wouldn't get far in that amount of time. The Alchemist dove into the ocean of night that separated him from his prey.

The clang of Caroline's cell phone ringing sounded like a cannon going off in the darkness. She lifted her head from the floor and glanced at the clock on her living room wall. Four in the morning. John never called at this hour.

What if Mrs. Hicks had suffered complications? Sandy and Ray would need her.

Weary of heart and stiff from head to toe, she sat up and scooted across the floor to the table where she'd left her phone. Her thoughts shifted in too many directions, from facing the day without Meical to the prospect of explaining to Sandy and Ray that their mom wasn't coming home as soon as they'd been told she would. She picked up the phone and said "Hello" before she realized she'd failed to check the caller ID.

"Good morning, Caroline."

An unfeeling, cultured voice. Terror rose inside of Caroline so swiftly that it nearly cut off her next breath. "Burke."

"Don't hang up," he said. "I assure you, the sheriff

won't get to your friends the Calvins before I do, and by the time he finds their bodies, I'll have paid you a visit. So, let's keep this between us."

Her mouth went dry. Where was he? She closed her eyes and probed the vicinity around the house. His sick soul stood out, like red on black. He was less than a mile away and headed in her direction.

What would buy her some time?

Relying on the power of the inner shield Meical had built within her, she braced herself for the plunge into Burke's tainted soul. His delusions remained unchanged. Yes, there was a lot there to use against him. If he'd been sane, she'd be dead.

She took a deep breath. "I know you can hurt my friends. You don't have to prove it to me. It's me you're after."

His smooth, calm tone of voice sliced through her like daggers. "I can see you're going to be reasonable. We've danced around with this long enough. We have to give Rivera what he paid for. But how I do that is your choice. I want to make it painless for you, so I'm going to give you a chance to cooperate with me."

Caroline responded in a passive voice, "But I know what a sportsman you are, Burke. Deep down, you don't really want me to cooperate, do you? It will be more satisfying for you if I give you trouble."

The arousal in his voice was audible enough to gag her. "Yes, you do know me. That's why I'm going to enjoy you so much. You're as skilled in your discipline as I am in mine. There's a lot of psychology to what I do. You're going to like that part. Just don't think you can play me."

"I know I can't get away with that. You'd see through it. I'm only asking you to consider a few things. Someone as powerful as you doesn't need to threaten nonhostiles outside his target's perimeter. Isn't that right?"

"Your behavior will determine how safe your friends are."

"I understand." She switched the phone to her other hand and wiped her sweaty palm on her jeans. "But powerful people don't have to lie. If you tell me you won't hurt my friends, I can believe you. Can you show me that kind of power? Can you give me your word you won't hurt them, if I give you my word to keep this between you and me?"

She held her breath and waited. He could just as easily prove his power by driving straight to the Calvins' and killing them while she listened. If she'd learned anything from staying one step ahead of him it was the fact that he never made idle threats.

"Your terms are acceptable. You have my word. Your friends are safe."

"I believe you," she murmured.

Caroline heard the sound of his car pulling up in the driveway and slipped behind a chair. He left the motor running and stayed in the car. Good. That meant he didn't want his fun to be over too quickly. That was her only hope. If he got out of that car, it meant he was finished playing.

At this proximity, she could pick up on his emotions more clearly. She felt the fraternal twins of abuse, waiting to send him over the edge. Suppressed rage and abject terror. The first would get her killed in a heartbeat; the second was her only viable weapon against him.

But she needed a better battleground than this cabin and more time to prepare for a confrontation.

"Powerful people can compromise," she said evenly. "Like your willingness to give me a head start. I've shown you how well I understand you. Isn't that worth something?"

"You know I can't let you go."

He turned off his motor.

"No, no," she said. "I'm not asking for that. I'm asking for time to prepare my defenses."

She sensed his surprise at her boldness, followed by suspicion. "I think I've made it clear, if you go to the police, I'm going to have to kill all your friends."

Wrong turn. Don't challenge him. "I know the police can't keep me safe from you."

"No, they can't. And if you go to them, Caroline, or try to get help of any kind, I'll have to hurt you for it when I catch up with you. And someone you care about will suffer."

He said it so deliberately…what was he hiding from her? Caroline tried to reach deeper into him, but she couldn't get past her own fear. She had to stay calm. She had to get rid of him long enough to think. And she had to be sure she didn't give him a reason to retaliate against her friends.

"No police," she whispered. "It'll be just the two of us."

"So, you just want me to wait until you're ready for me?"

"The alternative is that you come in here right now and kill me. That's not much of a challenge."

Take the bait. Take the bait. Come on. Take it.

His voice dropped to a breathy whisper, as if he were holding the phone too close to his mouth. "I'm ready to get this going, now. You're making it very hard for me to wait."

"On the other hand, I won't be much fun if I'm dead."

He laughed again. "Oh, all right. I'm listening."

"Give me that head start you promised. Give me three days to get out of here. I just want to take this fight where we won't be disturbed. And I give you my word, when you catch up with me I'll meet you face-to-face. No more running."

That much she meant. She was finished running from him. This ended now. But she had to get him away from here, so he couldn't use her loved ones against her.

He didn't say anything for a moment.

Caroline lowered her voice to a submissive purr. "Powerful men have their own rules. I can play by your rules, Burke. Give me three days, and I'll prove it to you. I'll make this an experience you won't forget."

Or survive.

"I'll give you until sundown. I'll call you. If you don't answer, I'll assume you've gone back on your word and the people you love won't survive the night. But if you can show me you can be trusted to keep our bargain, you can take comfort in knowing all your loved ones will still be alive when this is over."

He hung up.

Caroline let her hand dangle at her side. The phone slipped from her shaking fingers and clattered on the floor. Sundown?

How far could she get by then? Not nearly far enough away to keep her friends safe, if Burke decided to use them as leverage. She'd have to choose her battleground somewhere close.

And then she'd make him wish he'd never been born.

Gasping for air, Meical swayed to a halt in the darkness and braced himself against a tree to rest, almost too weak to stand. Dawn was only moments away. Something in the way his flesh stung at the thought of it told him he probably wouldn't survive it this time. He closed his eyes for a moment. When he opened them again, the Alchemist stood on the path ahead of him.

Neshi wore the half-amused, half-deadly look on his face that always prefaced something unpleasant. "Do you think you can just walk away like this? Abandon your prey to others?"

Meical poised for a fight, weaving on his feet. He ground his teeth together, nearly choking on the words. "If I have to become her worst nightmare to survive, then I'd as soon rot. I am the *last* person she needs."

"You're quite wrong. She needs you now more

than ever. But apparently, I'm going to have to prove it to you."

Meical growled. "I'm warning you. I'm finished. It's over."

The ancient vampire quirked a brow at him, and the corner of his mouth twitched. Meical never felt the blow.

Nothing had surprised him in at least a millennium. Not like this. Badru hung in the air above the forest and watched Benemerut shoulder his ill-gotten creation and vanish out of sight, as oblivious to Badru's proximity as a fledgling.

What could possibly account for this sudden and atypical lack of caution in one so ancient?

Moments ago, something had distracted Benemerut so completely that he'd let his powerful shield fall, allowing his signature vibration to break from the mass of mortal life like the moon broke from the clouds on a clear night. Badru had found him within seconds.

Why? He tapped into the age-old connection that hummed between them, taking care to avoid detection, and found Benemerut alight with some newfound discovery. He was so utterly engrossed by it that he didn't even feel Badru's presence.

This horrific enthusiasm did not bode well. It could only mean Benemerut was contemplating something worse than the abominations he'd already committed.

And if he is, whose fault is that?

Gods, that voice…honey-sweet with possession and soft with reprimand… Who was she? Badru spun in a circle, looking for her, turning the night upside down to find her.

The breeze lifted his curls and caressed his cheek, bringing him fragrances he hadn't smelled since his mortal youth.

Who are you? he demanded. *Show yourself to me. Now.*

You know me. I called to you long ago, in happier times for both of us. Have you been nightbound so long that you cannot remember the warmth of Osiris rising in the east and the rhythm of the Nile coursing through your soul?

The scent of incense and the hush of murmured prayers enveloped Badru, as powerful to him now as in the hours he'd spent prostrate on the cool stone of the temple floor, surrounded by the sacred cats of Bast. How he'd pleaded with the goddess Bast to grace him with a sense of direction and duty like Benemerut had. Badru swallowed a bitter taste at the back of his throat. Tears burned his eyes.

Do you remember what else you asked of me? Bast whispered.

Badru closed his eyes and nodded, as consumed with her presence now as he had been that night—his last night as a mortal. *I asked you to show me a way to serve you. I asked you to make me yours forever.*

And what did I tell you?

To remain with you for another hour, there in the temple. But...my friends came and...they found me there...

And they were intent on their mischief that night, off

to meet a passing caravan of travelers outside of town. Magicians, they said. Seers and sages who could work forbidden wonders before your very eyes.

They dared me to come with them. They said I was a coward if I didn't.

And you didn't have the humility to remain with me. So you went. And that night, the "magicians" worked their dark miracle for you, to be sure. You were their forbidden wonder. Now we will see if you have the patience, at last, to bide with me, or if you will turn your back on me as you did that night.

It's too late for me. This hunger will destroy me. Benemerut will go the same way. I intend to see an end to both of us before that moment comes. He will pay for what he has done.

What he *has done? The original crime was yours. This you know. You took everything from him. In my eyes, you are the author of all his wrongdoing.*

What about his "experiments"? I didn't set him on that path. Better that he should cease to exist than go on with his transgression.

You would do well to take a closer look at this "transgression" of his. There is honor in Grabian, and the woman Grabian loves is kind and brave. She has shown herself capable of generosity toward those who are beloved by me.

Badru caught sight of a small black cat meandering closer. Its gold eyes twinkled in the darkness like holy embers.

I have appeared to each of them in my own way, Bast went on. *I have tested them and found them worthy of life and happiness, just as Benemerut is worthy of forgiveness.*

Bast's hand came to rest on the crown of Badru's head, soft and soothing. The small black cat blinked at him in the darkness.

Forgiveness? Never. Please. You are my last hope for justice.

But I am his last hope for mercy. Go now. Keep an eye on him, but do him no harm. I need him. And I will not suffer my plans to be undermined.

Badru sighed. *I make no promises. For now, he is safe, but when the moment comes, I will do what I must.*

He rose in the air, floating along above the treetops in the direction Neshi had taken, and vanished.

Caroline stared into her coffee and gave John and Millie time to think. She'd offered them no explanations about why she had to leave. It was a lot to expect of them to just take her dog and not ask questions, but the less they knew, the safer they'd be.

Sunlight poured through the cream-colored curtains of their familiar kitchen, making everything feel right and normal. The light brought out the silver in Millie's auburn hair and the lines in her roseate face. Caroline loved the vibrations she got from Millie. She was the Cosmic Mother type.

She hadn't realized until now, how much she would miss Millie's company, or how much she ached to stay here, with these two dear people who cared about her.

Their friendship was a luxury that had made the insanity of the past few months easier to bear.

"But where will you go?" Millie asked.

"I can't really say," Caroline answered with a quick smile. "I don't want to be around people right now. You know I'm so messed up. I need to get away. I just need you to look after Dash while I'm gone. It could be two weeks. Maybe less."

John's face was ruddier than usual from sleep, but his clear blue eyes were as sharp as always. "I don't have to know what you've been through to realize you need protection. Stay here with us. Let me go get the sheriff."

She stood up and kissed his cheek. "Big mistake."

When Dash rose to follow her out, Caroline bent and cradled the shepherd's head in her hands. "You have to stay here, baby."

"Hold on, Caroline," John murmured. "If we could give you someplace to go, somewhere you'd feel safe, would you take it?"

"No, because then you'd know where I am," she replied.

"Forget that for now. Answer my question."

She didn't dare. "I think I'd just better go."

"Now, just wait." John turned to Millie. "What do you think, honey? Your family's old place?"

"I think Caroline has to be the one to decide that." Millie turned to Caroline with a hopeful smile. "Our old house is only a short way from here, but it's sitting on five acres of woodland, and no one ever goes out there. Mama moved out last month to live in Glenmore

Senior Lodge, just down the road from John's clinic. But she had me keep the utilities on in case she doesn't like Glenmore and wants to come home again. You'd be comfortable and safe there, and no one would be the wiser."

It was so very tempting, not to leave John and Millie behind. But anyone who knew her could be used as hostages to find her. She couldn't stand the thought of putting them in danger like that.

Millie reached across the table and took Caroline's hand. "If we don't try to help you, we'll regret it for the rest of our days."

Caroline's face flushed warm, and she placed her hand over Millie's. "The farther away I can get from here, the better."

"Not necessarily," John said. "Not if someone's after you, and someone obviously is."

"I can't tell you—"

He cut her off with a wave of his hand. "Just hear me out. If you're on the run, it's not how far you can get that matters, it's how unpredictable you can be. The last thing anyone would expect you to do in this situation is stay put."

She had to admit, it made sense in a typical John Calvin way. But if she was any kind of friend to them, she'd leave. She shook her head. "I can't risk it."

Millie squeezed her hand. "I can't stand the thought of you being out there on your own, dealing with something dangerous. At least stay somewhere within reach."

John nodded. "Like Millie's old place. The sheriff

could get to you in about six and a half minutes. Come on, honey, it just makes sense if you're in some kind of trouble. You don't have to be alone."

Alone. Was she strong enough to live on the run and face possible death in places where not a soul would even know what happened to her? If she stayed here and Rivera's men caught up with her, she had a better chance at survival than she would on her own. And if they killed her, at least she'd die where she had been happy, where people knew her, where she felt like she had had a home.

Maybe if she stayed in the area, but didn't make contact with anyone, and let a little time go by, and stayed out of sight for a while longer...

She met their waiting, hopeful gazes. "If I agree, you absolutely cannot tell a single soul where I am. That goes for Meical, too."

John gave her a chiding grin. "Whatever you say. But that boy's head over heels in love with you, and if he takes 'goodbye' for an answer, I'll be surprised."

"Just promise me you won't tell him anything about this," she said. "And under no circumstances can you contact me."

Millie smiled. "We won't, if you promise to let us know somehow if you need anything."

Caroline nodded. "It's a deal."

John set his cup aside and stood up. "Millie, call the office and ask Tabby to reschedule my morning appointments." He smiled at Caroline. "Got something for you, kiddo. Give me a second to go upstairs and get it, and then I'll help you pack up and get relocated."

John left the kitchen.

Caroline turned to Millie. "What's going on?"

"We've never had children of our own, you know," she said. "You're the closest thing to a daughter we'll ever have."

John came back in carrying an elongated case in his hands. It was big enough to hold a violin or long-stemmed roses.

He balanced the case on one arm and thumbed the brass closure open. "We've been meaning to give this to you for two months, but we weren't sure if it was the right time."

As he opened the case slowly, Caroline felt the rush of his angst, the hope that she would accept their gift, and her throat tightened up so hard she couldn't speak. Then she saw what lay inside, and she couldn't stop the tears from coming.

She reached into the case and ran her hand over the smooth, skin-toned calf of the prosthetic leg. From the brochures they'd handed out to her at the hospital during her recovery, she knew it had cost at least fifteen thousand. How many people in her situation longed for one of these and couldn't afford it?

John leaned over and kissed her forehead. "It'll feel a little weird until you get used to wearing it, and there may be some initial discomfort, but knowing you, you'll be running circles around Dash in no time at all."

Caroline hugged him tight. "I don't know how to thank you."

"Just promise us you'll call us if you're in danger."

Chapter 13

Thirsty...so thirsty...he was on fire...

Meical opened his eyes and peered around at bare rock walls. The light of a single lantern burned his eyes. Even that feeble flame seemed hot. He could make out wooden beams here and there. It was damp, and the air would have been soothingly cool if not for his feverish thirst.

It looked like he was in an old coal mine.

Meical jerked his aching limbs to attention and heard the clang of chains. He found himself shackled to the wall behind him at the wrists.

Good old Neshi, thorough to a fault.

Thank you.

Meical curled his lip and snarled in the darkness. "You'd better be glad I can't get to you."

Your actions have made it clear, Grabian. You're disinclined to survive. You made that decision all on your own. I'm merely acting on it. But you've done so much better than your predecessors, I think you deserve something more merciful than termination.

Bitter amusement ebbed beneath Meical's anger. "How generous. I don't care what you do with me, you maniac—"

I gathered that, yes.

"—but leave Caroline alone. She's finished with this."

Finished, yes. Done for, in fact. It's a pity.

Meical's heart stuttered, then pounded. And it had nothing to do with his weakening body. "What?"

The human who's tracking her now is a formidable foe for her to face. It's doubtful she'll survive.

Meical hung his head and closed his eyes. "Rivera."

Not Rivera, but the one Rivera has sent to kill her. He's professional, twisted and powerful. For a human, that is. Too bad for her.

Meical yanked at his chains and growled. Why hadn't he stayed with her?

Neshi's sigh of exasperation sliced through Meical's thoughts. *Because, fool that you are, you decided she could not love you, and in doing so, left her choiceless in the matter of her own fate. Your protectiveness blinded you to the fact that she was yours already. Of course, none of this will matter when she's dead.*

"Let me go to her, Neshi."

And what good are you to her in your current

condition? No, all you can do for her now is decide if you want to live for something or die for something. You wasted most of your human life and your existence as a vampire trying to choose between the two. You'd best decide soon, or she will perish.

Meical shook his head. *Damn you.*

The Alchemist laughed. The sound curled around Meical's senses like an icy breath. *The feat of my damnation rests in more powerful hands than yours. Heed me: I'm going to give you two ways out of this. Either way, you may have time to save Caroline.*

Despair drove Meical's breath away. "Neshi, please, don't let him hurt her."

Silence taunted him.

"Neshi!"

An impenetrable fog closed the connection between them.

Drifting on the edge of the deep sleep, though his body lay dormant in repose, Neshi pushed back the oblivion that sought to close his mind as it had closed his eyes and stilled his heart. There were things to be done if Grabian was going to survive whatever choice he was about to make.

Across the long miles Neshi expanded his consciousness, until he found the two for whom he searched. They lay entwined in the darkness of Ellory Benedikt's cellar room. Neshi regarded the serene scene of vampiric domesticity. Talisen lay in the arms of her dormant mate, as still and silent as he, though she was merely dozing. Revenants never slept.

She had given up the restoration of sleep, along with everything else in her that was human, just as Grabian had given up his existence as a vampire. All for the sake of Benedikt and his fledglings. So much sacrifice. So much devotion.

Neshi brushed Talisen's mind with a feather touch.

She stirred, pouty-mouthed like a sleepy child. He allowed himself a glimpse of the riches that belonged to Benedikt, just before she sensed that she and her mate were not alone and reached for the blanket at her feet.

Forgive the intrusion, he whispered in her mind.

Her eyes widened and she looked around the dark room as though she expected him to be there in the flesh. *Neshi?*

Soft, madam. I need to tell you where Grabian is and how you must help him. Are you ready to do the work of a revenant?

She frowned. *What have you done to him?*

I'll spare you the details. Listen carefully because I may not be able to communicate with you again. The key to Grabian's survival is his mate.

She blinked. *Meical has a mate?*

Yes, and at some point, you're going to have to help her get to him because he's going to do something very stupid, and she won't be able to reach him in time to save him without some help.

Talisen sat up. *Okay, I'm listening. What do I do first?*

I knew I could count on you.

That seemed to surprise her. Neshi watched her

expression soften. *Hey...I think you should know... there's an Ancient called Badru hunting you.*

I know. We have no time to discuss it. The sun is climbing, and I'm weakening. This is what you need to do for Grabian. There is a human you must contact.

Okay, just show me.

He filled her mind with phone numbers, locations, faces and voices, everything she needed to know, everything she needed to do, everything she needed to tell Ellory when he revived, and a myriad of tasks only a revenant could do in a vampire's place.

Who's the doctor for? she asked. *Meical's mate?*

Yes, and...there is someone else who may need his help before this is all over. I will explain everything to him. You just do what I have asked you to do.

Wait. What about Badru? Is there a way to get rid of him?

Neshi couldn't help but laugh. *You're asking me, the one you regard as your enemy?*

Better the devil you know...

Neshi laughed again. *There is nothing you can do about Badru. But I can vouch for his nature. He is high-minded, but not evil. I know him well, and have, for a very long time.*

Neshi, who is this guy to you?

He withdrew from her without answering. Sleep was upon him.

What were these "options" Neshi had mentioned? Meical wondered. His only way out was to strengthen himself.

Impossible.

The least he could do was warn Caroline. If he could pick up on her life force from here, he might connect with her long enough to do that much. He rested his head against the icy wall and closed his eyes.

There. Wrapped around his soul, a thread of her very essence vibrated between them. He had their oneness to thank for that. He followed the fragile trail, lost it and fell back into nothingness, then tried again.

The brilliant colors of a sunset filled his mind's eye, and the image of a large, rambling edifice shimmered and firmed into gables and windows. Meical could sense Caroline's presence inside the house. He clung to the vision, trying to ascertain its location. Woods. That was all he could see beyond the clearing that surrounded the old house.

A tainted cloud blotted out the sunlight, darker than the coming night, and Meical focused on its source. Her enemy was approaching, but Meical was too weak to discern how soon he'd reach Caroline. He focused his will on touching her mind.

Caroline.

He sensed the way she paused as though to listen. He could almost see her…touch her…

Caroline, you're in danger. You must hide. I can't get to you yet, but…I will…

The effort to push the words at her mind bled his strength from him and he had to let it all go. The image faded except for the darkness that crept closer to Caroline.

He had to find the strength to get to her, whatever

Janet Elizabeth Jones 221

the cost to him. It didn't matter. Nothing mattered but seeing that she was safe.

A hushed whisper sounded from the darkness of the mine.

Meical fell still and eyed the blackness beyond the lantern. Suddenly the whisper rushed past his face. He gasped and jerked aside. Someone was here with him.

A warm fragrant breath touched his cheek. *Here, sugar boy.*

Meical found himself staring into a pair of glinting black eyes six inches away from his face. Beautiful, winsome eyes.

She glimmered from head to toe, not quite opaque, and slowly materialized, crouching beside him in a long lavender gown of wispy, nearly transparent material. Exquisite…an angel with chocolate-colored skin…and that fragrance…it lulled his mind into thoughts of…

Meical sucked in his breath and felt his head spin. *"What are you?"*

"I," she replied, "am a succubus. Benemerut asked me to look you over and see if there was something I could do for you."

"So, you're like me, then?"

"No, sugar boy. I'm the real thing. You're a conversion model." She crossed her arms and gave him a meticulous once-over. Her gaze touched him as though her hands would follow in their wake. "I see Ben hasn't lost his touch for the dramatic."

Meical drew his legs together and winced. "Neshi mentioned two ways out of my predicament. You're one of them?"

"Yes, and you'll like me better than your other choice."

"All I care about is saving Caroline."

"You'll have a chance to do that, no matter what choice you make."

"You're sure?"

She nodded. "So, shall I fix you?"

Fix him? Meical cleared his throat. "Doesn't that mean we have to…um…"

"Yes, doll, it does." Her eyes glittered like gold for an instant. "But you can think of her every minute, if you like. It won't hurt my feelings. I'm doing this as a favor for Ben."

It was tidy. Smart. Foolproof. He'd be strong enough to save Caroline. He'd have the rest of his existence to protect her…love her…

Except for one problem.

He smiled slowly at the ethereal beauty before him. "I'm sorry. I can't…be with another woman. Only Caroline."

She quirked a brow at him. "You sound surprised."

"I want to survive long enough to protect her. That's all. But I have to do it with a clear conscience."

The succubus tilted her head and looked at him with true sorrow in her eyes. "Are you sure? I am your chance to survive forever. Your other choice…" she frowned and stood up with an air of queenly impatience "…will make you unfit for her. And then you'll die."

Unfit for her? What did that mean?

"Life or death?" she prodded.

Meical let his gaze fall and eyed her brown bare feet.

His gaze caught on the silver ankle bracelet she wore. It twinkled in the light of the lantern like Caroline's eyes.

Life or death? Neshi was right. He'd existed between the two for centuries, and all the while, honor had seemed so far from him. Once it had been as important to him as his very soul. He had let it go over these long years past, as though it were merely some earthly vestige.

Until Caroline. She had brought out the best in him.

But saving himself at the cost of what little honor he had left seemed the coward's way out.

"She'll be all right without me," he murmured. "She'll be all right. She just needs my help now, in this moment."

The succubus crouched again, her eyes alight with a fire almost too robust for Meical to bear. It seeped into his mind, his body—but not his heart.

She flattened her hand on his chest and leaned closer. Meical felt her sift through his thoughts, memories, feelings…his very soul…as delicately as a surgeon with a scalpel. Whatever she was looking for was a mystery to him, but she nodded, as though she'd found it.

"Listen, sugar boy, this girl is your heart's song. No matter what happens, you just remember, you've saved her once already."

"I have?" Meical swallowed hard. "When?"

Her eyes twinkled, but she shook her head. "I can't tell you that. But this I know. If things go badly for you tonight, don't lose hope. You won't always be without her. The two of you are meant to be together."

Meical's heart ached to believe her words. "Thank you."

She looked him up and down again. "I told Ben I wouldn't toy with you. And I won't. But I didn't tell him I wouldn't help you along a little. It won't be enough to get you out of this, but it might help you with your second choice."

Before Meical could draw his next breath, the succubus pressed her lips to his and poured an ancient flame into every inch of him. Fire and power. In an instant, he was fit to burst. He gasped in an exquisite heat that boiled his blood.

All for Caroline. Only for her.

His strength flooded into his muscles and bones so fast that his head spun. He was still gasping with relief when he realized the succubus had gone. Satiation brought restful sleep he couldn't escape. His eyes closed, and he laid his head back and drifted in and out of gossamer mists, fragrant with Caroline's scent. He didn't know how long he slept, but when he came to, he wasn't alone.

"You thought you were tough. Now look at you, freak."

Meical's senses cleared enough for him to recognize who that voice belonged to. What was *he* doing here? He peered through the half light. Before him swam a trio of human-looking apes. He concentrated on the one in the middle, and a moment later, his triple vision cleared and he could see.

"Hicks, you have a knack for being in the wrong place at the wrong time."

Hicks snorted. "You're the one who's chained to a wall. *I'm* working for Neshi now."

Neshi wouldn't. Not Hicks. What was he thinking?

"The Alchemist doesn't make servants out of vermin; he dines on them."

Hicks curled his lip up at Meical and swaggered closer—close enough for Meical to see the glint in the little snake's eyes. The flushed face, the gleaming gaze, the bounce in Hicks's tread…he nearly floated off the ground with every step he took. But it couldn't be possible.

How many centuries had come and gone since the Alchemist had created a revenant? His staunch determination to guard the power in his veins was the one reassurance the vampire community had that he was still sane, unlike others who had lived longer than a millennium. Like every revenant, Hicks was now a dangerous weapon against vampires, a deadly hybrid with a human's imperviousness to the sun and whatever power and abilities his maker had bequeathed him. Even if Neshi had withheld most of his power from Hicks, it was madness to choose such a vessel for that kind of treasure.

Or was it?

Neshi never did anything without a reason. Hicks was somehow part of his endgame, here to serve a purpose in Neshi's plans for Meical, a purpose he could only serve as a revenant.

When the realization hit him, Meical smothered a

bitter laugh. This was Neshi's plan B. He'd said that
pure human blood would kill Meical, but the blood of
a new revenant was both human and that of his vampire
creator. With that potent mix, Meical could survive to
save Caroline.

But only until sunrise. This was what the succubus
had meant when she said his second choice would
mean his death. The Alchemist's fail-safe would be
inescapable. But at least he would die as he lived. As a
vampire.

It was just like Neshi to leave his wayward lab rat a
morsel, something to tempt him to gnaw and claw his
way out of his cage, even though it could end only in
one way. It was no less than the proverbial "gentleman's
way out"—a loaded pistol that provided an honorable
death.

Hicks, then, was his loaded pistol.

He followed the revenant with his eyes. "I see you've
been recruited. Congratulations. You have a stunning,
if brief, existence to look forward to."

Hicks pounded his chest with his fist. "No way. I'm
going to live forever. He said so."

Meical watched the beads of sweat on Hicks's face
glint under the lantern light. "He lied."

Hicks's face contorted with rage. "He wouldn't lie to
me! He needs me. And after I'm finished helping him,
I'll help myself—to anything I want. Nobody can stop
me. Things are going to change around here."

Meical gave his chains a subtle pull. He could feel
them give way a little. At least some of his strength had

returned, thanks to the succubus's kiss. "If Neshi needed you, he would have made you an incubus like me."

Hicks looked petulant. "He refused to."

"That's because you're not cut out to replace me. But you make a useful slave."

Grumbling to himself, Hicks came nearer. There was too much caution in his face, for Meical's comfort. He sank down on his haunches and leaned in close—but not close enough—and his face flushed red-blue with a sheen of new sweat. "I don't have to wait on him to give me what I want, freak. I can do whatever I want."

"Except make an incubus out of yourself."

Hicks eyed him with less confidence.

Meical closed his eyes and said no more. At the moment, the only thing keeping Hicks's greed in check was his spinelessness. That wouldn't last long. A revenant's natural inclination to test his limits would lead the idiot right over the edge.

"Ouch!"

Caroline gasped as she hit the hardwood floor. Rolling onto her back, she stared up at the shadowy vaulted ceiling of the living room in Millie's old family home.

She sat up with a wince and scowled at her prosthetic leg. One screwup like this while facing off with Burke, and she'd be dead. Her only hope was to stay out of his reach long enough to use his fear against him. And she couldn't do that on crutches.

The attic. That was her only high ground. She eyed the long stairway that rose from the living room upward to the second story. There was a third story above that. And then the attic.

The last time she'd climbed stairs, she'd had both legs.

She'd have to slow Burke down, weaken him somehow, if those stairs were going to be as hard for him as they were for her.

Dragging herself to her feet, she held her hands out in front of herself and took a few careful steps, trying to ignore the pain in her swelling half-leg. It felt so weird to trust her weight to a foot she couldn't feel.

The sound of her cell phone ringing nearly made her fall again. So soon? She needed more time.

She plucked her phone from the table by the couch and answered it. "I'm here."

"I must say," Burke murmured, "you've chosen a strange place for us to do this. I'd have thought you'd want to spare your friends the heartache."

He must have tailed her from John and Millie's cabin. Of course. He wouldn't risk losing her by letting her out of his sight for even a minute.

Time to sharpen her ax.

"No one comes out here," she coaxed. "There will be no interference. Nothing to mar our moment. You've scanned the area by now. So you know I haven't got anyone watching for your arrival. No tricks. No surprises. Just you and me, Burke. One. On. One."

Caroline was quick to pick up on the fleeting trace of fear in him. What chord had she struck? Was it the thought of being alone with her?

She tested him. "You aren't walking into an ambush."

His fear morphed into icy rage, and his whisper sliced through her. "Better not be."

Was that what he was afraid of? An ambush? She dug deep, absorbing the sickening fear that drenched him. She could practically feel him sweating. Trauma, old and deep, provoked the rage in him. She followed it to its source, to a memory from a time before Burke saw himself as someone powerful.

A little boy ran through a jungle, dodging rubber bullets. Faces covered with camouflage paint peered at him through the bushes as he ran past them. Guns rang out. A bullet nicked his ankle, and he screamed but ran on.

Caroline let the boy's terror suck her into the memory just long enough to catch a panted whisper of his thoughts, and then she recoiled from the scene as quickly as she could claw her way out of it.

She had a way to fight him now. "Trying to ambush you would be a mistake."

"One you'd pay for."

"Just like they made you pay for *your* mistakes."

His silence was both scary and satisfying.

She pushed him. "Little boys who made mistakes were used for target practice, weren't they, Burke? You were fast enough to survive, so they let you live. Then they made you a killer."

He was close to exploding, barely hanging on to his balance. "They made me a warrior, strong enough to deserve the right to live."

"But you aren't strong. You depend on guns. *I don't.* I'm going to beat you my way."

He recovered his composure way too quickly. "I don't know how you know these things about me, Caroline. You really understand me. I won't enjoy killing you."

"But you never enjoy the killing. You have a panic attack seconds before you pull the trigger. Panic, pleasure and pain. Yours. Your victim's. It doesn't matter. It feels the same to you, and you crave it. But as much as you want to be powerful, you're not. You're just scared and angry."

"You have until sundown. To show you how lenient I am and how fair I can be, I won't wear my night gear."

"I tried to warn you. I won't kill you because I'm not like you. But I'm going to make you wish you were dead."

Even as he laughed, Caroline felt the tendrils of fear twisting around his throat. She pressed the phone closer to her mouth and shoved her anger at him, "I'll be waiting for you."

She slammed her cell phone down.

Sundown. What did that give her? Three hours? Maybe four? She glanced out a window and then at the mantel clock and eyed the stairs with a sinking feeling in the pit of her stomach.

She had to slow him down and make him feel vulnerable. That was the only way to make him susceptible to his fear.

She began by raiding the kitchen.

The pantry yielded a few canned vegetables, a cracked

glass vase and an empty fire extinguisher. The cabinets revealed two place settings of chipped china and some plastic forks. She rifled through the silverware drawers, hoping to find a carving knife. No luck.

But she did find a screwdriver, along with a rusty, Y-shaped cheese cutter missing its cutting wire, and a huge rubber band that still had some stretch to it.

Caroline dragged her finds into a heap in the kitchen floor. There was a garage out back. What would she find there?

Still wobbly, she half hopped, half stepped her way out the kitchen door and into the garage. The stench of old grease and rusty car parts assailed her nose, too similar to her memory of the basement where she'd nearly died.

Caroline fought for her control, shoving past the traumatic memories that flew at her. If she couldn't control her own emotions, how could she expect to control her adversary's? She had to keep her head, or she'd be paralyzed by fear.

She stepped into the smelly darkness and felt for a light switch on the wall. One bare bulb in the ceiling. Way too much like that basement had been. She slammed it off and clung to the wall, willing herself to breathe.

When she was sure of herself again, she explored, keeping her hands in front of her as she went along. A little sunlight shone in through greasy windows in the weathered double doors. This place was more like an old carriage house than a garage.

There was one car and a boat. She spent one precious hour going through them and returned to the kitchen

with her treasures: a pulley, a sizable coil of rope and a
very dull ax. She eyed the ax blade for a long moment.
The obvious possibilities ran through her mind.

But she'd meant what she said to Burke. She wouldn't
kill him. She wouldn't stoop to his level. The only thing
that made the difference tonight, between the hunter and
the hunted, was her refusal to cross a line he'd erased
long ago.

As she piled all her defenses on the kitchen floor and
set to work, a twinge of animosity, mixed with hope,
made her face flush hot.

Look out, Goliath.

Chapter 14

The sun had all but gone. Burke cocked his rifle and proceeded up the driveway toward the house. He passed through a green-black tangle of shrubs that closed in on the yard and shuddered. The memory of rubber bullets whizzing overhead and hard gazes watching him from the trees drove him on.

As he crossed the yard, he schooled his mind to focus on the job at hand, and only that. But the trees seemed to be alive tonight. Watching him.

He mounted the porch. The door stood slightly ajar, welcoming him. That was cocky of her. Noise poured out of the house. He listened. It sounded as if she'd turned on every radio, stereo and TV she could reach. Smart. Being less than nimble, she wouldn't be very quiet on foot; hence, the noise pollution to cover the sounds of her movements. She would put up a delicious fight.

Not that it would last long.

He walked forward, gripped the doorknob in his gloved hand and pushed the door open slowly. In the instant between training his eye on the dark interior of the house and hearing a scraping noise above his head, Burke realized he had underestimated Caroline.

A heavy metal object crashed down on his head, crushing the light out of his eyes and jarring him with pain. He staggered across the threshold and caught himself on a wall that kept turning sideways. Seeing double, he felt for the bleeding lump on his head, scowled at the fallen fire extinguisher at his feet and tried to adjust to his double vision and pitching stomach.

"Very good, Caroline," he called out in the emptiness. "You've struck the first blow."

No pain. No sickness. Move. Move. Carry out the mission. Find the target. Terminate her.

Burke proceeded unsteadily into the noisy, shadowy room. The place was oppressive. His chest felt as heavy as his pounding skull did. He swallowed and wiped the sweat from his upper lip as senseless dread unfurled in the pit of his stomach, leaving his limbs icy and heavy and unresponsive.

He hadn't felt this way since…

The terror that had ruled his childhood erupted inside him, setting his heart pounding. The room stifled him with his boyhood horrors. He turned his face toward the window and tried to breathe, tried to separate himself from his emotions as he'd been taught to do.

A board creaked in the darkness behind him. He turned and lashed out, felt his fist connect with a sinewy arm, as something sharp skidded from his ribs all the way down to his thigh. A gouging pain in his leg tore the breath from his lungs. What had she skewered him with?

As he collapsed to his knees, he felt her lithe little body tumble past him in the gathering grayness. A scuffling noise could barely be heard above the roar in his ears, and a hard jerk on his shoulder thrust his forehead to the floor. His gun was gone. Fear shook him again. His prey was armed.

Burke clamped his eyes and teeth shut as nausea swept over him. He waited for the shower of bullets from his semiautomatic. When she didn't fire on him, he lifted his head and looked around. He saw no sign of her.

Cursing, he felt along his wounded thigh. His groping fingers found the handle of a screwdriver. The rest of it was buried in his flesh. He yanked it out and fought to stay conscious.

She should have shot him when she had the chance. Her determination to play by her own rules would lead her right into his hands.

Burke slid his belt off, wrapped it around his bleeding leg and pulled it tight. Reaching into his flack vest, he pulled out a loaded M9 and pushed himself to his feet with a groan.

The curtain in the window across from him billowed in the night breeze. Burke approached the window carefully, dragging his leg as he moved. He nudged the curtains aside with the tip of his pistol, expecting to see a hobbling figure retreating to the woods.

A shard of something sharp pelted him from behind. Whipping around, he ducked as another sliced his forehead. Turning that fast on his feet made his head spin again, and his stomach gurgled and pitched. The room duplicated itself in a sickly swirl of black and white and flying glass.

With a roar, he emptied his pistol in all directions, until the humiliation of her attack stopped. Looking around him, he scrutinized the best hiding places in the room. There was only one. The sofa near the front door.

Hiding herself in this room had been a serious error on her part. He had her trapped now. There was no way she could get past him. Let her have time to realize he'd pinned her down. For ordinary people, the shock alone usually immobilized them. No need to hurry now. She was his. He kept his gaze on the sofa while he reloaded and picked as much of the glass out of his back and shoulders as he could reach.

"You know, Caroline, usually when my target gives me this much trouble, even though I admire their stamina, I make them suffer for it when I catch up with them. But not you." He took a breath, reveling in the power over her that his next words gave him. "If you give yourself up now, I can keep a promise I made to your father. I told him your death would be painless."

Burke stalked to the sofa, thinking he'd find her huddling behind it, ready to beg for her life. He shoved it aside. She wasn't there. He staggered in a circle. There were only three directions she could have gone. Out the front door, into the kitchen and up the stairs to the second floor.

He had never made the mistake of hemming himself in like that. If he had, they'd have hurt him for it.

The dread he had felt moments ago budded inside him again. For a moment the wallpaper on the walls seemed to resemble eyes watching him from forest greenery. It woke every ounce of caution he had. He wouldn't underestimate her again.

He scarcely heard the chopping noise and soft whir of movement over the sound of the blaring radio nearby. He turned in time to see Caroline rising into the darkness like an angel. He leaped toward her, but missed. She'd taken the high ground. Panic seized him. He'd expected a tearful, pleading Caroline to come forward and give herself up to him to save her father's life. Nothing moved above him. He couldn't hear her. He couldn't see her. He waited, holding his breath.

The sound of a cell phone ringing behind him nearly made him waste more of his ammunition. He answered it.

Her voice was icy. "You lied to me. You wanted this to be between you and me. You said none of my loved ones would be hurt if I gave you a good hunt. But now you've involved my father. A real warrior accomplishes his objective without using hostages. *We're playing by my rules now.*"

She hung up.

An instant later, something careened out of the

darkness, nicking his shoulder before it hit the floor-boards behind him with a thunk.

He turned. An ax was lodged in the floor.

He threw the cell phone down and waited, gun ready. She could have killed him anytime. Why hadn't she?

Something swung out of the darkness and slammed into his chest, knocking him backward. He ricocheted against the wall and landed facedown on the floor. He came to his feet, firing at the ceiling. Another magazine spent. Another loaded.

A rope dangled in front of him. He caught it, bleary-eyed and feeling sick, just as he heard the same whirring sound as before. This time he ducked and covered his head. He caught the sound of a bare foot hitting the second-floor landing only yards above him and fired toward the sound.

She yelped and clamored down the hallway, just ahead of his next barrage of bullets.

She was definitely wounded. Burke began his slow ascent.

Watching Hicks pace was enough to drive Meical mad.

Suddenly the revenant halted, squeaked out a laugh and turned to Meical with a gloating smile. "I've got Neshi's blood in my veins. There's nothing you have that can make me stronger than I am now."

Meical gathered his composure, his desperate thoughts all for Caroline. "Yeah. Right."

The revenant looked at him more closely. *Really*

studied him. Meical shielded his intentions, just in case Hicks could read him better than he thought.

Hicks crept closer and leaned against the wall, just out of reach. Meical could almost taste the revenant's blood now. He yearned for it. The thought woke an ache in his gums. This time, he welcomed the pain.

"He didn't give you his blood," said Hicks. "That's not how he made you an incubus. So what did he give you?"

Meical answered offhandedly. "Some kind of herbal crap."

"I could get some if I wanted it, freak."

"No, he has to give it to you. And he didn't. And he won't."

Meical watched Hicks seethe.

"Where does he keep it?" asked Hicks.

"You think I'd tell you? I'd rather rip out your spinal cord and strangle you with it."

Hicks's eyes reddened and glowed. He slipped a knife out of his boot and held it up in the lantern light. "I bet you'll tell me if I bleed you a little."

Meical bade his entire body to relax, while underneath, he gathered his energy. "Bad idea, Hicks. Don't do this."

The pain caught him by surprise, but another pain, very familiar, followed swiftly on its heels. When Meical opened his eyes, the knife was buried in the palm of his manacled hand and a new set of fangs had emerged from his gums.

As Hicks plucked the knife out of his hand, Meical

clamped his mouth shut to keep his canines out of sight and freed the beast inside him at last.

Hicks's gaze was fixed on the blood that ran down Meical's sleeve. Meical summoned his strength, ripped his hands free of the manacles and grabbed Hicks by the head. The revenant tried once to gouge him with the knife, but Meical caught his wrist and twisted it a half turn to the right. The knife clanged on the floor, and Hicks howled with pain.

Even as Hicks twitched and struggled, the might of Neshi's blood in his veins manifested in the unearthly speed of his healing. Before Meical's eyes, his twisted hand righted itself and knit together again.

Meical shook Hicks hard and jerked his head up to make him look him in the eyes. "Well, well, well. Here we are, two of Neshi's recent accomplishments. Abominations, both of us."

Hicks screamed again. The scream ended in an animalistic squeal.

"If it's any consolation to you," Meical growled, "I probably can't kill you, since Neshi created you." He wrenched Hicks's head back. "Not that I won't try."

Meical plunged his fangs into the translucent, scrawny throat and drank. The first three gulps went down like acid and came back up again. He managed to hold on to his squirming prey while he emptied his stomach. When he quit vomiting, he jerked Hicks upright and drank again. He had to make this work.

This time he tasted Neshi's blood. It went straight to his head. Yesssss…the red darkness slipped over him and finally…finally…euphoria.

The same thing that would finish him hours from now swept like a river through him now. Meical felt himself shatter beneath the weight of the sheer timelessness of Neshi's power until there was no more Meical.

The succubus had said he'd be unfit for Caroline. Surely this was what she had meant. Nothing left of him, not the man he'd been once so long ago…not the vampire he had become…

All that remained was the beast of appetite within him, a gift from Neshi's ancient, insatiable hunger.

He'd make it serve him well.

Caroline got as far as the last bedroom and slipped to the floor with her back against the wall. She could see the attic stairway just beyond the door. It was as good a place as any to make her last stand. Then let him find her. He'd regret it forever. No more running.

Focus. Focus. Where was Burke now?

She sought out the red-hot mass of rage and fear that filled the house and followed it to its epicenter. He was coming upstairs. His search for her below had bought her time. But now he knew she could only be somewhere up here. If she hesitated another minute, the only thing that would separate them was the length of the hallway. Move. Move now. Now, now, now…

Caroline dragged herself to her feet, wobbled on her prosthetic leg and leaned in the open doorway of the bedroom to take a look down the hallway. He was just coming into view as he topped the stairway, intent at the moment on managing those last few steps. By the way he was struggling, it looked as if she'd made that climb harder on him that it had been for her.

She slipped into the hallway, keeping an eye on him as she moved, and made it to the short stairway to the attic. She took her gaze off him long enough to get to the narrow doorway and reached for the doorknob.

A bullet hit the wall just over her right shoulder, then another at her feet, and the stair beneath her seemed to explode. Suddenly she was on her knees, clinging to the doorknob. She twisted it in all directions. The next bullet wouldn't miss. The door flew open, and she rolled into the waiting darkness, slamming the door shut behind her with her good foot.

Her prosthetic leg was gone. He would pay for that. Pushing herself up from the floor on her knee, she felt and fumbled in the dark for a lock on the door, a sliding bolt, anything. She just needed time to recover her focus and work on him.

But there was nothing.

She could hear him just outside, kicking aside the debris from the attic steps, moving closer.

Caroline turned and eyed the warm, dark room. She just needed a little time and something to put between her and his gun. She lay down on her belly and dog-paddled over the floor to the back of the room, around and between an assortment of discarded furniture, until she found the back wall. Once she had a forest of inanimate objects around her, she rolled onto her back, scooted behind an old wardrobe and leaned against the wall for support.

She got a moment of blessed silence, a respite in

which she could just breathe and renew her grip on her runaway emotions, and then the door crashed open.

She clutched at the gunman's psychotic fear and stoked it like a fire. She sensed his inward flinching, his attempt to cast off the mounting terror she built inside him. She could almost feel him gripping his gun more tightly, turning this way and that, fighting the loss of control over his emotions.

When he was close enough for her to feel the vibration of his boots on the floor, she peeked out to get a look at him.

Yes, she was definitely getting to him. He was loading a second pistol, so he'd have one for each hand.

"I promised your father," he said, "that I'd give you a painless death. Don't make me go back on that promise."

He was toying with her.

"Come out now, Miss Olek, and let's do what we have to do. Do it now, and I give you my word I can keep that promise to your father."

The thought of what her dad might have endured at this maniac's hands turned Caroline's anger to rage. She gave her attacker a psychic shove, using the memories of his old abusers and bore down on the hot thread of his terror, feeding it until it escalated to panic.

When he gasped a couple of times and groaned, she knew she had him. She surrounded him with endless trees and a gauntlet of armed men who fired at him from all sides until that became his only reality, and his inner demons pushed him toward his breaking point.

In an effort to rid himself of his invisible enemies, he yelled and sprayed the attic with bullets.

Caught between the wardrobe and the wall, Caroline flattened herself on the floor and covered her head, as the furnishings around her splintered in a thousand directions, toppling in on her one by one.

The next thing she knew, someone yanked her off the floor, knocking the breath out of her. She came up fighting, slinging her fists and kicking with her leg. An iron-strong arm squeezed her close, and a hand closed on her mouth before she could scream. She opened her watering eyes to find herself looking down at the attic from the ceiling.

Caroline had just enough presence of mind to realize she was dangling from a familiar arm before a wave of energy clapped like lightning in her head and she passed out.

She came to on the floor of the attic, thirsty and shaking. Where was he? Where was Meical? She felt his presence, but he didn't feel right.

The shuffle of a shoe on the floor reached her, and she opened her eyes to look for him. A splash of moonlight from a window on the far side of the room illuminated two figures in the corner nearest her. Caroline blinked and stared.

Meical clutched the motionless gunman close and ripped into his neck with his teeth, catching blood in his mouth as though drinking from a fountain. He'd slipped over the edge.

"Stop, Meical!"

His head shot up. "Better him than you."

What did he mean by that? "Let go of him. Just listen to me. Look, I'm not hurt. I'm safe. You came in time. Just let him go."

A sigh escaped him, and he leaned against the wall with his head back and his eyes closed. His voice resonated through the room as though it came from somewhere else. "That's better. Much better."

Suddenly he slammed Burke against the wall and pressed his hands on either side of the man's head. In the red glare that shone from Meical, Caroline watched Burke's eyes become glassy and his mouth hang slack.

"Are you listening?" Meical whispered to him.

Burke nodded, zombie-like.

"I have a new assignment for you."

"Anything."

Meical leaned close to Burke's ear and murmured words Caroline couldn't hear. Burke nodded, and when Meical released him, he limped out of the attic.

"What are you doing?" Caroline demanded.

"Making sure you never hear from Rivera again."

"But Rivera's men are holding my dad. If anything happens to Rivera, I'll never see him alive again."

"Neshi is on his way to rescue your father."

But of course there was no way *Neshi could know what was happening to her father. He certainly couldn't rescue him.*

"Yes, he can," Meical murmured. Evidently his condition had done nothing to dampen his ability to read her mind. "That maggot Burke was most obliging.

He told me where your father is, and I told Neshi. Neshi is on his way there now, and there are others coming to help you. They'll be here in a moment and…then I'll go."

Go? Where? To get the police? Oh, no. "Meical, listen. No police. Burke will have my dad killed if you do that. No one can go to the police. I have to handle this myself, understand?"

"Neshi won't need the police."

She had to reach him somehow. "Come here and let me hold you. Please."

She held her hands out to him. A moment passed, while the darkness careened around her.

Meical's words were almost too soft to hear. "I can't."

"Just let me help you."

"I'm beyond your help. What I need now is…"

"Anything you need from me. Just ask. Anything."

He sounded more coherent now, as though he'd taken a drug that had restored his sanity. "I need you to forgive me. And I need you to let me go."

When his words penetrated the fog of exhaustion and dread in Caroline's mind, adrenaline poured into her bloodstream, waking her completely. He'd made a decision. He'd committed himself to an action. He was saying goodbye. That could only mean one thing. His anger had turned inward.

Her heart thudded hard and she shook her head. She needed to get herself under control, so she could deal with this. She needed to. But this was Meical. She couldn't compartmentalize him. She loved him.

She tried to clear her throat to get the wobble out of her voice, but she couldn't. "No, Meical, don't. Please."

"Caroline," he sighed, "look at me."

He pushed himself away from the wall and stood over her. A red light rose from him, enveloped him, shone from him like a murderous aura. It radiated from his eyes, from his very soul. He was violence. He was death. He was power.

And she'd seen him like this before. She'd seen him in the basement when she'd lain there on the floor, nearly unconscious, sure she was about to die. The red light had flashed before her eyes, and her attackers had vanished as if by magic. And just as it hadn't mattered to her then to know how he'd done it, it didn't matter now. All that mattered was making him see that he had saved her.

"It was you," she whispered. "You were there, the night of my attack. You were the one who kept them from killing me."

"I couldn't have been. I…" He fell silent. The reddish glow around him mellowed to orange. "Wait…"

"Take your time. What do you remember?"

"That must be it. That must be why. The night you found me, after I revived, I took the liberty of going through your memory of the attack. I wanted to understand you."

Caroline fought to hold on to her control, but the tears came anyway. She brushed them away with the back of her hand.

"I saw it all," Meical went on. "I saw what they did to you. I thought I was seeing it through your memory.

But then you blacked out, and from that moment I should not have been able to see anything more. But I did. I saw everything that happened after you lost consciousness. Now I know why." The red-orange haze around him turned to succulent purple. "It was my own memory I was reliving. I *was* there. But…how?"

Caroline pushed her bangs out of her eyes. "Think, Meical. You can remember. Just think."

He shook his head. The purple haze around him began to turn blue. "That's what she meant. She said I…I saved you once already…"

"Who said that?"

"Someone wise and powerful. She said…" The blue light around him turned hot white, and the red haze enveloped him again. His voice deepened and hardened. "She said a lot of things. None of it matters. Except she's right about one thing. I'm not fit for you now."

He took another step closer, and the room blazed brighter, as hot as a furnace. Caroline gasped at the heat.

She sensed pain surfacing in the pool of his rage. It was gone in the blink of an eye.

"If you doubt your own eyes," he murmured, "you have only to think of what you witnessed a moment ago what I've done, what I'm capable of." He pointed to the gunman on the floor. "*That,* Caroline, is what I am. I'll spend my final seconds of life craving every drop of blood in your body. Give me half a chance, and even now, I'll take precisely that from you."

She shook her head and held her hands out to him

again, pleading. "Delusions like this are common for someone who's—"

"For pity's sake," he snapped. "Wake up and realize what I've done to you. You were right when you said I used you."

"But I found a lost piece of myself in the dreams with you, Meical. And I found you. The real you."

He pounded his chest with a fist. "*This* is the real me. Compared to what I could do to you at the moment, you would think those dreams of ours were *nothing.* Don't you understand? It's not just your blood I need. It's your passion, your essence, your soul, your very life. And I have Neshi—may he rot in hell—to thank for that. He thought he could make us harmless, give us back the sun, but all he's done is create a more insidious way for us to kill humans."

He was out of control, beyond reality. He needed her to be calm and strong and professional. Caroline tried to rein in her denial and disbelief. "Let me help you calm down, and then we'll talk this through."

"Caroline, I'm dying."

The words sliced through her mind and heart. She shook her head. He couldn't be. He looked so powerful and alive. She'd thought he meant to take his own life, but…what if…

He added hoarsely, "If I stay much longer, I won't go. I will spend my last moments on this earth making you wish you'd never known me. There won't be enough left of you for Dr. Calvin to save by the time I'm finished and death finally catches up with me. So don't…please… don't ask me to stay."

"But I love you."

In the red-and-black darkness, she saw him bow his head. She thought he whispered to her tenderly, sweetly, but when he looked up again, his expression was as unmoved as ever. "Perhaps I should just give you a taste of what will happen if I stay."

He scooped her up in his arms and shot straight up from the floor. Caroline's breath left her. Pure emotion, raw and devouring, swallowed her. She felt the wall at her back, and Meical's face close to hers.

In the glow of his own glaring ethereal light, she saw his gleaming canines. "Meical, stop. Stop."

He ran the tip of his tongue over one fang, and his eyes glinted as he let his gaze travel down the length of her and up again. "I'll wager you'll think I'm outstaying my welcome inside of two minutes."

He bent his head and nuzzled her neck, giving her little nips that made her breath catch in her throat. When he caught her close and shoved them away from the wall, Caroline braced herself for a fall, only to find them floating above the floor.

The weightlessness worked like a drug on the last of her strength. She mouthed his name, but couldn't speak it. She had lost him.

Meical kissed her as gently as if they were in one of her dreams again. In the next instant, he sank his fangs into her throat and drank.

Euphoria spread through Caroline's mind and body. No fear. Only pleasure, deep and dark and ancient, all that waited for her at the heart of him. His red-hot anger remained on the periphery of her world, doused like a fire by the cooling deluge of their love. As fast as her life essence bled out of her, Meical swallowed it down, along with her hunger.

Something made him lift his head. He grew still, as though listening. "Here comes the cavalry, baby, just in time to prevent me from pushing my point."

Caroline filled her lungs with air and pressed the word past her throbbing throat. "Coward."

His gaze riveted to hers, and his mouth parted.

"You heard me right."

She made a weak attempt to slap him. He caught her hand and ran his tongue over her palm.

"Don't you get it?" she moaned. "You've done what I thought no one could ever do. *I love you.* Whatever you call yourself, whatever's happening to you, I still love you. And no matter where you go, I'll find you."

He held her close while she cried. "Then I'll have to make sure you can't, won't I?"

"There's nowhere you can go that I can't find you."

"Yes. There is." He eased her onto the floor, even while she clung to him. "I love you, Caroline. Goodbye."

The instant she slipped out of his arms, the room became dark again, except for the moonlight. Silence settled in every corner. Empty darkness. He was gone.

Caroline clasped both hands over her mouth as her grief unwound inside her. She tried once to call him back to her, using every ounce of her empathic abilities, but there was a solid door between them, as indomitable as eternity itself.

Chapter 15

Caroline? Help is on the way. Just hang on.

She looked around her in the pitch-black attic, shaking all over, unable to contain her sorrow. "Neshi? Is that you?"

Yes. Your father will be safe in no time. I want you to concentrate on Meical. You're the only one who can save him.

He was talking to her inside her mind just the way Meical had. His voice reverberated through her, making her dizzy.

Caroline clasped her hands to her head and doubled over. "This can't be real…"

The bark of Neshi's voice arrested her panic. *I suggest you put logic aside. Now. You need to believe what's happening. Believe and accept it. Believe what Meical is and what he's capable of, or neither of you will survive the night.*

She'd seen enough tonight to believe almost anything. It wasn't faith she lacked; it was reassurance. "How can you save my dad? You don't even know where he is!"

I'm looking at him. She caught the sound of his laughter, as though he were in the room with her, but his laughter was strained with pain. *Although he's not sure how he managed to kill most of his captors and get away, he's headed for the nearest town. He left only two survivors, and they think he's a one-man army, so they're not chasing him.*

She held her breath. Could Neshi be that powerful? He could, if he was like Meical. "Are *you* okay?"

Let's concentrate on Meical. You don't have a lot of time. You must get to him before sundown, and Caroline…it's going to take all the courage you have.

His voice was strained, as though he were fighting for his life, but the conviction in his words resounded in her soul.

I flatter myself to think I chose you for him. In truth, you've always been his, just as he's always been yours. That's why you're the only one who can save him. That's why he was the only one who could save you.

Suddenly the dark surrounded her with a memory laden with the greasy smell of blood and the sound of her own sobs. The abandoned house. The basement. The last place on earth she wanted to be. "I know where he is."

He's gone there to die.

She nodded, barely breathing. "That's what he meant

when he said he was going to a place I couldn't go. He thinks I'm too frightened to follow him...to go back there..."

Is he right, Caroline?

She swallowed hard. Her stump throbbed at the thought of it. "It's miles away. I'll never get there in time."

Leave that to Ellory and Talisen.

"Okay. So when I get there, how do I save Meical?"

His voice gentled. *I think you know that, too, Caroline.*

She rubbed the throbbing bite Meical had left on her throat, trying not to panic as Meical's words filled her mind. *It's not just your blood I need. It's your passion...* "Yeah."

Any questions?

"Yes. Where do you fit in? Are you a—"

Vampire, yes.

She exhaled slowly, while her heart raced and her head kept spinning. "The night John and I found Meical, you were there. I felt you. You thumped my shield like it was made of paper and made sure I took Meical home with me. That was you, wasn't it?"

Yes. I couldn't take a chance on his not being able to get to you during his first few hours. He needs you now just as much as he did then.

I need him, too.

Yes. In fact...you're going to need him more than he has ever been needed before...nine months from now.

Nine months? "W-what are saying?"

Perhaps I shouldn't try to speculate on the gestation period. I really have no way of knowing. This has never happened before. It wasn't supposed to ever happen.

The night caught up with Caroline, and her stomach pitched and rose. A baby. She was going to have a baby. With Meical.

Not without him.

Her scattered thoughts congealed into one. She flattened her palm on her abdomen and reached inward with all her empathic might. A pinpoint of life stirred in response, deep within her.

"Okay," she whispered. "Okay. I can do this."

Ellory and Talisen should arrive any second. Just rest.

"Thank you, Neshi."

No, Caroline. Thank you.

"Hey…are you okay?"

He didn't answer.

He had done the right thing to tell her.

Doubling over, Neshi leaned against the wall and eyed the crimson splotch he was contributing to the yellow carpet of the room Olek had been imprisoned in. The bullets had struck his spleen…perhaps also his liver…or a lung… Not that he needed them anymore, but the blood…

The sound of combat boots could be heard on the stairs beyond the room and in the hallway. Neshi gathered his waning strength and dematerialized, just as the rest of Burke's men filled the room.

They saw the empty chair where Olek had been bound and gagged a moment ago and flocked to the open window, stepping over their dead comrades. One of them shrieked orders into a two-way radio to the men who patrolled the grounds. When there was no answer, he led all but one of his followers out of the room.

Clinging to the ceiling, Neshi tried to remain invisible. When he couldn't manage it, he settled for remaining silent. He needed blood, and he needed it fast. He eyed the guard below him with torturous hunger. It wouldn't be a clean kill, but he couldn't afford to be graceful at the moment.

The thug stationed himself at the window with his back to the room. Neshi hovered closer, until he was directly over him. Gunfire sounded in the distance. Was Olek safe? He took his focus off his own dilemma long enough to see that the old man had made it safely to the highway.

"What the…?"

Neshi looked down at the human below him who was now gaping at him, wiping drops of Neshi's blood off his forehead.

Neshi bared his fangs and let the red haze of his hunger swallow him. No mercy. Feed. The human screamed, dodged and stumbled backward over a bullet-riddled chair. It broke beneath his weight, spinning him around so that he landed on his stomach.

Neshi sprang. The man rolled over, brandishing something in both hands. Neshi saw it a second before he felt the bite of the wooden chair leg pierce his chest. Just like a wooden stake.

A whoosh of sound filled his ears, like the wind in the rushes on the banks of the Nile. He saw the human's mouth move, inches from his face, but didn't hear the words. Pain eclipsed everything.

The room tumbled around him, and then he lay on his back, with the chair leg pointing upward to an afterlife that was surely beyond his reach. The man filled Neshi's vision, staring at him while he spoke into his two-way radio. Neshi was vaguely aware of the human nudging him with the toe of his boot, as one would nudge a fallen enemy to see if he was dead yet.

Colors grew brighter, then faded to black, and the darkness brought merciful numbness. Dawn would bring the pain again, but only for a moment, while his body burned.

To rise no more.

When the humans had departed in search of their escapee, Bast materialized in the room wherein her favorite priest lay.

Benemerut's *ka* yet remained, tethered to his corpse by his stubborn will, floating in a void, unknowing and unseeing.

She stood over his lifeless form, held out one hand and whispered. The wooden chair leg rose slowly from the vampire's chest and clattered to the floor. Blood bubbled from the wound. She murmured a prayer. The wound healed, and energy flowed through muscle and bone again.

Kneeling beside him, she studied his beautiful face

for a moment, then closed her eyes and pressed her hand to his bloody chest. *Benemerut Neshi, you are not yet dismissed from this life.*

The air around Caroline snapped with electricity, raising the hair on her scalp. Her muscles tensed as she waited, looking around her.

Meical had called them "the cavalry," but most people she would look to for help didn't arrive by way of a shower of gold sparks. The sparks died and left them all in the dark.

"I take it you're Talisen and Ellory."

"Yes," came a female voice in the dark. "We've come to help. Ellory, the lights, please."

"Certainly, love."

Caroline heard Ellory snap his fingers, and every light in the attic came on, and every light in the hall beyond, and as far as she could see with the spots in her eyes, every light in the house.

She blinked at the gorgeous pair before her, took one look at their translucent skin and gleaming eyes, and for the first time since she'd pulled Meical out of the snow, understood why he and Neshi were so physically beautiful, so perfect and so impervious to the elements.

Except for the sun.

"We don't have much time, do we?" she said. "It'll be sunrise soon. I have to get to Meical before the sun comes up."

Ellory nodded and swept her up in his arms. "First

things first. Neshi's calling the shots for us this evening, and his orders are to wait for Dr. Calvin."

He floated out the door with her and down the stairs.

"We can't wait. Meical needs me now."

"Neshi was adamant. You're going nowhere before Dr. Calvin has the chance to check you over."

"I can't thank you enough for your help. I'm glad we have you to count on."

"Meical and Ellory are like brothers," said Talisen. "Ellory helped Meical survive his fledgling days."

"So Meical hasn't been completely alone?"

Talisen shrugged. "Meical is Meical. He's a loner by nature, and that's a part of him that didn't change when he was turned. He's like family to us, but he has his secrets. He's very much on his own."

Ellory settled her on the living room couch and put a hand on her forehead. Her stomach ceased its gurgling and settled down. She felt a calm slip over her, but when she looked up at the vampire, he was as white as a sheet and staring at her belly.

She pulled a pillow over her middle. "Please don't freak. I don't think I can handle vampire hysterics. I have enough of the human kind, all right?"

A smile touched his mouth, and tenderness shone in his eyes. He straightened and exchanged a glance with Talisen, who suddenly clasped her hands to her mouth and started crying. She sat down and pulled Caroline into her embrace and held her.

"If it's the last thing we do on this earth," said Talisen, "we'll see that you and Meical survive."

Ellory cut a glance at the door. "Ah, there he is now."

"Who?" asked Caroline.

Ellory waved his hand at the door. It creaked open. John, physician's bag in hand, stood on the porch with his free hand still poised as he reached for the doorknob. Caroline beamed at him. The sight of him was a balm to her nerves.

He cleared his throat and strode in, shooed Talisen aside, set his bag on the coffee table and sat down beside Caroline.

When he met her gaze, she saw something in his eyes that hadn't been there before. "Hectic night we're having, isn't it?"

"Sorry we don't have time to compare notes. I guess Neshi sent for you?"

"Something like that—besides the surprise visit I got this morning from Talisen here. Let's just say, thanks to Neshi, I'm now on the same page with you, give or take a couple of special instructions for me. Doctor stuff, you know."

He rolled the leg of her jeans up and examined her stump. Satisfied, he folded the leg of her jeans and safety-pinned it in place above her knee. Taking a pungent-smelling disinfectant and swabs out of his bag, he examined the place where Burke's bullet had nicked her good leg. He cleaned and bandaged it, checked her blood pressure and finally turned his attention on the bite wound on her neck.

Caroline half turned away from him and covered the bite with her hand. "It's okay."

He pulled her hand away from her neck. "No, it's not."

"Actually," put in Ellory, "there's no need to clean a vampire's bite. We don't carry germs."

"With all due respect," John replied soberly, "Caroline is in no condition to take a chance on an infection."

After doctoring her neck, he disappeared into the kitchen and returned a moment later with a shot of seltzer for her. "Where's your prosthesis?"

She downed the seltzer. "Upstairs somewhere."

"I'll find it."

"If it's all shot up, I'm going to cry."

"You and me both, kiddo."

John headed up the stairs.

"So, where to?" Ellory asked.

"An abandoned house on the outskirts of El Paso." She ran her hand over her half leg. "This is part of what happened to me there; Meical is the reason I survived it. He's gone there because he thinks I don't have the courage to follow him. I just don't see how we'll get there in time."

Talisen gave her a half smile. "You won't like our method of travel, but it works really well when you have to be somewhere in a hurry."

John hollered from upstairs, "Found it. And it's in one piece. Now get going."

He appeared at the top of the stairs and lobbed Caroline's prosthetic leg down to Ellory, who caught it and handed it to Caroline. She put it on, and Ellory picked her up again.

"Deep breath," he warned. "It's better if you close your eyes."

Caroline filled her lungs with as much air as she could hold and kept her gaze on John, who stood at the top of the stairway, looking down at her with a world of worry in his eyes. He disappeared in a shower of gold and silver.

For a moment she felt as though she were being sucked through a straw. Then the entire world blurred together, collapsed around her as though it would crush them all, and she found herself looking down an endless tube of color, light and deafening sound. She thought her lungs would explode.

Neshi stood atop a barren desert mesa, five miles away from Meical's location—close enough to keep Badru away, if necessary. He had no doubt that Badru would come. It was only a matter of how fast his little brother could replenish himself and get there. Badru would also have reckoned—and rightly—that the only way to get to Meical was to go through Benemerut.

His little brother appeared almost within reach of him. He looked so young and impetuous. It was as if he'd come to goad Neshi into a wrestling match in their father's vineyard. He sprang like a young lion, but Neshi caught him and held him at arm's length.

"Let me give you back the sun, Badru."

"I can't let them survive. You know that."

Whispering an incantation, Badru vanished. Seconds later, he dropped out of the dark and slung Neshi to the ground. Neshi turned himself into sand and whisked himself away on the wind. When he materialized, his brother locked arms with him again in midair.

The bloody tears in Badru's eyes caught his gaze. He wanted to clasp Badru in his arms and hold him until his rage was spent, just as he had done so many times when his little brother's temper had gotten the best of him.

Badru's slashing blow caught him by surprise. Blood spurted from his belly, and he plummeted out of the sky. Badru caught him before he hit the ground and wrestled him down, murmuring an enchantrex.

Neshi felt his strength drain away with every ancient word.

Too late, Neshi felt his brother's nimble-fingered divination spell exposing the one secret he'd resolved to take with him to the afterlife.

Badru's eyes widened, and his voice sounded hoarse with disbelief. "How could you do this?"

Neshi made a weak attempt to catch him by the throat. "Where is your mercy? We speak of a child's life!"

The pain and weakness of the enchantrex eclipsed everything, striking him mute. Neshi lay motionless while his brother opened the earth beneath him. He felt himself fall backward, as though he would fall forever. The last glimpse he had of his brother was to watch him shoot off in Meical's direction.

The earth closed over Neshi, bringing darkness. The incantation wove through every vein, threading every sinew with numbness as hard as concrete. Icy fingers reached deeper into his body and soul than the day-death. His heart stuttered, jerked and stuttered again. One beat. Two.

Meical...Caroline...forgive me...

The icy dark consumed him.

Caroline gulped down the desert air, feeling like she'd been trapped underwater.

"Sorry. It's hardest on the stomach, I'm afraid."

Caroline looked up at Ellory, who was still holding her. "No, I'm okay."

He set her on the ground and held her up until her legs quit wobbling. "Just breathe for a minute and get your bearings. Are you sure this is the place?"

Her legs felt like sponge cake. No time for that. Taking a deep breath, she switched on her flashlight and turned in a circle—slowly—to take in her surroundings. "This is it."

Her feeble gold beam made little peepholes in the darkness, revealing bits and pieces of an image terror had burned into her mind. The house looked so much the same, she thought for a moment she'd stepped back in time.

It could have been the same pile of tumbleweeds crowding around the front door. The broken-out windows stared back at her. The desolate, silent desert stretched to the horizon around them. In the distance, the yellow glow of El Paso's lights and the blue twinkle of Juarez's street lamps sparkled. The only other light was the white gleam of the moon.

Caroline tried to block out the panic that assaulted her and concentrated on searching the area for a hint of life. What she picked up on was a force of will, rage, anger and old, old hunger. Where was her Meical in that maelstrom? She had less than an hour to save him.

She drew a tremulous breath and opened her mouth to speak, but Ellory beat her to it.

"He's here," he whispered. "But he's definitely not right. I'm coming in with you."

She turned and shook her head at him, mortified. "You can't. I have to do this myself. Sunrise is coming. You've done what you can."

"He's not himself. I'd be a fool to let you do this alone."

Caroline turned a beseeching gaze on Talisen. The revenant studied her face for a minute, then tugged Ellory's hand. "She understands Meical better than we do. And she's right. The sun will be up in a few minutes."

Ellory caught Caroline's hand in his. "You carry our hopes with you. Save him, if you can. If you can't, you needn't mourn alone. For love of him, we'll watch over you for as long as you live."

He kissed her hand, and in the next instant, the two of them vanished.

Caroline curled her fingers around her flashlight, closed her eyes and sent her entire being into the house, straight to the pocket of misery seething in the dark, somewhere within.

Neshi was right. Meical wasn't ready to know about the baby. It could push all the wrong buttons inside of him.

Meical flinched and grew still. She could sense how stunned he was that she'd come to save him.

And how angry.

The clouds boiled overhead. The air around her grew heated. Lightning roared over the mountains in the distance. Meical's energy seemed to convulse, and for a moment she thought she caught the sound of his groan.

His voice poured into her mind, deepened by pain, dark with warning. *I didn't think you'd have enough courage to come here.*

At least he could still speak to her. *I don't. But I have enough love. That's how we learn to live in this world, Meical. Your world or mine, it works the same.*

She heard him sigh. He seemed so close she could almost feel his hot breath on her cheek. *I'll give you one chance to rethink this, Caroline.*

You're mine, Meical Grabian. I've come to claim you.

She took a slow step forward, watching her footing on the rocky ground. Suddenly the house spat a tongue of scalding energy out the front door. It wrapped itself around her, touching her everywhere. In the shock of feeling her feet leave the ground, she dropped her flashlight. The next thing she knew she was hurtling toward the closed door. Caroline covered her face and braced herself for impact. Just before she would have smacked against it, it flew open and slammed shut behind her.

She landed in his arms, with her face inches from his. The red glow that had emanated from him earlier now seemed confined to his eyes. Madness shone in his gaze, as clear to her as the feverish heat of his skin and the soft growl deep in his throat.

She steeled herself against an onslaught of tears. "I'll take that as a 'Hi, come on in.'"

He moved like a specter, suddenly gone, suddenly there again, and caught her from behind. He pulled her back against him until she felt the heat of his skin through her clothes.

Meical pressed his mouth to her ear, and she gasped at the dry heat of his breath on her skin. "What do you think is going to happen here? That we'll make love? In this place?"

She drew a ragged breath, already throbbing inside. "If you'll stop playing hard to get."

He vanished again, leaving her swaying on her feet, almost mute with her need for him. He was still there. Still listening. She cast a glance out the window. She could see the outline of the mesas against the sky now, where the black of night had begun to lighten to deep blue.

"I know what you are," she murmured to the listening dark. "I know you were trying to explain what Neshi did to you."

His words echoed around the room. "A miserable failure from start to finish."

"If that were true," she returned, "I wouldn't be here. I'd be dead. Rivera's men would have killed me, right here in this very house. You stopped them. I think you knew, in some part of your mind and heart, exactly who I was and that I needed you. With all my heart, Meical,

I believe you came here to save me that night because we belong together."

A moment or two passed. Caroline held her breath; she could feel his confusion, his frustration as he tried to remember and his desperation to believe it was true. She cast another glance out the window. The sky had turned to a grayish-blue. A swath of pink lay on the eastern horizon.

"I remember flashes of things," he murmured. "I wasn't all in one piece."

He became visible slowly, standing just six feet away from her. Caroline began to edge her way closer to him.

"Neshi was working on my body," he went on, staring at the floor. "I saw myself on his lab table, but only for an instant. Then there was nothing. I was trying to remember who I was, or where I was, or how I'd come to be there. There was silence. And then I heard you scream."

She took a step closer, just as he looked up. But he didn't back away.

"I didn't even think," he murmured. "I just knew I had to get to you, or I'd lose everything."

He covered his face with his hands, and Caroline closed the distance between them and held him close. "Nothing can keep us apart now, just as nothing could keep us apart then. I'm here to see you through this, or die trying."

"You're bound to know, it won't be like the dreams." He nuzzled aside the shoulder of her cotton T-shirt. His burning tongue glided up the nape of her neck, and then he nipped her. "I need too much."

Caroline closed her eyes. "It's my turn to make our dreams come true."

"Oh, Caroline…I do love you so…"

He lapped at her neck, waking a wave of desire in her, then locked his fangs on the side of her throat. The dance of emotions that enveloped them eclipsed the pain. Caroline lost herself in the river of life and light that was Meical. The whole world, the stars in the sky, the sleepy moon, the very ground beneath her feet, even the rising sun that she mustn't let reach him…all of it was Meical, and only Meical.

She scarcely felt it when he lifted his head. He dropped to his knees in front of her. She felt him pushing her shirt up and his hot mouth on her belly. Languid and weak all over, she looked down at him. He'd tossed his shirt aside. She ran her hands over his muscular shoulders and arms, touching as much of him as she could reach.

A glistening bead of light caught Caroline's eye on the periphery of her vision. She turned and stared at it, as though in a daze. It gleamed, trapped and reflected in a jagged point of glass that still remained in the windowsill. Her gaze rose from the tiny dagger of light to take in the room, which filled with the blue-pink of a new dawn.

"Meical, the sun. We have to get you somewhere dark. Now."

He searched her gaze. "There's nowhere to go."

She fought down the memory that rose in her mind, beat back the terror. "Yes, there is, and we both know it."

He shook his head. She hated the sound of resignation in his voice. "I won't finish this down there. Not there."

She caught his face in her hands. "Can you think of a better place for me to save you than the place you saved me?"

She saw it then, the love in his eyes she so needed to see. No monstrous aura, only the gleam of his devotion.

Even as he nodded his consent, smoke began to rise from his skin. He let go of her and held up his hands, staring at the tendrils that wafted from his fingertips.

"Funny. There's no pain."

Chapter 16

Caroline grabbed Meical's arm and dragged him to his feet, nearly tripping over her own. She shoved him toward the doorway that led into the hallway. "Remember the trapdoor. Straight ahead. That's where the basement is. Go."

He took three steps and fell, laboring for breath. Pale gray light followed them, streaming in through the living room window. She grabbed his arms and tried to drag him farther into the shadows that lingered in the hallway. Meical gasped, shaking, and rolled onto his back.

His eyes were solid white, his pupils gone. "I'll never forget…"

"Meical, honey, stay with me."

She caught him under the arms and half carried,

half dragged him a few feet farther down the hall. She slipped down and skidded under him, but kept pulling him along, scooting on her backside and dragging him by inches.

The trapdoor was just a few feet behind her. She let go of Meical and scrambled to it. Wrapping her hand around the withered pull rope, she gave it a tug. It creaked open, and the gaping, black hole below belched a cloud of dust and odors Caroline remembered all too well. Oil and old gasoline, dry rock and rusty metal. Anxiety unwound in the pit of her stomach.

The light in the house turned silver, then gold, as a tongue of sunlight traced its way across the hall floor in their direction. Sparks raced over Meical's chest and abdomen. His eyes widened and he gasped and shook again.

No more time. Caroline lay down, wrapped her arms and legs around Meical and rolled them toward the edge. Just as they tumbled into the darkness, she felt him jerk against her. He was dying.

Bumping down the stairs, she let go of Meical to shield her head and roll. When the world stopped rotating, she opened her eyes, flat on her back, staring up at the ceiling of the basement. Just like that night.

She could remember their faces. They hadn't concealed them. Why bother? She wasn't going to live to identify them. She had tried to crawl into the corner to get away from them, screaming and crying behind the duct tape they'd put over her mouth.

The darkness weighed her down, squeezing the life out of her. Caroline's lungs froze. Her stump throbbed like a living reminder, and every ache from her tumble down the stairs woke a memory of pain in her body.

Light poured in from above her and shimmered like an angel through her tears. She wanted the light. She wanted the air. But to Meical that light was death. She had to close that trapdoor. But that would mean she'd be trapped here in the dark. Caroline's heart pounded so hard that her head ached.

Maybe he was dead already. She might not even be able to help him. Meical would be the first to understand she couldn't do it. She wanted out. She couldn't be here.

She clamored to her feet, choking, trying to get her lungs to breathe around the knot of terror in her chest. She dragged herself up the steps. She wouldn't stay here. She wouldn't.

Sunlight blinded her, pale and translucent. In another moment, the sun would be all the way up.

She looked down at the pool of silver-blue that fell close enough to Meical's foot for her to make out the details of the loafers he'd borrowed from John.

Meical had nothing of his own in this world. And no one. Only her—and now the child she carried, a child who would need Meical's love and protection.

He'd been alone for so long, with no one to love him. There might be nothing she could do for him. But how could she let him die alone, down there in this hole? He had saved her from precisely that, the night of her attack.

How could she live with herself, knowing she would have died alone down here, if not for him, or tell their child how he had saved her, knowing she left him here to die by himself?

She looked up at the crusty adobe walls of the house and the brittle wood floor on her eye level, and watched the light creeping into the house through a hole in the ceiling just above her head.

She couldn't take the light down with her. She had to bring her own. And that was the light that had restored Meical before. Her light.

She jerked the trapdoor shut just as the house above burst into the light of a new day.

Easing herself down to the bottom step of the stairs, she shut her eyes tight to close out the darkness. In her mind, she built the image of the radiant glow inside her, her shield. She wrapped it around her, gathering it closer like a blanket, and recited her courage words.

I am Caroline. I control my own emotions. This fear is no longer mine. It belongs in the past. I won't accept it. I'm here and now. I am Caroline.

The faces of her attackers rose and fell, making shadows and gaps of darkness, but she visualized her light closing them out. She didn't move, scarcely breathed, until she could feel the warmth of that light inside her as clearly as she saw it glistening, downy soft and warm, on her skin. Air rushed into her lungs, but she made herself breathe slowly.

When she opened her eyes, they had adjusted to the darkness well enough for her to make out a face before her. On instinct she probed him. The only thing she could grasp before he shielded himself was that he wasn't human.

"Who are you?" she demanded. "What do you want?"

The stranger stared at her through matted ebony curls and began to murmur words that made no sense. He started toward her.

Caroline tried to back her way up the stairs, but he snapped his fingers, and every ounce of strength left her body. She opened her mouth to scream, but couldn't make a sound.

He was practically chanting now, in a language she'd never heard before. Catching her before she tumbled off the stairs, he leaned her back against him. He held out his hand, and the ceiling above opened for a split second, belched her flashlight, and sealed itself. He caught the flashlight, flicked it on and set it on the floor with its beam turned upward.

In the pale wash of blue light, Caroline watched his free hand rise as his voice grew louder, descending slowly to flatten on her belly. Suddenly he was silent. She felt a shudder pass through him.

"I can do nothing to save Meical," he whispered. "Only you can do that. What I *can* do is buy him time. But you need to understand, it will halt his transition. He'll be just as he is now, both incubus and vampire, and as such, he'll need both your passion and your blood to live. With his dual nature, he should be able to tolerate sunlight, but he will never relinquish his craving for the night. I hope you can live with that."

As long as she had a chance to save Meical, Caroline didn't care what it cost her. Whether heaven or hell or somewhere in between, it would be hers to discover with him.

"Forgive me," he murmured, "but what I'm about to do isn't for *your* eyes."

He blew softly in her ear, and the whole world faded away. Caroline found herself enveloped in her own white light again, spinning and drifting, alone in the warmth and brightness with the tiny life she carried.

The stranger's hushed voice brought her out of the ocean of white. She opened her eyes in the dim light of the flashlight to find herself propped against the wall.

He stood over her, wiping a rivulet of blood from his wrist. "It's up to you now. If he survives, tell him Benemerut is safe. This I swear."

"Wait. Who are you?" she asked.

He gave her a boyish grin. "A fool named Badru."

Before she could say another word, he dissolved into the floor like a ghost.

Caroline waited for her head to stop turning cartwheels and her strength to return. When her vision cleared and the roar left her ears, she crept closer to Meical's still form on the floor a few feet away. "Meical? Can you hear me?"

He didn't move, didn't make a sound. She touched his bare chest. His skin was icy to the touch.

"Come on, Meical, you know what to do. Just like you did the night I pulled you out of the snow. Remember?" She closed her eyes and reached for his being, trying to pour her love and light into him. "I'm not taking no for an answer. Feel my need for you."

She waited, attuned to the slightest pull on her soul that would tell her he was trying to take in the warmth she could give him.

Nothing.

She kissed his cold mouth. "Come on, I'm trying so hard."

She kissed him again.

Under her palm, where it rested on his chest, Caroline felt a pool of warmth. She lifted her mouth from his to look down at him. "Meical?"

She kissed him again. This time his lips were cool, not cold. She kissed him again. And again. Her Sleeping Beauty.

She felt a gentle tug at her soul. Yes! Caroline opened his mouth and swept her tongue around his, kissing him deeply. She filled her mind with her dreams, the power of their devotion and trust, and the pleasure of their lovemaking.

This is what you give me, she whispered to Meical in her heart. *This is who we are.*

Meical groaned. She lifted her mouth from his and looked down at him. "Oh, Meical, I almost lost you."

His eyes fluttered open, clear gray eyes with pools of black. "Caroline…"

She kissed him again and smoothed his hair out of his eyes. "I'm here. I'm here."

"Why aren't I dead?"

"You had some extra help. I'll tell you later. We'll have some things to work out, but first we need to get through this."

He lifted a shaking hand to her face. "If we don't do this right…"

Caroline sat up and pulled off her T-shirt, shivering

deliciously as Meical's gaze swept over her. "Since when have we ever not done this right?"

He sat up with a wince and looked around them. "I'm so sorry. I've tried so hard to make it beautiful for you, yet here we are."

She caught his chin and kissed him again. "Don't think about that. I'm not."

He rose up on his knees and pulled her close. Suddenly he was still. He looked left and right, as though searching the shadows around them. "Do you feel someone here with us?"

Caroline ran her tongue over her parched lips. That was, of course, her cue to tell him about the baby. But she had to be sure he was himself first. She couldn't risk anything going wrong now. "Meical, we don't have much time."

"There's someone here. In this very room."

He was definitely onto it. But could he handle it?

The silence hung between them while he looked this way and that. Caroline waited, spellbound by the beauty of what he was about to discover. He sat back on his haunches and stared at her abdomen. She wanted to remember the look on his face forever. He was terrified, but his hope shone in his eyes, giving them an unearthly silver gleam. That's when she knew it was all right.

He dragged in a deep breath and whispered. "Impossible."

She waited to hear how he was going to try to explain to her. Priceless words. Priceless man. "What?"

He lifted his hand to touch her stomach and closed his eyes, mouth parted, and smiled slowly.

She put her hand over his. When he looked up to meet her gaze, she was sure her tears would give away the fact that she knew, but he was still clueless.

"I'm afraid Neshi's methods resulted in…um… something neither he nor I anticipated. He must have gone farther than he realized, when he put me back together again."

"What are you trying to say?" she whispered, unable to maintain her pretense a moment longer.

He straightened his shoulders in an apparent effort to man up. "Caroline, you're pregnant."

She grinned and reached down to run her hand through his hair. "Scared?"

His eyes widened. "You know about it already?"

"Neshi told me." She ran her hand over his forehead. "I suggest we finish what we started."

He swayed a little, but his hands unerringly found the clasp of her bra. The cool air on Caroline's bare skin sent a shudder of need through her. His kiss deepened, and she felt waves of his hunger pour out of him and wash over them both.

He dragged in a deep breath and whispered, "Impossible."

He caught her by the elbows and helped her to her feet, kissed his way over her abdomen. He curled his hand over the back waist of her jeans and panties, and tugged. Before she could find her zipper, he had her unclothed.

Wrapping an arm around her good leg, he lifted her other leg over his shoulder, and mouthed his way

over her abdomen again, lower and lower, until tears of
anticipation sprang to her eyes.

Caroline cried out at the first touch of his tongue. He
groaned against her, rocking her in his grip as he made
love to her with his mouth. There was no room in her
for fear, no room in her for nightmare memories. She
was too full of love and pleasure and need.

He took her right to the edge, then moved away from
her. Caroline reached out for him to find him on his feet.
He picked her up, wrapped her legs around him and
sheathed himself inside her. He moved them together,
deep and swift.

Caroline opened her inner eye on a world of color and
light she had never seen before. Their oneness flickered
between them, blinding white one moment, as red as a
nova the next, while all around them, the whirlpool of
their combined emotions made a cocoon that separated
them from time and place.

The pleasure he needed, the pleasure she longed
for, wrapped around the muscles of her hips, delicious
weakness that spread through her body. She couldn't
get enough of him.

She gasped out the words. "Deeper, Meical."

He firmed his grip on her backside and pressed her
against the wall. "Oh, yes! This is what I need, all I'll
ever need for as long as I live. Say it, Caroline. Say it
now."

"I love you."

Caroline wrapped her arms around him and held on,
as he took her mouth in a long, hard kiss, hurling them
over the edge.

Somewhere between heaven and earth, Caroline felt the darkness relinquish her incubus, and the fear she'd carried with her gave up its hold on her. The haunting memory of this house withered like a weed in the sun, replaced by the memory of their new beginning.

* * * * *

nocturne™

COMING NEXT MONTH

Available January 25, 2011

#105 VAMPIRE SHEIKH
Immortal Sheikhs
Nina Bruhns

#106 TAKEN
Lilith Saintcrow

HNCNM0111

HARLEQUIN®

A Romance

FOR EVERY MOOD™

Spotlight on
Classic

Quintessential, modern love stories
that are romance at its finest.

See the next page
to enjoy a sneak peek from
the Harlequin® Romance series.

*Harlequin Romance author Donna Alward is loved
for her gorgeous rancher heroes.*

*Meet Wyatt as he's confronted by both a precious
little pink bundle left on his doorstep and his neighbor Elli
who's going to show him the ropes....*

Introducing
PROUD RANCHER, PRECIOUS BUNDLE

THE SQUAWKING QUIETED as Elli picked the baby up, and
Wyatt turned around, trying hard to ignore the feelings of
inadequacy as Darcy immediately stopped fussing.

"Maybe she's uncomfortable. What do you think, sweetheart?" Elli turned her conversation to the baby.

"What do you think is wrong?" Wyatt asked, putting the
coffee pot back on the burner.

A strange look passed over Elli's face, one that looked
like guilt and panic. But it was gone quickly. "I couldn't
say," she replied.

"But you were so good with her this afternoon." Wyatt
put his hands on his hips.

"Lucky, that's all. I just...remembered a few things."
The same strange look flitted over her features once more.

Wyatt took the coffee to the table. "You fooled me. You
looked like you knew exactly what you were doing." So
much so that Wyatt had felt completely inept. A feeling he
despised. He was used to being the one in control.

Elli and Darcy walked the length of the kitchen and
back. After a few moments, she admitted, "I haven't really
cared for a baby before. The things I thought of were simply
things I'd heard about. Not from experience, Mr. Black."

Her chin jutted up, closing the subject but making him

want to ask the questions now pulsing through his mind. But then he remembered the old saying—*Don't look a gift horse in the mouth.* He'd benefit from whatever insight she had and be glad of it.

"I don't really know what babies need," he said. "I fed her, patted her back like you did, walked her to sleep, but every time I put her down…"

Wyatt almost groaned. Of course. He'd forgotten one important thing. He'd been so focused on getting the formula the right temperature that he'd forgotten to check her diaper. Not that he had any clue what to do there either.

Pulling calves and shoveling out stalls was far less intimidating than one tiny newborn.

"She's probably due for a diaper change, isn't she." He tried to sound nonchalant. This was a perfect opportunity. Elli must know how to change a diaper. He could simply watch her so he'd know better for the next time.

Instead, Elli came around the corner of the counter and placed Darcy back in his arms. "Here you go, Uncle Wyatt," she said lightly. "You get diaper duty. I'll fix the coffee. Cream and sugar?"

Oh boy, Wyatt thought, looking down into Darcy's pursed face, his smug plan blown to smithereens. He was in for it now.

Will sparks fly between Elli and Wyatt?

Find out in
PROUD RANCHER, PRECIOUS BUNDLE

Available February 2011 from Harlequin Romance

REQUEST YOUR
FREE BOOKS!

2 FREE NOVELS PLUS 2 FREE GIFTS!

HARLEQUIN®

n o c t u r n e™

Dramatic and Sensual Tales of Paranormal Romance.

YES! Please send me 2 FREE Harlequin® Nocturne™ novels and my 2 FREE gifts (gifts are worth about $10). After receiving them, if I don't wish to receive any more books, I can return the shipping statement marked "cancel." If I don't cancel, I will receive 4 brand-new novels every other month and be billed just $4.47 per book in the U.S. or $4.99 per book in Canada. That's a saving of at least 15% off the cover price! It's quite a bargain! Shipping and handling is just 50¢ per book.* I understand that accepting the 2 free books and gifts places me under no obligation to buy anything. I can always return a shipment and cancel at any time. Even if I never buy another book from Harlequin, the two free books and gifts are mine to keep forever.

238/338 HDN E9M2

Name _____ (PLEASE PRINT)

Address _____ Apt. #

City _____ State/Prov. _____ Zip/Postal Code

Signature (if under 18, a parent or guardian must sign)

Mail to the **Reader Service:**
IN U.S.A.: P.O. Box 1867, Buffalo, NY 14240-1867
IN CANADA: P.O. Box 609, Fort Erie, Ontario L2A 5X3

Not valid for current subscribers to Harlequin Nocturne books.

Want to try two free books from another line?
Call 1-800-873-8635 or visit www.ReaderService.com.

* Terms and prices subject to change without notice. Prices do not include applicable taxes. N.Y. residents add applicable sales tax. Canadian residents will be charged applicable provincial taxes and GST. Offer not valid in Quebec. This offer is limited to one order per household. All orders subject to approval. Credit or debit balances in a customer's account(s) may be offset by any other outstanding balance owed by or to the customer. Please allow 4 to 6 weeks for delivery. Offer available while quantities last.

Your Privacy: Harlequin Books is committed to protecting your privacy. Our Privacy Policy is available online at www.ReaderService.com or upon request from the Reader Service. From time to time we make our lists of customers available to reputable third parties who may have a product or service of interest to you. If you would prefer we not share your name and address, please check here. ☐

Help us get it right—We strive for accurate, respectful and relevant communications. To clarify or modify your communication preferences, visit us at www.ReaderService.com/consumerschoice.

HN10

Try these Healthy and Delicious Spring Rolls!

INGREDIENTS

2 packages rice-paper
spring roll wrappers
(20 wrappers)

1 cup grated carrot

¼ cup bean sprouts

1 cucumber, julienned

1 red bell pepper, without
stem and seeds, julienned

4 green onions
finely chopped—
use only the green part

DIRECTIONS

1. Soak one rice-paper wrapper
   in a large bowl of hot water
   until softened.

2. Place a pinch each of carrots,
   sprouts, cucumber, bell
   pepper and green onion on the
   wrapper toward the bottom
   third of the rice paper.

3. Fold ends in and roll tightly
   to enclose filling.

4. Repeat with remaining
   wrappers. Chill before
   serving.

Find this and many more delectable recipes
including the perfect dipping sauce in

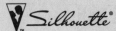

ROMANTIC
SUSPENSE

Sparked by Danger, Fueled by Passion.

NEW YORK TIMES BESTSELLING AUTHOR

RACHEL LEE

No Ordinary Hero

Strange noises…a woman's mysterious disappearance
and a killer on the loose who's too close for comfort.

With no where else to turn, Delia Carmody looks
to her aloof neighbour to help, only to discover
that Mike Windwalker is no ordinary hero.

Available in February.
Wherever books are sold.

Visit Silhouette Books at www.eHarlequin.com

SRS27709R2